ABRAM

SON OF TERAH

By

Brian J. Cahill

This is a work of fiction. Names, characters, businesses, organisations, places, events and incidents either are the product of the author's imagination or are used fictitiously. Any resemblance to actual persons, living or dead, events, or locales is entirely coincidental.

To Holy God

CONTENTS

CHAPTER 1

Star

There was no king greater than Nimrod in all the earth. He was fierce and strong and a mighty warrior. All the kings of the earth, knowing his fame, came to worship him and pay tribute, bowing down to the earth. Nimrod reigned supreme. He was the high king and all the kings of the earth, including Terah, were under his power and counsel.

Terah, the son of Nahor, was the king in the city of Ur of the Chaldeans. The city of Ur was situated in the land of Shinar, the land of the two rivers. These rivers were named the Tigris and the Euphrates. Ur received its water supply by canal from the River Euphrates. Ur became a very prosperous city; the people of Shinar called it the City of Light. Terah was highly esteemed by Nimrod, the king of Shinar. He was elevated to the position of prince of Nimrod's host, which meant that he commanded the whole of Nimrod's army. King Nimrod and his subjects loved Terah. There was none greater than Terah among all of Nimrod's princes, judges, and rulers.

Terah, at the age of seventy years, became the father of Abram. His wife Amthelo, the daughter of Cornebo gave birth to Abram during the night. Terah held a great celebration. 'I give my son the name Abram,' he announced to his guests. 'King Nimrod has raised me high in his kingdom. He has placed me above all his princes, I will reveal this in the name of my son; *Ab* meaning father and *ram* meaning raised.'

King Nimrod did not attend but many from his court were there. The household servants were busy tending the wise men and the magicians from Nimrod's court. The food was plentiful. No expense was spared on the banquet that Terah presented to his guests. The food was rich, with choice cuts of beef, mutton, and wild venison. There were dishes containing lentils, beans, and mixed grains. The servants presented breads of wheat and barley, leavened and unleavened. Dairy products included milk, cream, curds, whey, and cheese.

Terah presented many dishes, sweetened with honey and jam. The selection of jam was made from the choicest of fruits. The guests received many fresh fruits and vegetables. These included leeks, onions, garlic, pomegranate, melon, figs, dates, and grapes. Of course there was no shortage of drink, with plenty of beer and potent rich wine. The rejoicing was great with musicians playing their flutes and lyres and people dancing to the tambourine. After the eating and drinking everyone was happy. Wine always gladdens the heart.

It was late in the night when everyone left the house of Terah. The revellers, making their way home, stopped to look up at the stars in the heavens. Understanding the portents of the stars was of great importance to them. The astronomers and the astrologers prided themselves in their knowledge. The night sky was crystal clear and they gazed up at the constellations in the stars. They stood, marvelling at them for a long time.

They were astonished to see one bright star which rose up from the east and ran across the night sky. For a long time they stood in awe, watching this spectacle. In its path it swallowed up four stars from the four corners of the heavens. The onlookers stood transfixed, for they had never before beheld such an event in the stars. The significance of this event was not hidden from them. 'This betokens the child that was born to Terah this very night,' said one of the observers.

'How is this possible? What can it mean?' asked another, trembling. 'Did you all witness the star, turning ninety degrees on its journey across the heavens?'

'Yes. Three times it stopped and turned ninety degrees. It's completely unnatural.'

'Don't forget that every time the star stopped to turn, it devoured another star. These stars that were once living in the heavens are no more.'

'Yes. This can only mean that this child Abram will grow to be fruitful and multiply and conquer the earth. This child in his day will slay great kings and take possession of their lands.'

They each went home trembling at the significance of their discovery.

When dawn came the wise men met together. The astronomers and the astrologers joined with the magicians. They convened at the house of Anuki, the more senior sage. They intended to discuss their interpretation of the sign in the stars. The sign that they witnessed the previous night.

'What must we do about this sign?'

'We must inform King Nimrod.'

'What will be the outcome?'

'The outcome will be the death of the son born to Terah.'

'But Terah will never allow that to happen. Do you not realize that this will result in war? Have we not had enough conflict?'

'Listen, Terah is one of my closest friends. How can I bring harm to him or his son?'

'If we fail to inform Nimrod and he discovers that we have kept this hidden from him, it will not go well for us.'

'He will slay us. Throw us into the furnace.' They all fell silent, pondering the thought.

'But I have known Terah all my life; from my early childhood. We have grown up together. How can I abandon my love for him? And what of my bond of friendship?'

'You'll have to choose between your friendship and your life.'

'What do you think Nimrod will do to the child?'

'He will have the child destroyed. That's for sure.'

'But Terah is the closest to the king. He is the most highly esteemed of all the princes.'

'Yes and Nimrod may see him as a threat to his sovereignty. The child will certainly be seen as a threat. Have we not seen it for ourselves in the stars?'

After a long pause one said, 'So the child must die?'

'I see no other outcome.'

'And what of Terah? What will be his fate?'

'Terah has been loyal to King Nimrod. He has never caused any concern nor has he ever posed a threat to the king or to his subjects. He is a leading figure in the worship of our gods. He makes offerings on behalf of the people and gives good advice to those who worship them.'

'We know the outcome for the world. If this son of Terah lives, then he will be fruitful and multiply and take possession of all the earth. He and his children will kill the kings of the earth and there will be none to oppose him.'

'Who else can interpret this vision in the stars?' asked one brave soul. 'If we remain silent, how will King Nimrod ever know about it?'

'Shhh. Take care of what you say. If the king should hear you speak like this you will not see tomorrow.'

The company fell silent for a while. 'What will happen if a sage from another city should visit here? If he gives the interpretation of the sign to Nimrod, what will be the outcome? Nimrod will call us into his presence and we will have to give an account for ourselves. His anger will be fierce and we will all perish.'

'We cannot conceal this from Nimrod. We must go at once and tell him what we have seen and give him our interpretation.'

To this they all agreed and leaving the house of Anuki they made their way to the palace of the king. They had to wait for a long time but the time came and they were ushered into the king's presence. There they bowed down with their faces touching the floor.

'My Lord and King,' they announced together in one voice. 'May the king live. May the king live.'

'We have news of Terah son of Nahor, the prince of your host.'

'What news?' interrupted the king, he wondered if some catastrophe had occurred. The countenance of the sages and magicians was very sombre.

'My Lord, Terah had a son born to him last night.'

'Ah good news,' said Nimrod. 'And what name has his son been given?'

'My Lord, the name that he has given his son, is Abram.'

'Abram. What is the significance of this name?'

'His name means exalted father. Terah gave him this name because you have exalted Terah above all others in your house. He has been lifted out of the waters and placed high on dry ground.'

'Ah this means that he will be the father of many?'

'Yes, my Lord, it means that he will be a highly esteemed father.'

'Ah, that's good,' said Nimrod.

'But we have news, my Lord. Disturbing news.'

'What is this disturbing news?' He could see that they were extremely anxious.

'We were at the house of Terah last night and we were celebrating the birth of his son. We ate and drank well—'

'Is this the news?' interrupted Nimrod; he was showing his impatience.

'No, my Lord.' He paused.

'Then what is it?' said a frustrated Nimrod. 'Speak it now.'

'My Lord, when we left the house of Terah to go home our separate ways, we glanced up into the sky. The stars were shining bright and we witnessed a sign in the stars.'

'A most disturbing sign, my Lord,' the others nodded in agreement.

'And what is this sign? Too much wine?' mocked Nimrod.

'My Lord, no. We all witnessed this sign together and interpreted the significance of it. We are of one mind about it.'

'A very bright star travelled across the sky from the east. It moved in haste to the four corners of the heavens, swallowing four stars in its path.'

Nimrod was now intrigued enough not to interrupt and sat forward, resting his hands on his knees.

'We concluded, my Lord, that this sign must refer to the birth of Abram, son of Terah. The birth of this child will have grave consequences for the whole world. If this son of Terah should live then he will be fruitful and multiply and fill the earth with his seed. He and his children will kill all the kings of the earth and take possession of their kingdoms. He will be mighty and strong and none will be able to oppose him.'

Nimrod sat back in his throne and let out a heavy sigh. 'Terah,' he said to himself. 'The prince of my host. The commander of my army. He has been faithful to me,' he paused for a moment. 'I cannot believe it. This cannot be true.' The eyes of the king threw daggers at the sages and magicians. 'This cannot be. You must be wrong.'

'My Lord,' they shrieked, falling prostrate on the ground. They trembled violently, not daring to look up. Nimrod had flown into a rage.

'Stand up,' he roared. He watched them as they leaped to their feet, trembling with fear. 'Explain yourselves. How do you know that this interpretation is true?' Nimrod did not want to believe it.

'My Lord, this is what we do. We observe the stars. We know how they speak. We have advised you for decades and have never failed to guide you in all of your exploits. We have nothing to gain by telling you this. We have known Terah for many years. We would do anything to protect him. But we cannot conceal the importance of this sign and its interpretation from you, our king. We have observed it together and have reached the same conclusion.'

'Tell me again,' said Nimrod, who seemed to be calmer. 'What happened in the sky?'

'My Lord, a new star was born in the heavens last night. We have never seen this star before. It was very bright and rose in the east. The same night a son was born to Terah.'

'We laid eyes on the child for the first time last night, the night of his birth. This star represents Abram, the son of Terah. Quickly this star crossed to the four corners of the heavens and devoured four stars in its path. This child will grow strong and powerful. He and his offspring will fill the earth, as the stars fill the heavens. He will destroy kings and take possession of their kingdoms. None of the stars were able to resist this star and nothing will be able to resist Abram should he live.'

'If you destroy him,' said another. 'Then you and your kingdom will be safe.'

'Ha. Can a child overcome me and my kingdom?' mocked Nimrod.

'My Lord, no. But if you allow him to live, he will grow up into a man and then what will happen? The power of the gods is with him and Terah presents offerings to the gods.'

The impact of this statement hit Nimrod a heavy blow. Nimrod left his throne and paced up and down. 'Leave me,' he roared. 'Now.'

The men scurried out of the presence of the king.

CHAPTER 2

King

Two men arrived at the house of Terah. He was summoned to appear before Nimrod. They exchanged few words between them. The two men simply escorted Terah in silence to the king's palace. Approaching the throne Terah assumed that Nimrod had heard of the birth of his son Abram. 'He must have called me to his palace to congratulate me,' reasoned Terah to himself.

He was right. King Nimrod did congratulate him on the birth of Abram, after all he had heard the news from Terah's guests of the previous night. But something was not right. Terah could see it in the eyes of Nimrod. The look of evil. The look of malice. The presence of another spirit looking down at him.

'What is this all about?' said Terah to himself.

'The wise men witnessed portents in the stars,' said Nimrod.

'What portents did they see in the stars?' asked Terah.

'The stars revealed that your son, born to you last night, will grow up wicked. This evil must be stopped. If he is not killed now he will overthrow kingdoms throughout the earth. As you know well enough, I am the high king of all the earth. I will not allow the kingdoms of the earth to be taken away from me.'

Beads of sweat appeared on Terah's forehead and a cold shiver went up and down his spine. His heart leaped in his chest and he could hear a loud drumming in his ears. He was so overcome that he was not able to speak.

'Now give me your son,' went on Nimrod. 'So that I may slay him before his evil rises up against us. I will give you value for his life. I will fill your house with silver and gold.'

'How may I answer this king?' thought Terah. 'He wants to kill my son. He wants to kill a baby. How can I let him do this? How can I prevent him from doing this? I cannot let him kill Abram. I need to think. I need time to escape. I must play along for the moment.'

'My Lord and my King, I hear what you are saying. Your wisdom is great.' Terah felt prompted to speak a parable to the king. He wanted to see his reaction. But he was taking a risk. He could lose his life over it if he was not careful.

'I will do all that you wish. Only listen to my story of what happened to me a few nights ago. I need to hear what advice my king will give to his humble servant. If it pleases you, my Lord, then I will give you my answer.'

'Very well,' responded Nimrod. 'Speak.'

'My Lord Nimrod, you must remember the beautiful horse that you gave to me as a gift.'

'Yes of course I do. What about it?'

'Well, Ayen, the son of Mored, came to me a few nights ago and asked me to give him the horse that you gave to me as a gift. He offered to give me silver and gold to cover the cost. I said to him, "How can I give you my horse, the one given to me by the king? It would not be right to dispense with a royal gift. What would King Nimrod think of me for doing such a thing?"'

A smirk crossed Nimrod's lips.

'I said to him, "Wait until I speak to the king concerning this matter. He is wise and he will know what I should do. I will obey the king." So now, my Lord, I have made known to you this event that took place recently. What advice would my Lord give to his humble servant?'

The king was enraged. His cheeks flushed red and his eyes flared. 'What kind of fool are you that you have to seek my advice? How could you even consider for one moment parting with such a gift? The beautiful horse that I gave to you. All the silver and gold could never match the value of the horse. There is no other creature like it in the earth.'

He paused, looking at Terah in bewilderment. 'No. Do not sell your horse. How can you even think about it?'

'Thank you, my Lord,' answered Terah. 'Your wisdom is great,' he paused. 'But my Lord, what is this that you ask me to do concerning my son Abram? You ask me to give you my son for silver and gold, enough to fill my house, so that you can slay him. He is an innocent child who has done no wrong. What will I do with silver and gold? My son will be unable to inherit from me. He will be dead and when I am dead you will take it back.'

Nimrod flew into a rage on hearing the words of Terah. He knew that his own judgement had been thrown back at him. Terah buckled when he saw that the king's rage was kindled against him. Nimrod was a cruel character and greatly feared in the land of Shinar. Terah knew of many men who had been killed for a lot less.

To calm Nimrod's temper, Terah said, 'All that I have is in the power of my Lord and King. Whatever the king desires to do with me, let him do. You even have power over my son since you are his king. I will give you my son. Take him. Take all of my sons, even without exchange of silver and gold. I give them to you freely,' Terah trembled.

'No, I will not take your son. I will purchase your son. I do not need all of your sons, just your youngest.'

With a trembling voice Terah pleaded with the king. 'I beseech you, my Lord and King, please permit me to speak further and let my King hear the words of his servant.'

Nimrod nodded his consent.

'My Lord, please allow me three days to consider this matter, so that I can come to terms with your decision. It will give me time to consult with my wife and family.'

Falling down on his knees he pleaded with King Nimrod.

'Very well,' said Nimrod. 'You have three days. Consider carefully what I have decided to do. I will not be persuaded otherwise. So do not speak another word. Leave me now. Go home to your family. I expect you to return in three days with your son. I will slay him,' he paused. 'If you do not return in three days with your son, I will kill you and everyone else in your household. I will kill all of your servants. Not even a dog will be left standing.'

Terah bowed down, touching his forehead to the ground. He left the presence of the king, moving backwards as he bowed to the ground. He arrived home, greatly disturbed. He revealed the news to his wife and family and they were terrified.

Terah's wife, Amthelo, the daughter of Cornebo, considered the matter in tears. She was fearful for her son Abram and her entire family. 'What will happen to our family if we fail to surrender Abram to Nimrod? Curse him,' Amthelo screamed. 'Curse Nimrod. May his head be sliced from his body,' she trembled violently with tears flowing down her cheeks.

'He is only one day old,' she wiped her face with her hand. 'And curse those soothsayers. To think, they ate and drank here and celebrated with us yesterday evening. And then they went and told Nimrod to kill Abram. They have given a wicked interpretation of the stars,' she paused while she wept.

'Have they nothing better to do with their lives than to make up stupid stories? How do they know if he will grow up and kill Nimrod?' Looking directly at her husband she said, 'Maybe I will kill Nimrod myself, since you are unable.'

Terah hung his head. He did not know what to say or do. 'How can I comfort Amthelo?' he asked himself. 'She has every right to be angry.'

'Those soothsayers will never darken this door again,' she said. 'If they do I will kill them. With my own hands I will kill them. We must run,' her eyes widened. 'We must escape from here and go into hiding.'

Gripping Terah by the arm she said, 'You must get us out of here. Get us away from here, where Nimrod can never find us. I am still in pain,' she said almost to herself. 'I am not strong enough to travel but I cannot delay. I must go tonight, under cover of darkness. I must go with Abram without anyone knowing of it.'

'You must arrange it,' she said, turning to Terah. 'I will go into hiding with Abram in the wilderness, where Nimrod will never expect to find us. A baby will be easily noticed in a town or village. Word will get back to Nimrod, he will find Abram and kill him. We must be wiser than Nimrod and we must act fast. Tonight, we must leave tonight.'

'I can't get you out tonight. Do you think that Nimrod is a fool? He is a hunter. He will easily track us down and we will all die. We must think of another way because he will be watching us, expecting us to run. He will pay our neighbours to spy on us and report our escape. We must be shrewd and outwit him, play along with his plan,' he said, looking Amthelo in the eye. 'We must be clever and think carefully. We have three days.'

Amthelo's eyes filled with tears. Abram cried out with hunger. She left Terah to tend to her son. She comforted the boy and wept through the night.

Terah prepared a roasted offering and presented it to his god, his idol made of wood. He worshipped before the god, appealing for wisdom and guidance. This god of many other gods, he believed would listen to his plea. This god, Anu, was the supreme god in the heavens and all the stars in the universe centred upon him. Terah believed that Anu would manipulate the stars regarding his own circumstances and empower him to overcome Nimrod.

'O Anu how can I save Abram? How can I prevent his death? And should I cheat Nimrod or defy him in any way, how can I avoid my own death and the death of my entire household?'

Terah knelt down on a rug on the floor before the idol that he had fashioned out of the limb of a tree with his own hands. 'Speak to me, O Anu,' pleaded Terah. 'I need your help.'

The wooden idol remained silent, perched on the shelf in the alcove built into the wall. Terah gazed upon the idol, but the eyes of the idol were blind and unable to see. Terah spoke to the idol, but the ears of the idol were deaf. The idol made no response because it could not speak and had no mind of its own. For the next couple of days Terah prayed to the idol, laying roast offerings before it. On the eve of the third day, the final day, he devised a plan to thwart Nimrod.

Amthelo's face was disfigured by the tears. Terah sat down beside her and told her, 'You will be leaving with Abram in the morning. I have made arrangements with the household servants. They have been instructed to take you and Abram with some maidservants to a place of safety.'

'How will we get out without being seen? We must not allow anyone to follow us,' said Amthelo, terrified. 'And what is to become of you?'

'There is no need to worry about me,' answered Terah. 'I am going to fool Nimrod.'

'But how?' cried Amthelo.

Terah lifted his hand to silence her. 'You will be taken to your father Cornebo. He will take you to your mother's family and they will take you to the place of safety. So not one of our own servants will know where you have been taken to. They will think that you are simply visiting your family.'

'But if you don't bring Abram to Nimrod he will kill you and the rest of our family.'

'I have a plan.'

'Well,' she enquired of him. 'What is it?'

Terah cast his eyes down and shook his head. 'I can't tell you. It's better that you don't know everything,' he cleared his throat. 'I will leave the house first and go to Nimrod. You remain by your bed in the room, but get dressed and be ready to leave. Don't show yourself to anyone until you're called for. When I'm at Nimrod's palace, only then must you leave with Abram. I've already made preparations with the servants. You must move with haste and speak to no one.'

'What of you?' asked Amthelo. 'How will you escape with your life?'

'My plan will work,' answered Terah. 'But you must do exactly as I've instructed you. I won't visit you immediately, but in time I will. All of this we must do to fool Nimrod. If you do exactly as I tell you, we will be successful.'

Amthelo looked him in the eye and then they embraced. 'I'm so afraid,' cried Amthelo. 'I'm afraid that someone's going to die.'

Terah's eyes gazed into the distance. His heart was thumping wildly in his chest. 'It's the only way,' he said to himself. 'It's the only way the plan will work.'

CHAPTER 3

Plan

Amthelo had a fitful night's sleep. The anxiety kept her awake. She thought that at any moment she must flee with her baby under her arm. The door to her room remained closed but she could hear muffled voices in the house. This made her even more anxious and she was tempted to open her door to see what was happening. But she decided not to open the door and spoil the plan of her husband Terah.

'I must remain hidden,' she said to herself. 'I must wait until I'm collected. That will be long after Terah has gone to Nimrod.'

It seemed like she had to wait for eternity. When the time was right the trusted servants hurried her outside the house. With haste and without making a sound they led her to the waiting camels. They managed to leave the city without drawing any attention to themselves.

In her father's house Amthelo felt that she would be safe but she knew that her father was no match for Nimrod. The last thing she wanted to do was bring trouble to her father's house. She knew that she would only be able to stay for a short time. Soon she would have to flee again.

On the road Terah encountered armed men dispatched by Nimrod. They had a severe warning for him. The chief guard announced, 'A message from the Lord Nimrod, King of the Earth, to Terah son of Nahor. "Today you will send me your son Abram for the price agreed in silver and gold. In exchange for your son you will be richly rewarded and will never be in want, all the days of your life. If you do not do this, as agreed three days ago, you will be punished. You will be put to death. You and your entire family will be slain. You and your wife, your children and their children, all of your household servants and slaves. All of your cattle and sheep will be slain. All of your worldly possessions will become mine." What is your answer?'

'I will obey my Lord and King. Even now, as you can see, I am travelling on my way to his palace to deliver my son to him.'

'Show me your son,' demanded the guard.

Turning around Terah beckoned a maidservant who rushed forward. 'Reveal my son Abram to the palace guard,' said Terah.

Nimrod's man stripped the baby to ensure that it was a boy and nodded his head. 'Follow me,' he said.

Before Nimrod, the maidservant lay the baby boy on the ground at his feet, as she was commanded.

'See,' said Nimrod to Terah, pointing out sacks and chests of silver and gold. 'As promised I have purchased your son for a price. There is silver and gold, enough to keep you in wealth for the rest of your life. You'll want for nothing.'

'I'll want for nothing except my son,' answered Terah.

Shrugging his shoulders, Nimrod answered, 'In time you will forget.'

The baby began to cry because he felt the cold. The handmaid covered him up.

'Why bother to cover him?' said Nimrod. 'He won't feel the cold for long.'

Reaching down, Nimrod uncovered the boy. The baby involuntarily urinated over the hand of Nimrod.

'Your last defiant gesture,' laughed Nimrod.

Gripping the child by his ankle, he swung the infant into the air. With all of his might he brought him down, splitting his head open on the floor. Blood splashed on Terah's feet and hit the handmaid in the face. She shrieked, backing away. In haste she wiped the blood from her face on the sleeve of her garments. The crunch of bone chilled Terah to the core. Nimrod was delighted.

'It's done,' he said, looking down with satisfaction at the thick pool of blood forming under the body of the child. 'So,' mocked Nimrod, licking the urine and blood from his hands, 'this is the child that was to grow strong and multiply and fill the earth with his seed. This was the child that was going to kill all the kings of the earth and take possession of their kingdoms.'

Nimrod laughed, saying, 'This child was foretold in the stars in the heavens to be mighty and strong. The stars revealed that none might oppose him. Ha, ha, ha. Not anymore. He has been wiped from the face of the earth. He is no more.'

Turning to Terah he said, 'You have done well to obey me. You have saved your life and the lives of everyone in your household. I know that it was difficult for you but you have been richly rewarded for your obedience and loyalty.'

Pausing for a moment he said, 'Terah, son of Nahor, you will drink some wine with me to steady your nerves. You have witnessed something shocking. I understand.'

The wine was served and Terah drank some to steady himself. It warmed him as he swallowed it down. But Terah was trembling and he excused himself from the presence of Nimrod. He returned home, realising the terrible deed that he had done. Because in the place of Abram, Terah had taken a new-born boy from one of his slaves, pretending that he was his own son. Terah had given instructions for this woman to be removed secretly and she was never seen again. Terah knew that he had matched the cruelty of Nimrod.

Abram and his mother Amthelo, along with a few trusted servants, went into hiding. They were taken to a secluded place far from the trading routes. In this place there would be little chance of discovery. There they lived in a cave and remained there for ten years. Terah came to visit them occasionally. He was very careful to travel secretly, so that no one would discover their place of concealment. He made arrangements for them to receive regular deliveries of food.

Abram was seven when his eldest brother Haran was married. In the same year Haran's wife gave birth to a son. Haran called his son Lot. Haran's second child was a girl and he called her Milca. When Abram was ten, Haran had a third child, a girl, and she was given the name Sarai.

It was at this time that Abram and his mother Amthelo came out of the cave. Abram was to be introduced to a society greater than he had ever imagined possible. Cities, roads, animals, people – he had never seen the like of it before. This new experience fascinated him.

Abram was gone from Nimrod's memory but Terah was still anxious for his son's safety. So he sent Abram to the house of Noah and his son, Shem. There Abram remained in safety and he learned the way of Yahweh Elohim, the one true God. Noah and Shem remained faithful to God and had not turned to false gods, as did most of mankind, especially those under the influence of Nimrod.

CHAPTER 4

Nimrod

Forty years before the birth of Abram, Cush had a son born to him in his old age. Cush was the son of Ham and the grandson of Noah. Cush named his son Nimrod. He was given the name Nimrod, which means rebellion, because at that time the sons of men began to rebel against God. Cush greatly loved his son Nimrod. Cush gave Nimrod the garments that God had made for Adam and Eve, and at the age of twenty Nimrod put on the garments.

These garments had been passed down through the generations. Before he died Adam gave the garments to Enoch, the son of Jared. Enoch lived a holy and blameless life and he was taken up into heaven, without seeing death. Before rising up into heaven he passed on these garments to his son Methuselah. At the death of Methuselah, Noah received the garments onto the ark. But upon leaving the ark, Ham stole the garments, fashioned by the hand of God. He immediately hid the garments from Noah and his brothers, Japheth and Shem. Ham secretly passed on these garments to his firstborn son, Cush. Cush likewise concealed these garments, keeping them hidden from his brothers and sons.

When Nimrod clothed himself in these garments, he was endowed with strength and power. He was the first to wear these garments since Adam and Eve wore them. He was a mighty hunter and captured animals in the field. These animals he sacrificed to God, Yahweh Elohim. In those days after the flood everyone believed in and worshipped Yahweh Elohim, the one true God.

Nimrod rose up as a mighty warrior among his people. He fought battles for his people against their enemies. All the enemies of his people were delivered into his hands. It was Yahweh Elohim who prospered Nimrod in his endeavours and he reigned upon the earth.

In those days, when men were trained for battle, they would be encouraged by their leader. 'May Yahweh Elohim strengthen us and deliver us this day from our enemies. He did so with Nimrod, who is a mighty hunter in all the earth. Nimrod always managed to defeat his enemies, delivering his own brethren from the foe.'

It so happened that the Cushite's were tormented by the sons of Japheth. They were greatly tormented and under their power. Nimrod was forty years old at that time. He rose up and assembled all the sons of Cush and their families, numbering four hundred and sixty men.

'We must end this torment and we must finish it today,' declared Nimrod. 'There are four hundred and sixty men here and I can raise eighty more and I will pay them their hire. Will you join me and go into battle against the sons of Japheth? They have tormented us, far too long. They have crossed the Great Sea, leaving their own land, given to them by Noah. And have descended upon us, taking what is not theirs.'

The Cushites declared, 'We will join you in battle against our enemies, the Japhites.'

'Don't be afraid or discouraged,' announced Nimrod. 'Because all of our enemies will be delivered into our hands, for Yahweh Elohim is with us.'

So into battle they went, the Cushites and the men that Nimrod had hired for the battle. They were strong and powerful and they subdued the sons of Japheth. The sons of Japheth came under the authority of Nimrod. He placed officers over them to keep them under his power.

For added security Nimrod took some of their children. These children became servants to Nimrod and his brothers. In this manner Nimrod ensured that the sons of Japheth would not rebel against him to save the lives of their children.

The Cushites turned home and they celebrated their victory over their enemies. In their enthusiasm they made Nimrod king over them and forgot to give the glory to God, Yahweh Elohim. Nimrod appointed princes, rulers, and judges over all of his people. This included those that he had subdued. Terah, the son of Nahor, came from the line of Shem. Nimrod elevated Terah because of his loyalty and service. He was dignified above all of Nimrod's princes.

Nimrod was the reigning king and all of his enemies had been subdued. He decided that he wanted a city to be built to house his palace. So he sent his counsellors to search for a suitable place to build his city. They found a suitable place, fit for the king, in the land given to Shem and his descendants by Noah. This was in the fertile valley of the great River Euphrates.

So Nimrod and the Hamites infiltrated the land and took possession of it. The Semites were ousted by force from the land that had been given to them by Noah. Nimrod was pleased with the location and he commanded the construction of his city to begin. Because he had violently shaken his enemies and destroyed them, he called the name of his city Shinar. Nimrod lived in his palace in the city of Shinar and he reigned with authority. He was secure and he fought with all of his enemies and put them under his power. He became a ruthless ruler and none could oppose him.

All of the neighbouring kingdoms heard of his fame and might. Ambassadors came to him with gifts and bowed down to worship him. He became the supreme king of all these nations and he reigned over all the sons of Noah. But Nimrod became proud and he turned away from Yahweh Elohim. He declared that it was by his own power and authority that he had succeeded in overcoming his enemies. He became more wicked than all of the men that had lived since the flood.

CHAPTER 5

Noah

The sign in the stars was not hidden from Noah. He called his son Shem to witness the event. Looking up into the sky their hearts were stirred as they saw the new star rising in the east. It slowly but steadily crossed to the four corners of the sky, swallowing up four stars in its path.

'What does this mean?' asked Shem, excitedly.

'Yahweh Elohim is telling us something,' answered Noah. 'Something great is happening now and something greater is going to come of it.'

'What could it possibly be?'

'Well son, there's only one way to find out. We must pray before Yahweh Elohim and seek his counsel.'

After the sunrise they lifted up a ram sacrifice on the altar. They first gave thanks to Yahweh Elohim and then offered him praise. Confessing their sins they washed themselves with water. This was an outward sign of inward grace. Then they approached the altar to make the sacrifice, in a pure and righteous manner. Noah, Shem, and the entire household took part in the sacrifice. They performed all of the rituals. They all paused to listen to Noah, the priest, petition

Yahweh Elohim.

'How great is Yahweh Elohim, the God of heaven and earth and the whole of creation. He is the almighty saviour of mankind. We come before you now to seek your face and ask for your answer to our prayer. We witnessed a sign in the stars during the night. A sign which was thrilling and exciting but also daunting and perplexing. We don't understand the meaning of this sign. But we are bold to ask for your guidance, so that we can truly interpret the meaning of what you are revealing to us. We place all our trust in you and abandon ourselves to your holy will.'

In silence they waited in the presence of God. They listened to the crackling flames of the fire. The flames danced and the smoke rose up high into the sky. They could smell the smoke and the burning of the flesh on the altar. They waited patiently. There was no hurry, no anxiety. Peacefully they surrendered themselves to the loving embrace of the living God of creation.

The worshippers spent time singing praise to the glory of God. 'O Yahweh Elohim you have commanded the stars to speak, the objects of your creation. You wield authority over all that you have created. Send us your spirit. Let your spirit stir in our hearts. Come spirit of truth and reveal yourself to us.'

They waited upon Yahweh Elohim and he breathed upon them. He sent his spirit upon them. Like a gentle breeze he stirred among them. They welcomed him in to stir up their minds, to stir up their hearts and to fill their intellect. The breeze of the spirit of God blew away all doubt, all fear, and all uncertainty. The spirit of God filled them with truth, with faith and trust.

'Yahweh Elohim forever remains with his people, with the ones that he loves. God has come,' announced Noah. 'Yahweh Elohim has spoken to us this day. He has answered our prayer.' Everyone listened in silence to the voice of Noah. 'Salvation has dawned upon the world. A child has been born and he will rise up, as the sun rises up in the eastern sky. This child is not the saviour, but from his seed will come the saviour. This child is anointed by God and appointed to fill the earth with his descendants. He and his descendants will be strong and mighty and will follow Yahweh Elohim, the one true God.'

'Who is this child?' was the question on everyone's lips.

'In time,' continued Noah, 'his people will be tormented, deceived, and afflicted but Yahweh will not abandon them. Yahweh will encourage them. They will prevail and they will bend to the will of Yahweh. Even now, the life of this child is in great peril. We must pray for his protection, trusting in the salvation of Yahweh.'

Some lifted their hands and closed their eyes to pray silently in the depth of their hearts. Noah continued, 'The kings of the earth will rise up against him, but he will defeat them. Nothing will stand in his way. The ways of Yahweh Elohim are just and he will reveal himself to this man. Yahweh will make known to this man what he must do. He will be filled with the spirit of Yahweh and be endowed with perseverance and endurance. From his fidelity to Yahweh a great nation will arise. Other people, who do not know Yahweh Elohim, will come to know the true God. They will be grafted into this nation and inherit the promise of eternal life.'

Noah finished speaking the prophecy from the lips of Yahweh Elohim. Everyone wondered at this news. Silence fell upon them as they pondered the impact that this man will have upon the world. They all considered the meaning of eternal life.

At the appointed time Abram was received into the house of Noah. He was aged ten and Noah knew in his heart that Abram was the child that was written in the stars. Noah felt the conviction in his heart to rear this boy and bring him up in the way of Yahweh Elohim.

In the course of time Abram learned much in the house of Noah. It was there under the guidance of Noah that Abram was introduced to Yahweh, the creator of heaven and earth. Noah explained, 'It's believed that it was Enosh, the grandson of Adam, who first called upon the name of Yahweh. God must have revealed his divine name to Enosh in his day.

'We spell this divine name with four letters. These are Yod, Hey, Waw, and Hey. As you know Abram, each letter in our language has several meanings. Yod is the image of an extended forearm and hand and can mean arm, hand, work, deed, and worship. Hey is the image of a man with his hands raised high and means behold, see, look, reveal, breath, and sigh. Waw is the image of a nail and means nail, secure, fasten, and add. So when put together YHWH could mean the hand, behold; the nail, behold. The true meaning of his name still remains a mystery. But I believe that the true meaning will be revealed to us by God in the course of time.

'We believe that Yahweh means: I am who I am. But in some way he is saying to us that his name is: I am he, whom you can never know. Our understanding and knowledge of God is beyond us. Another translation means: he exists. Yahweh also means: he causes things to be. So when we call upon his name we are reminded of our reason for being. We exist because God has designed us and has created us for a purpose. Yahweh has come close to us and wants us to draw close to him, but at the same time he is hidden from us. He has placed in us a desire to seek him and we will never be at rest until we rest in him.

'Many more names have been revealed to us by God. As time progresses he will reveal himself in more ways under new names. Some of these names are already known to us. El is a known name for God which means Power. Elohim is another name which means the Greatest of all Powers, the Mighty One. We also call him Adonai and this means Lord; there is no lord greater than Adonai. His name El-Elyon means God Most High. El-Shaddai means the Breasts of God, All-Sufficient and All-Bountiful. And Elohei Tzeva'ot means

God of Hosts, God of Armies.'

'Why does God have so many names?' asked Abram.

Noah answered, 'He is known by many names to describe his nature to us for our benefit. He reveals himself according to the limits of our understanding. When we call upon the name of God it is right that we use the appropriate name to fit our circumstances. So if we need comforting we call upon El-Shaddai and if we are facing conflict we call upon Elohei Tzeva'ot.

'God is infinite and powerful and all of his names cannot be known by us, because our minds are limited by our nature. We are created by him, and how can the created beings fully understand the creator? As time goes by he will reveal himself to us in his way. He will reveal new names of himself when he considers us ready to receive them. Some of the names of God are known to him alone and will never be revealed to us until the end of the age.'

'But why would he keep his names secret?'

'Some people believe that if they know the name of God then they will have dominion over him. They imagine that they will be able to invoke his name in a magical rite to suit their own purposes. In knowing his name we would also have full knowledge of him. But we will never have full knowledge of him and we will never have full knowledge of his name. We can only know God when he draws us close to him.'

'How will God draw me close to him?'

'The only way is for you to surrender to him. You must not try to force the hand of God, to make things happen your own way. Ask God to draw you close to him and allow him to act in your life. Place your trust in him and listen to his voice. He will speak to you. Let there be no doubt in your heart.'

'That's what I want. I know that God is with you and you hear his voice. I want to hear him and follow him like you do.'

Noah drew the young boy Abram to himself and he embraced him. 'It will happen, Abram. God has you in his mind and he will honour your request.'

'Tell me,' asked Abram, 'what was the world like before the flood?'

'The world was so different than it is today,' Noah paused as he remembered the past. 'Today the world has become much more arid. The canopy of vapour that shielded the earth has disappeared and now the earth is scorched. Since the flood the length of the life of man has diminished. Adam lived for nine hundred and thirty years. The oldest man that ever lived was Methuselah. His age was nine hundred and sixty-nine when he died; the same year as the flood. I was six hundred years old when the great flood came upon the earth. And the year you came here, when you were only ten years old, I was nine hundred and two years of age.

'If only man had stayed away from sin. It was because of the sinfulness of man that Yahweh sent the flood. I spent one hundred and twenty years trying to turn people away from sin, but they wouldn't listen to me. They laughed at me, considering me a fool. But they laughed at all of the prophets that preceded me also.

'The ways of man became more violent and wicked and Yahweh became saddened at their conduct. There were many times when men turned back to Yahweh but they didn't remain faithful to him. They were infected by the same perversions of the wicked. They worshipped idols, false gods fashioned by their own hands. They committed murder and went to war against each other.

'They cross bred the animals which was forbidden by Yahweh and their sexual conduct was perverse. They even had sex with animals, creating wild and repulsive creatures. But Yahweh was patient and he sent more prophets to encourage the people to turn from their wicked ways. There came a time when Yahweh decided to wipe the wicked off the face of the earth. So he gave me instructions to build the ark.'

'Ark? What is that?'

'Yahweh told me to build a very large ship which he called the ark. In the ark I was to save the beasts that walk upon the face of the earth and the birds that fly in the sky. God commanded this so that after the flood the world might be repopulated with his creatures. The rest of creation was destroyed. Yahweh saved me and my family and it is from my sons that the world has grown in number again. It was Yahweh's plan for us to remain holy and live peacefully together. But sin has remained in the world and wickedness has grown among us again.

'We gathered the creatures at Yahweh's command and we entered the ark before Yahweh brought the disaster upon the earth. Very quickly, the heavens opened and the rain poured down in torrents. We were terrified because the world had never seen rain before. The water vapour that covered the earth kept the soil moist and enabled the crops to grow. Then the earth below us shook and great fissures opened up beneath us, pouring out fire and smoke. The ground broke apart and the pillars of the earth shifted. The land mass broke up and the continents drifted apart. They separated from each other, pushing in opposite directions. The water of the oceans flooded the growing void between the continents.

'And the rain kept falling. We were floating adrift for a total of one year and ten days and in all that time there was no sign of land. All we could see was the water and the sky.'

'I've never been on a ship. It must have been exciting. Were you not afraid?'

'I must admit, I was terrified. I completely trusted in Yahweh but it was a time of great anxiety and most of the time we were exhausted tending to the animals. Feeding them and cleaning up after them was not an easy task.'

At this remark Abram made a face as if he had encountered a bad smell. They both laughed at his joke.

'Eventually the ark came to a halt because we had entered shallow water. The water level began to drop and the earth appeared below us. At the appointed time Yahweh told us to leave the shelter of the ark and release the animals into the world again.'

'Where in the world did the ark come to land?' asked Abram with his eyes wild with excitement.

'The ark settled in the land between the Asken Sea and the Jabus Sea upon Mount Ararat.'

'Where is that? Is it far away? Can we go there to look at it?'

'Mount Ararat is far from here, to the north of us. Maybe we will go there some time for you to see the ark. But do you know that much of the ark has been stripped by the people who now live there? They are foolish and because of their superstition they believe that it has powers to bring good fortune and ward off evil spirits. So they have pulled it apart and they sell off pieces of it for profit, especially the bitumen which they use to make amulets for protection.'

Abram hung his head, thinking that by now there would be nothing left of it. 'What year did you come out of the ark?' he asked.

'We came out of the ark one thousand six hundred and fifty-seven years after Yahweh created the world.'

Quickly doing his calculations Abram said, 'Oh no. That's over three hundred years ago. The ark; there will be nothing left of it by now,' he announced as his eyes filled with tears.

'Come on, young fellow. Let us go for a walk. We can spend some time walking through the vines. Wouldn't you like to taste the grapes? You can tell me which grapes you find tastier, the red grapes or the green grapes.'

In the vineyard they sat on the ground under the shade of the vines. Without a doubt Abram preferred the sweeter taste of the red grapes. Abram was eagerly filling his mouth with more grapes when Noah said to him, 'When we all came out of the ark I built an altar to Yahweh. And taking some of the clean animals and birds I presented a fragrant burnt offering to him. The fragrance reached heaven and was a pleasant aroma before Yahweh. He accepted the offering and declared that he would never again curse the earth. Even though man is sinful, through and through, he declared that he will never again destroy all the creatures that walk upon the face of the earth.'

After some time Noah became very quiet. He hung his head in sorrow and Abram reached out to comfort him. 'Abram,' said Noah. 'Sin is in the world. This is our greatest enemy and we must constantly be on our guard to resist the temptations of the devil.'

'What is the devil?'

'Yahweh created the angels. These angels have no physical bodies, they are spirits and they worship and serve Yahweh in the heavenly realms. One of these angels, called Lucifer, was the most beautiful, the most luminous of all the angels. It is believed that he is a spiritual, musical instrument and he was created to sound praise to God throughout heaven.

'But he was filled with pride, the worst sin of all. He wanted to be like Yahweh and he became jealous of Yahweh, his creator. He rebelled and turned against Yahweh. He thought that he was as good as Yahweh, if not better than him. He wanted to take the place of Yahweh on the heavenly throne. So he was banished from heaven but not before he managed to persuade a third of all the angels in heaven to rebel against God and follow him.'

'What happened to him?'

'He was banished from heaven and was cursed by God. He is the one who managed to entice Adam and Eve to commit sin by disobeying Yahweh. He lied. He is known as the Father of Lies. He told them that they would have great knowledge and be equal to Yahweh. They were foolish enough to listen to him. And so they sinned and, because of their sin, they alienated themselves from Yahweh. Yahweh does not tolerate sin and so he banished them from Paradise where they used to walk in the Garden with God.

'They were thrown out of the Garden of Eden. They were once very close to Yahweh but their sin raised a barrier between them and Yahweh. Because of this, they lost sight of him. The Archangel Michael banished them from Paradise and the Cherubim, spinning their fiery swords, stand guard, preventing them to enter there again.

'You must be on your guard, Abram. Get used to listening to the voice of Yahweh so that you will not be deceived and enticed into sin. We are all weak and can be tempted to stray from the path of Yahweh. But don't despair, even if you do go astray, Yahweh is always ready to forgive you for your sins. It is our own pride that often keeps us from repenting. Don't be afraid to call upon the name of Yahweh, the Lord God, for help. He will never forsake you. He will always come to your aid.'

'Noah?' asked Abram with enthusiasm, 'Did you ever meet Adam, the very first man? What was he like?'

'I regret, Abram, that I never met Adam. He died nine hundred and thirty years after creation. I wasn't born until one hundred and twenty-six years after his death. He was a holy man. Even though he brought original sin into the world, he always regretted his sin and he sincerely followed Yahweh all the days of his life. During his lifetime, he prophesied that because of the sin of man, the world would be overcome by flood and fire. The flood has already taken place and it will not happen again because Yahweh promised so. But the destruction by fire has yet to be fulfilled.

'When we left the ark, Yahweh made a covenant with us. He put his rainbow in the sky as a sign to remind him of his covenant to never flood the earth again. This covenant he made not only with mankind but with every beast that he rescued from extinction and that came out of the ark. For the first time we were allowed to eat the flesh of animals. I established seven laws that we must all live by for righteous conduct.'

'What are the seven laws?'

'The first law states that we must worship Yahweh, the one true God, and we must not worship idols. The second law states that blasphemy is forbidden and we must not curse the name of Yahweh.'

'Do some people do that? Do they really speak against God?' asked Abram.

'They do indeed and it's very sad because they don't realise the great love that God has for them. Some people are very foolish. The third law states that we must not commit murder, we must respect all that live. The fourth law says that sexual sin is forbidden. The fifth law states that stealing is forbidden. The sixth law forbids us to consume the blood of any creature and the flesh of a living creature must not be eaten. The seventh law states that courts of justice must be established in order to uphold the entire law.'

'So Noah, are you now the father of the whole world?'

Smiling at Abram's question Noah answered, 'Yes Abram. That's true. All of my sons have fathered all who live. Including you.'

'Well, from which of your sons do I come?'

'As you know, I have three sons. They are Shem, Ham, and Japheth. You have been born to the house of Shem. Arphachsad was born to Shem and Shelah was born to Arphachsad. Shelah fathered Eber and he fathered Peleg. Reu was the son of Peleg and Reu fathered Serug. It was Serug who fathered Nahor and he is your grandfather. Nahor fathered Terah and Terah fathered you, Abram.'

CHAPTER 6

Idolatry

Nimrod became more wicked in the land. He ruled the land and governed the people with tyranny. His punishments were cruel for those who refused to obey him. Long before Nimrod ruled the earth everyone believed in Yahweh Elohim, the one true God. But when Nimrod governed the land, he declared that God was not a person but a force, a source of power. People were encouraged to fall away from the truth and they stopped praying to God. Over time Nimrod declared that the aspects of God had been divided.

Nimrod created twelve idols. These idols he presented to his people, declaring that God had placed a different aspect of himself into them. These idols were established to be worshipped. A different aspect of God was present in each idol and each idol had to be worshipped at the respective month of the year. Anyone who refused to worship these wooden idols was punished and the punishment was severe. The worship of the one true God was now forbidden.

Before the birth of Abram, his father Terah, the son of Nahor abandoned God and adopted the false beliefs of Nimrod. Terah promoted the worship of these idols and implemented the harsh regime throughout Mesopotamia, the land governed by Nimrod. In his own house Terah had twelve idols and he worshipped each one in the appropriate month, according to the constellation of stars in the sky. He presented meat offerings and drink offerings to these gods, hoping that he could manipulate them in his favour.

Shortly after the flood, Ham, the son of Noah, in his travels came upon a rock, on which he discovered writing that had been carved. Ham read the writing and discovered its meaning. He secretly wrote down the writing, keeping his discovery from his father Noah and his brothers Shem and Japheth. This writing had been carved upon the rock before the flood and it led Ham into sin.

The writing preserved the teaching of the Watchers, the fallen angels who inhabited the earth as demons. It was their teaching among other wicked ways that provoked God to flood the earth and wipe out sinfulness. This teaching of the fallen angels had led men to mock God and turn to occult practices, observing omens in the heavenly bodies and the use of magical spells and incantations to manipulate the demons to obey men.

Ham secretly passed on this discovery, this knowledge, to his sons Cush, Mizraim, Phut, Canaan, and Nimrod. All of his sons preserved this knowledge and put it into practice, passing it on to their own children and through the generations. In this rebellion against God, all of the Hamites went astray.

New religions sprang up, devised by man but influenced by Satan, the devil. Satan's wicked demons served him by tempting men to turn away from God. The heavenly bodies were the first to be deified. The sun and the moon were the most visible and were held in high regard by the astronomers and the magicians. The sun god, the god of justice and truth, became known as Shamash or Utu, though he was known under other names in different places. The moon god, the god of fertility and cattle, was known as Sin in the land under Nimrod's influence.

The planet Sagmegar (Jupiter) revealed the god Marduk, the

patron god of the city of Babel. Inanna the goddess of sex and warfare, resided in the planet Dilbat (Venus). The god Ninurtu was considered to reside in the planet Lubat Sagus (Saturn), he was known as the god of healing and agriculture. The planet Lubat Guud (Mercury) revealed the god Nabu, who was the god of wisdom and writing. The god Nergal was revealed in the planet Lubat Dir (Mars), he was the god of death, the underworld, and plague.

The stars and their positions in the night sky told a story of their own. The astronomers and the astrologers spent much of their time studying these heavenly bodies and they took measurements and made calculations from the movements of the stars.

The astronomers and the astrologers held a high position in the court of Nimrod alongside the magicians and sages. They discovered that there was a link between the position of the stars in the heavens and the events that occurred on the earth below. In reading the stars well, the astrologers were able to understand and even predict the future events in the earth. Because of this knowledge, men were forewarned of possible events that would be either good or bad. The priests were then guided to offer sacrifice to the appropriate god, to encourage prosperity, or to avert disaster.

In the course of time other gods were created. The god who presided over the heavens was called An, he was also known as Anu. The god of the earth and the atmosphere above the earth was called Enlil; and Ea was the name of the god who governed the deep. The astronomers and the astrologers divided the heavens into three parts and this division became known as the Three Ways on the Heavens. Of the three ways Anu ruled the north, Enlil governed the middle, and Ea presided over the south.

Anu was the supreme god and he held the ultimate power, presiding over the entire universe, because everything revolved around him, the North Star. His centre of worship was in the temple called the House of Heaven and he possessed the Anutu, the heavenly power. The name of Anu was known as the One on High and he ruled with his two sons Enlil and Ea.

Enlil literally means Lord Wind. He was not considered to be the lord of the wind but was considered to be the wind itself. So whenever and wherever the wind blew, there was the god Enlil. He was also god of the earth, the air, and the storms. The Ekur temple where he was worshiped was known as the mooring place, where heaven was tethered to the earth and it was also called the Mountain House. He was worshipped as the god who watches over and cares for man.

Ea was known as the god of the deep, that is, god of water. He was the god of creation, knowledge, crafts, magic, and mischief. His centre of worship was in the city of Eridu. His star sign in the heavens was Iku, also known as the Field; in time the Greeks called this Pegasus. Ea travelled from Iku and was also associated with the star signs Suhurmasu and Gula. The temple where he was worshipped was called the House of Water. Because he was the god of water the two great rivers were seen to emanate directly from him, these are the River Tigris and the River Euphrates. This water, being creative, was seen to bring life and sustain life, making the fields fertile to produce crops. Ea was the lord of the Absu, the abyss where fresh water encircles and flows beneath the earth. This was the place where the dead were gathered.

Many more gods were created by man and some were replaced by newer creations. Ninursag was a fertility goddess known as the Lady of the Sacred Mountain. The goddess Inanna was known as the Queen of Heaven and was seen in the planet Dilbat; she is associated with love, beauty, sex, war, and power. Just like the planet Dilbat could set in the west and rise again in the east, so too could Inanna descend to the realm of the dead and rise again to life.

Some of the gods were male and some were female, some were good and some were evil. Some had to be appeased and others were praised. Some of the gods married each other and gave birth to sons and daughters who also became gods. The gods helped each other and some fought and killed each other. Some were popular and others fell out of favour. The gods who were worshipped more often, were the ones that were seen to most benefit the worshiper.

The zodiac was developed in the land that Nimrod governed. This zodiac was the map of heaven, where the gods were visible in the constellations of the stars. The original zodiac had between seventeen and eighteen periods. This was later changed to correspond with the twelve calendar months of equal days numbering thirty. This amounted to three hundred and sixty days in a year.

The zodiac sign for the month of Nisan was Agru, the image was the Hired Man and it was known to the Greeks as Aries, the Ram. The sign governing the month of Iyar was Gu, the image was the Bull of Heaven and was commonly called Pleiades (The Stars), it was also known as Taurus to the Greeks. Mastaba, commonly called the Twin, which was also called Gemini in Greece, was the sign for the month of Sivan. Allutu bore the symbol of the Crayfish and ruled the heavens during the month of Tamuz and was also known as Cancer to the Greeks.

The sign for the month of Av was Nesu, symbolized by the Lion and was also known to the Greeks as Leo. The sign governing the month of Elul was Sisinnu, represented by the Furrow and later the Barley Stalk and was also known as Virgo to the Greeks. Zibanitu, the Claws which became the Scales and was called Libra in Greece, was the sign for the month of Tishrei. Zuqaqipu bore the symbol of the Scorpion and ruled the heavens during the month of Cheshvan and was also known as Scorpio to the Greeks.

Pabilsag, the image of the Anzu Bird (a bird with the head of a lion) was the sign for the month of Kislev and was also known to the Greeks as Sagittarius. The sign governing the month of Tevet was Suhurmasu, an image of a Goat-Fish and was also known as Capricorn to the Greeks. Gula, the Great One (the Water Bearer god,

Ea) which was also called Aquarius in Greece, was the sign for the month of Shevat. And Zibbatu, the Tails of the Swallow ruled the heavens in the month of Adar and was also known as Pisces to the Greeks.

CHAPTER 7

Babel

In their defiance and rebellion against God, Ham and his children Cush, Mizraim, Phut, and Canaan and their families, along with the kings, princes, and governors showing allegiance to Nimrod came together. They decided to found a city and make it great upon the earth, to make it the greatest city ever built. In the heart of the city they planned to build a tower, taller than any tower that had ever been built. This tower was to reach heaven. In doing so their enemies would know how great they were and God would also know how great they were. In this way they would reign over the whole world. They were determined that they would not be scattered over the face of the earth, going to their allotted place as God had intended.

They came to the king and assembled before him. Nimrod listened to them as they laid out their plan; he received their scheme with delight. He granted them the authority to go ahead and find a suitable place to build this city. So all the families, numbering six hundred thousand men, assembled and went out in search of a place upon the earth, large enough to hold an enormous city. They searched throughout the earth and found an expanse of ground in the land of Shinar, by the River Euphrates.

They began to build the city and the tower, and the building material that they decided to use was brick. The slaves and the children of slaves were forced to make the bricks, pressing the ingredients into moulds to dry in the sun, before being fired in the furnace, where the heat baked them hard and strong. Thousands upon thousands of bricks were needed and the slaves were forced to work seven days every week with no day of rest. They were worked to the point of exhaustion and many of them died at a very young age. There was always a furnace burning to fire the bricks. The heat was ferocious and smoke always filled the sky.

For many years they continued to build the city and the tower. The tower grew so tall that it took an entire day for the bricks and mortar to reach from the base of the tower to the top. The men would ascend on one side and descend on the other so that progress might not be hindered. If a brick fell and broke, there would be so much weeping and frustration and whoever caused a brick to fall or break would be beaten. But if a man fell from the tower and died, not a tear was shed.

It was Nimrod who laid the foundation stone and established the cult of masonry. Using the symbolism of the plumb-line, dividers and square, all the masons had to participate in a series of ritualistic ceremonies, swearing an oath of allegiance to Nimrod, the Grand Master. Each mason was led blindfolded with his hands bound and a rope around his neck. Secret knowledge of the occult was revealed to him and he had to promise not to reveal this knowledge to anyone on fear of death. Should he break his oath of silence he would suffer the penalty of death by strangulation and disembowelment.

The families involved in the building of the city and tower were of three minds. The first group said, 'We will ascend into heaven and fight against God for destroying the earth by flood, so that he will never flood the world again. If he should flood the earth again, we will be high above the water.'

'We will ascend into heaven and place our own gods there and we will serve them,' said the second group.

The third group said, 'We will ascend into heaven and strike God with arrows and spears and destroy him.'

Yahweh Elohim knew their evil thoughts and could see all the works of their hands, the city and the tower that they were building. This work, known as Babel, the Gateway to the Gods, was a transgression, for in their pride they had fallen into sin. When they were gaining in height, some cast arrows toward heaven and these arrows fell down from heaven covered in blood.

'Surely we must have slain everyone in heaven,' they announced joyfully. 'We're almost there.'

The building continued now at a frantic pace, because heaven was within striking distance of an arrow. But it was Yahweh who covered their arrows in blood, to thwart their plans and lead them astray. Many times the builders paused to cast arrows into heaven and every time Yahweh returned the arrows in blood. The builders continued this ritual every day.

Yahweh laughed at them and turning to the seventy angels who stood before him in heaven he said, 'Come. Let us go down and confuse these men. Let us give them confusion, so they will not know what they are doing.'

So they descended from heaven and changed the language that everyone spoke into seventy different languages, so that one man might not understand the other. From that moment every man forgot the one language that they all used to speak and they began to speak in different tongues, as Yahweh Elohim gave to them. They could no longer understand each other. Instructions and orders could no longer be obeyed, because there was no understanding between them anymore. This led to fights among themselves and one turned on another and many killed each other. Many of them died in this manner.

'Of the three divisions,' said Yahweh, the Lord God., 'I will punish them according to their works and designs. Those who declared that they will ascend to heaven and fight against me; I will scatter them throughout the earth. Those who said that they will ascend to heaven and place their gods there and worship them; I will alter their appearance, changing the colour of their skin, so some will be as pale as the snow and others will be as black as the night sky. One will not be able to tolerate the heat and the other will not be able to tolerate the cold. For those who said that they will ascend to heaven and strike me with arrows and spears, so that they will kill me; I will strike them, each one through the hand of his neighbour and kill them.'

This, Yahweh, the Lord God, accomplished. Those remaining among them who witnessed these events as they were fulfilled understood the sin that they had committed. They realized the punishment that was about to fall upon them and they abandoned the building work and fled from that place. Yahweh scattered them over the face of the earth.

The earth opened its mouth and a third of the tower was swallowed up. Then a fire descended from heaven and destroyed another third from the face of the earth. All that remained of the tower was a third of its completed size. The circumference of the remaining third of the tower was a three days' walk. The number of men who died in the tower on that day is without number.

Many, however, refused to participate in the construction of the tower because they knew that it was an affront to God. Eber and his household refused to obey Nimrod. For this crime, those who refused to obey Nimrod were held under house arrest and were refused the means to buy and sell their goods. This caused great hardship for them and many suffered hunger. Yoktan, the son of Eber, was fortunate to escape with a company of men and they found refuge in the mountains. It is said that Yahweh did not alter the language for Eber and his family. It was retained in its original form and was named Hebrew after the name of Eber.

CHAPTER 8

Nations

When God dispersed the sons of men on account of their sin, he scattered them to the four corners of the earth. The men were dispersed with their families and settled according to their new languages, in the lands that had been allocated by Noah, many years ago, to his three sons and their descendants. Some of these people built cities and called them after their own names or the names of their children, or after the events that had occurred to them.

The sons of Japheth, the son of Noah, were scattered into many lands in the north of the world and there they settled according to their languages. These are the sons of Japheth; they are known as Gomer, Magog, Media, Javan, Tubal, Meshech, and Tiras.

The children of Gomer were known as the Gomerites and later became known as the Francum and were also known as the Gauls or Galatians in other tongues. They lived in Franza, which is also known as France; they settled by the River Senah, also called the River Seine. Gomer had three sons; Ashkenaz, Riphath and Togarmah.

Ashkenaz and his family became known as the Ashkenazi people, they were also known in another tongue as the Rheginians. Their territory stretched from the Ma'uk Sea in the north to the banks of the River Dubnee, which is also known as the River Danube.

Another name for the Ma'uk Sea is the Baltic Sea.

Riphath and his family became the Ripheans and the Bartonim, they were also known as the Paphlagonians. They lived in the land of Bartonia, by the River Ledah which flows into the Gihon Sea or Oceanus; this is Brittany by the River Loire which flows into the Atlantic Ocean. They had originally settled in the land of Armenia with Togarmah before migrating away from there.

Togarmah had ten sons and they became the Armenians and were also known as the Phrygians. Seven lived by the River Hithlah and the River Italac and their names are Buzar, Elicanum, Ragbib, Tarki, Bid, Zebuc, and Tilmaz. Three more of his sons, Ongal, Balgar and Parzunac lived by the River Dubnee.

The sons of Magog were Elichanaf and Lubal. The children of Magog, the Magogim, settled in the land called Scythia; in the course of time they migrated further north into Russia as far north as the Me'at Sea, which is also known as the Arctic Ocean. As their numbers grew they migrated further afield out to the west as far as the island of Ireland and out to the east, reaching Mongolia.

The sons of Media were Achon, Zeelo, Chazoni, and Lot. The land allotted to Media was in the north between the Jabus Sea and the Asken Sea, that is, the territory between the Caspian Sea and the Black Sea. However, Media did not want to go there. He had married a daughter of Shem and preferred to remain in the company of the Semites. He went to Elam, Ashur, and Arphachsad, the sons of Shem, and appealed to them to allow him to reside in their territory. They granted him his request and so Media settled with his family in the land of Curson, this is in the north-west of the land of Persia, that is today known as Iran and they were called the Orelum, also known as the Medes.

Javan and his people, known as the Javanim, settled in the land of Makdonia which also became known as Greece and Iona. Javan had four sons and they were called Elishah, Tarshish, Chittim, and Dodanim. The people of Elishah are known as the Almanim and are also called the Aeolians. They settled between the mountains of Job and Shibathmo; the Lumbardi are his descendants who conquered Italia. Tarshish and his family settled in the land known as Cilicia and the capital city of the land was given the name Tarsus.

The Romim are the family of Chittim and they dwelt on the island of Cethima which is also known as Cyprus and it was there where a city was established and was given the name Citius. They migrated from there and later settled in the valley of Canopia by the River Tibreu, also known as the River Tiber. Dodanim settled in the land of Bordna by the Great Sea, which is also considered to be the island of Rhodes in the Mediterranean Sea. This is the largest of the Dodecanese islands and the Trojans are descended from the Dodanim.

The sons of Tubal were Ariphi, Kesed, and Taari. Tubal established his home in Tuskanah by the river Pashiah; his people also became known as Iberes. They founded the city of Sabinah and were neighbours of the Romim. War broke out between them after the rape of the Sabine women by the Chittim.

The sons of Meshech were Dedon, Zaron, and Shebashni. The family of Meshech became known as the Shebashni and were also known as the Cappadocians; some of his family settled by the Jabus Sea where the River Cura flows into the River Tragon. In the course of time, some of his family migrated out to the north and founded a city named Mosocha, also called Moscow, after his own name Meshech. Some members of his family migrated to the east and settled in Mongolia.

The sons of Tiras were Benib, Gera, Lupirion, Gilak, Rushash, Cushni, and Ongolis. His family was known as the Rushash and his people were also called the Thracians in another tongue; they lived in the same territory as some of the family of Meshech, by the Jabus Sea. Some of the family of Tiras moved out to the east with members of the family of Meshech and they settled in the territory called Mongolia which was named after Ongolis

The descendants of Japheth settled in a vast area of land from as far to the west as Ireland, an island in the Gihon Sea, that is the same as the Atlantic Ocean; to Russia in the north bordering the Me'at Sea, that is the same as the Arctic Ocean; and out as far as Mongolia and China in the east Me'at Sea; also to the Rafa Mountains, bordering the land known as India in the south by the Gihon River, which is also known as the Ganges River.

The sons of Ham were given land in the continent known today as Africa. His son Cush, the father of the Cushites, settled in the land called Cush after his own name. In the course of time it became known as Ethiopia. Cush had five sons. Sheba fathered the Sabiens; Havila fathered the Getuli; the Sabthens were also known as the Astaborans and were fathered by Sabatah; Raamah fathered the people of Sheba and Dedan; and Sabtecha was the father of the Sabactens.

Mizraim, son of Ham, became the father of the people of Egypt. The children of Mizraim are the Ludim, Anamim, Lehabim, Naphtuchim, Pathrusim, Casluchim, and Caphturim. The Pathrusim and Casluchim intermarried and gave birth to the Azathim, the Gerarim, the Githim, the Ekronim, and the Pelishtim. The Pelishtim became known as the Philistines. They all founded cities of their own and lived by the River Sihor, which is also known as the River Nile.

The sons of Mizraim crossed over the border into the territory of Libya; these were the Ludim, Anamim, and Lehabim. The Naphtuchim and Caphturim also settled inside Libya near the border with Cush. These settlements inflamed the Libyans and conflict broke out between them. The Cushites forced the Libyans back, ending the conflict, but many people were killed. Fearing another war the Pelishtim decided to leave and they migrated to the island of Crete in the Great Sea. In the course of time they sailed from the island of

Crete and headed for the southern coast of the land inhabited by Canaan and his family and settled there.

Phut, son of Ham, fathered the people of Libya, and lived in the land bordering the west of Egypt, and the coast of the Great Sea. His sons were Gebul, Hadan, Benah, and Adan. Canaan, the son of Ham, refused to settle in the land to the west of Libya, that he received by lot from Noah. Instead he settled in the territory allotted to Shem, the son of Noah and his descendants. This land is north of Egypt and is on the coast of the Great Sea. He called this land Canaan after his own name and his descendants were known as the Canaanites. Canaan's sons were known as Zidon, Heth, Amori, Gergashi, Hivi, Arkee, Seni, Arodi, Zimodi, and Chamothi.

His first son Zidon founded a city in the northern territory and named it Sidon. Four of his sons founded the cities of Sodom, Gomorrah, Admah, and Zeboiim. Arodi settled in Arodus Island and Arce near the forests of Lebanon. Amori founded the city of Amathine, also known as Amath and his people were also known as the Epiphania. Seir, the son of Hur, son of Hivi, son of Canaan, founded the city of Seir, opposite Mount Paran, and he had seven sons and fathered the Seirites.

The sons of Shem were given the centre of the earth. These five sons were called Elam, Ashur, Aram, Lud, and Arphachsad. Elam had three sons called Shushan, Machul, and Harmon. The Elamites settled in the land called Elam after the name of their father and later became known as the Persians. Ashur had two sons named Mirus and Mokil, they all settled in a land which they called Assyria and built four large cities called Nineveh, Resen, Calach, and Rehobother.

Two years after the tower fell a man called Bela from the house of Ashur left the city of Nineveh. He wanted to escape the oppression of Nimrod and after searching for a long time came to the land to the south of the city of Sodom. There he built a small city and gave it the name Bela after his own name. The city was free from paganism and it became known as Zoar because it was a small city and Zoar means small.

Aram had four sons and they were named Uz, Chul, Gether, and Mash. Aram fathered the Aramites and they are also known as Syrians in another tongue. He founded the city Uz, naming it after his first son. Uz built the city of Trachonitus and the city of Damascus. Chul settled along with the sons of Togarmah in the land to the north called Armenia. Gether, son of Aram, fathered the Bactrians, and Mash, son of Aram, founded the Mesaneans. The Mesaneans were also known as Charax Spasini in another tongue. Lud fathered Pethor and Bizayon and his people were known as the Ludites and were also known as the Lydians in another tongue.

Arphachsad fathered the Arphachsites who were also called Chaldeans in another tongue. They settled and lived by the River Euphrates. His sons' names were Shelach, Anar, and Ashcol. Arphachsad's line of descendants leading to the birth of Abram are given that he fathered Shelah, who fathered Eber. It is said that the Hebrew language was named after Eber. Two sons came to Eber and one was named Yoktan because, in his day, the length of days of the sons of men were reduced. Yoktan fathered many sons and their names were Almodad, Shelaf, Chazarmoveth, Yerach, Hadurom, Ozel, Diklah, Obal, Abimael, Sheba, Ophir, Havilah, and Jobab. The sons of Yoktan moved out to the east and settled in the land of Havilah by the Cophen River. This land is known today as India.

Eber's other son was called Peleg and he was so named because Eber prophesied that in his day the sons of men would be divided by Noah and be given their allotted territory; and in the latter days the earth would also be divided by violent volcanic eruptions. Peleg became the father of Reu who fathered Serug. Serug became the father of Nahor who fathered Terah and Abram was born to Terah in the city of Ur, one thousand nine hundred and forty-eight years after the creation of Adam.

The sons of Noah continued to fill the earth with people and the migration of people throughout the world continues to this day. Some of the lands were already populated and well established before the fall of the Tower of Babel. Roots were laid down in Africa, Europe, and Asia as people in their respective families migrated and found places to settle and build cities.

CHAPTER 9

Hayk

Nimrod remained in the land of Shinar and he built four cities, naming them after the events that took place concerning them. His first city, he called Babel, because this is where God confounded the language of all in the earth. Erech was the name given to the second city because God dispersed the people from there. The third city he called Eched which means that a great battle took place there. The fourth city he named Calnah because his princes and mighty men transgressed and rebelled against God and they were consumed there.

In these cities Nimrod forced his people to live and he placed his princes there to govern them. Nimrod lived in Babel and re-established his reign over them all. His people called him Amraphel, because at the Tower of Babel, his men fell at his hands. Nimrod was not contrite and did not return to God, but he continued in wickedness. His son Mardon was even worse than his father and enticed the people to fall further into sin. Because of this there was a saying among the sons of men, 'From the wicked goes forth wickedness.'

There was much discontent at that time, regarding Nimrod and his wicked behaviour. The king of Elam distanced himself from Nimrod, the king of Babylon, and he refused to continue serving him. The name of the king of Elam was Kedorlaomer and he fought with the Hamites. He fought with the kings of Sodom, Gomorrah, Admah, and Zeboiim. He was victorious and he subdued them, putting them under his control. They were forced to pay him a tax every year.

Hayk, as he is known in the Armenian tongue, was the son of Togarmah, son of Gomer, son of Japheth, son of Noah. He served under the command of King Nimrod and for many years he remained loyal to him. Hayk's sons stood by him in service to the king. Looking at Nimrod with the crown of divinity upon his head, gave Hayk a bad taste in his mouth.

He remembered the day that Nimrod had placed the crown on his head with his own hands. All the people who were assembled cheered, they were chanting, singing, and dancing with joy. 'The god Nimrod reigns,' they chanted. 'May the king live. May the king live.'

The story was told that Nimrod had received a dream in which a crown clothed in black cloth, festooned with jewels, came down from heaven and landed on his head. Nimrod called for Sasan, the weaver, and commanded him to make such a crown. This he did and he presented it to the king. Holding the crown in his hands Nimrod beheld its beauty. Nimrod was pleased with the craftsmanship of the weaver Sasan, who received a rich reward.

Nimrod assembled his people and in a public ceremony placed the crown upon his head with his own hands. Sitting upon his throne the crown was visible on his head from a long distance away. The gilded horns of an ox were fastened to the left and to the right side of the crown and perched upon his head the jewels sparkled in the sunlight. He declared himself divine, commanding the people to worship him.

Convinced that Nimrod's empire was becoming more and more corrupt, Hayk, along with more than three hundred members of his family, decided to leave the service of the king. Hayk and his family travelled north to lands that had fallen by lot to the sons of Togarmah. They settled in a land which Hayk named after his first born son, Armaneak. There he built a city called Haykashen. Soon other settlements developed around this city.

Nimrod was not pleased that Hayk and his family had left his service. 'I'm the king and more than that, I'm god of the Babylonian Empire. Who is Hayk that he should walk away from me? I'm the king. He must obey me. When I command him to stay he must stay. He must serve his king and his god. His knee must bend to me. I'm divine and I must be worshipped.'

One of the sons of Nimrod named Bel said that he would find the whereabouts of Hayk, 'I will visit him and entreat him to return to serve you.'

With the approval of Nimrod, he set off on his journey. He brought a few men with him and they searched the travel route north, following the River Euphrates. After some time they came upon an outpost. This was governed by Kadmos, the grandson of Hayk. Kadmos made them welcome, according to tradition, by offering water to wash their feet. Then he made arrangements and prepared food and gave it to them to eat. He sent a messenger to Hayk asking him to come and meet the son of Nimrod, who had requested a meeting with him.

Hayk arrived and welcomed the men to his territory.

'My father Nimrod, King of Babylon and god of the Babylonian Empire, has sent me to speak to you,' announced Bel. 'By the command of the king, you are to abandon this place where you live and you must return to the city of Babel. There you will present yourself to the king and surrender yourself to his service.'

'No,' answered Hayk.

'No?' questioned Nimrod's son. 'What do you mean, no?'

'It's very simple,' said Hayk. 'My answer to you is no. I will not return to the city of Babel. I will not leave this place. This land is now my home.'

Bel, the son of Nimrod, flew into a rage, 'I demand that you obey your king and return to Babel.'

'Nimrod is no king of mine,' replied Hayk. 'He is nothing to me anymore. How can I serve a king who is corrupt and has, in time, become more evil? This place is my home. It has been allotted to me by Noah and I will not leave. I'm here to stay, both myself and my family.'

'How dare you speak to the king's envoy in such a manner,' said the son of Nimrod, who was red in the face. 'If you will not return willingly, then you will be forced to obey,' his nostrils were flaring. 'There will be severe consequences if you fail to obey.'

'Go home,' replied Hayk. 'I will never return to Babylon and my knee will never bend to that evil despot again.'

Kadmos was now on high alert and had the approaching road and all alternate mountain passes watched. Sure enough, the day came when, in the month of Av, when the summer fruits had been tasted, a large body of men was witnessed heading north to Hayk's territory. Hayk had plenty warning of the advance of the army of Nimrod from Babylon. The Armenian army assembled on the shore of Lake Van where Hayk encouraged them. 'Be fearless and stand your ground. Show your strength and defeat Nimrod's army. Or die trying. Nothing, let me remind you, would be worse than being enslaved by the Babylonians. The outcome for us will be torture and death if Babylon wins the battle.'

The invading army was discovered in a mountain pass near Julamerk and Hayk set a trap for them there. The same son of Nimrod returned, leading the Babylonian army. He was determined to bring Hayk and his family back to Babylon as slaves. But Hayk had plans of his own.

Hayk was a skilful warrior and was expert with the bow. Seeking out the son of Nimrod, Hayk raised his bow and pointed his arrow. He watched carefully, listening to the wind and feeling it toss his long curly hair. His men remained silent, waiting for the command from Hayk. He waited patiently. The invaders did not know that they were being watched. There was no hurry on Hayk's part. He judged the direction and speed of the wind; he calculated the distance to his target and adjusted the elevation of his bow. His muscles were strong and when the moment was right, with all of his might he pulled back on his bow, his familiar instrument of war, and released the arrow.

Silently, with ferocious speed, the arrow flew through the air. The son of Nimrod dropped dead before his army. They were overcome with shock. None of them were ready for battle because they were unaware of the presence of the Armenian army. Hayk and his men had remained hidden in strategic places, waiting for the right moment to rise up and attack.

'This is the right moment,' said Hayk. 'Attack them now.'

The Armenians rose up from their place of concealment and descended upon the dismayed Babylonian army. The Armenians destroyed them. This battle became known as Dyutsaznamart, which means the Battle of Giants. The hill where Nimrod's son and his soldiers fell was called Gerezmank, which translates as tombs. The corpse of Nimrod's son was embalmed and Hayk had him buried in a high place, which was visible to all.

CHAPTER 10

Terah

In his fiftieth year Abram left the house of Noah and returned to the house of his father, Terah. In all the years that Abram was away, Terah remained the prince of the host of Nimrod, the king of Babylon. Upon returning to his father's house, Abram was dismayed to see the twelve gods in his father's temple. His heart sank at the sight of them. Twelve idols, made from wood, stone, and clay stood glorified, each one on a shelf in its own alcove in the wall.

Being in the house of Noah for most of his life, Abram knew Yahweh Elohim, the one true God, and he walked in his way. He knew that Yahweh Elohim was with him. Abram opened his heart and cried out to God for help. 'How am I to help my father to mend his ways, to abandon these false gods and to walk in the path of righteousness?'

Abram's anger burned within him and he was determined to turn his father away from wickedness. He determined that within the next few days these idols would be destroyed. Leaving the temple in his father's house he stepped outside and came upon Terah, sitting in the outer court with the servants of his household.

Sitting before his father, Abram asked him, 'Where is God? Where is he who created heaven and earth and all the creatures upon it, the birds in the air and the fish in the sea? And where is the God who created the sons of man who walk upon the earth, including you and me?'

Terah was stunned by such a question. He did not know what had provoked Abram to ask such a thing. 'Why they are all around us. They are here in this house. They are in the temple. Have you not seen them?'

'Show them to me that I may see them and understand them.'

Rising up, Terah led Abram back into the house and brought him into the temple, where a lamp, filled with oil, was burning before the idol of the present month of the year, according to the star signs in the heavens. The room was full of idols, some large and some small. Some were made of stone, some of clay, and some of wood.

'Behold the gods,' said Terah, gesturing with his hand. 'These are the gods who created heaven and earth and all the creatures of the land, the sea, and the air. These are the ones who created the sons of men, including you and me. These are the gods who give us success and fruitfulness and riches and power and happiness. These are the gods who watch over us every day.'

In saying this Terah bowed down to his gods and left the temple, with Abram following him out. Abram parted company with his father Terah and decided to go and find his mother Amthelo. He wanted to speak with her. When he found her he asked her if she believed in the idols in his father's temple.

'Yes, my son Abram. I follow the gods of your father Terah. Every month we worship the god who is represented in the stars of the night sky. We place his image on the shelf in the alcove and burn a lamp before him as we offer up our praise.'

'What of the God of heaven and earth, the creator of the whole world? What of him?'

At this point their conversation was interrupted by the arrival of

Haran, the eldest brother of Abram.

'Shalom to you, mother,' said Haran, as he embraced his mother.

'Shalom Haran,' she smiled. 'Your brother Abram is here.'

With a beaming smile Haran embraced his younger brother Abram, who he hardly knew at all. Haran had only glimpsed him briefly after his birth, because only three days later, Abram was taken away into hiding. Tears filled his eyes as he embraced his younger brother.

'Shalom Abram. It's good to meet you again after so many years.'

'Shalom Haran. Peace be with you. I have come home from the house of Noah.'

'How is father Noah? You know, in all my years I've never met him.'

'Nor have I,' announced his mother Amthelo. 'Sit down, Abram, and tell us all about your time in his household.'

They spoke for many hours. Abram was eager to speak about God. Noah was a good and upright man, who never wavered in his faith and continued to follow Yahweh Elohim, the one true God. He refused to turn to worship false gods. Abram's mother and brother Haran worshipped the idols in his father's temple. They did not know of Yahweh Elohim, the one true God.

'The one God divided himself and came down to put some of himself into each one of your father's gods,' said Amthelo. 'The one God is here but he is of a different nature in each one of the gods.'

'Can he see you?' asked Abram.

'Of course. With his eyes.'

'But the eyes are made of wood, or clay, or stone. Have the eyes even blinked?'

Both Amthelo and Haran laughed.

'No they haven't,' answered Amthelo.

'Then how can these idols be God?'

'This is our belief.'

Haran smiled to himself. He was enjoying this conversation with his younger brother. 'No harm to stir up the pot,' he thought to himself. Then he said to Abram, 'Why don't you ask the gods a question? They are in father's temple.'

'I will prepare a savoury meat offering,' suggested his mother.

Amthelo called a servant to her and gave instructions for a sheep from the flock to be slaughtered and prepared as a savoury meat offering to the gods. When the meat offering was ready, it was served up on a dish and placed in the presence of the gods. Haran accompanied his brother Abram into the temple but their father was away and not aware of their presence in the temple.

So Abram sat and waited and nothing happened. The savoury meat offering remained on the dish and the gods remained on their plinths, in their alcoves in the wall. The gods made no sound, no movement, and the meat offering remained on the dish, untouched, getting cold, wasting away.

'Speak to me,' asked Abram. But there was no answer. 'Can you hear me? I have set before you a savoury meat offering, so that you can listen to me. Are you real?' he paused. 'Can your ears hear and can your eyes see? Can you smell the savoury meat offering that has been prepared and set down before you? Does it not make your mouth water?' There was no response. 'Why don't you reach out your hand and take from the dish and eat? This dish has been prepared especially for you.'

There was no sound, no blink of the eye, no flaring of nostrils to take in the smell of the savoury meat offering. No mouth opened and no hand reached out to take the food.

'Perhaps you don't like to be watched while you are eating. I will leave you now and I will return later to remove the empty dish,' said Abram as he rose to leave. Haran, his brother, followed him out.

'There's no god in that room,' announced Abram.

'Why do you say that, Abram?

'Can you not see? There are figures carved out of wood and stone and figures moulded in clay in that room. The wood is cut from a tree, but a tree is not God. A tree didn't create you and me. The stone comes from the mountain and the mountains can't create us. There are other idols made from clay and the clay comes from the soil of the earth. The clay did not create the sons of man.'

Haran was amused to see Abram so fired up.

'None of these idols created the sun, the moon and the stars, nor the land, the ocean, and the sky. They didn't create the beasts of the earth, nor the fish in the sea, nor the birds in the air. And they certainly didn't create the sons of man. They didn't create you. I was not created by them.'

'So who did? Who created all these things?'

'The one true God did. His name is Yahweh Elohim. He created everything. The whole world and everything in it. I pray to him. He is the only God who is real. These things,' he made a gesture with his hand, 'these idols made by the hand of man would not exist unless the craftsman had fashioned them with hammer and chisel. How can they be God if they are made by man? It is God who creates man, not man who creates God.'

'That sounds reasonable, I suppose,' said Haran. Inwardly his heart was stirring. Abram had made a good point and had given him something to consider. 'That savoury meat offering is making me hungry,' he announced. Putting his arm around Abram's shoulders he said, 'Let's go, my young brother, and eat,' so off they went, laughing and joking, enjoying each other's company.

Abram and Haran returned to the temple after they had eaten. There they found that the savoury meat offering had not been touched at all.

'Their lips are clean,' laughed Haran. 'And there are no crumbs at their feet.'

'Maybe there wasn't enough food for them all to eat and they were embarrassed, not wanting to appear greedy.'

'Why not prepare another savoury meat offering for them tomorrow?' suggested Haran. 'They will certainly be a lot hungrier by then.'

'That's exactly what I'll do,' said Abram.

The next day Abram approached his mother and told her that the gods did not eat any of the food that had been prepared for them. 'They must be very hungry by now.'

Smiling in agreement, Amthelo said, 'So you want me to prepare more food for the gods to eat?'

'Yes. That's right. But this time we must present them with much more. Why not slaughter three sheep from the flock this time and serve them a much larger and satisfying dish. Surely this will delight them and they will eat and be satisfied.'

Amthelo arranged for the much larger dish to be prepared and when it was ready she presented it to Abram. This dish was set before the gods and presented to them as a savoury meat offering. Abram sat down in their presence. Haran was not with him this day and his father Terah was not aware that Abram was in the temple.

All day Abram remained in the presence of the gods and he observed that they could not see the meat. Neither could they smell the meat nor taste it. Not one of them reached out his hand to take the meat, to eat it. In the evening Abram cried out in frustration.

'What foolishness is this? My father has wasted his life

worshipping wood, stone, and clay instead of Yahweh Elohim, the one true God, creator of heaven and earth. Instead he is guided by idols who have eyes that can't see, ears that can't hear, mouths without speech, hands with no feeling, and legs which can't move. And yet my father trusts in them.'

In anger, Abram left the room and went in search of an axe. Taking the axe in his hand he returned to the temple. Swinging the axe wildly, he smashed all of the idols except the largest one. He split the wooden idols down the middle, broke the idols made of clay into small pieces, and smashed the stone idols.

When he had finished venting his anger and frustration on the idols, he placed the axe in the hands of the largest idol. This one he did not break at all. It was the largest of all the idols in the temple in his father's house. Abram left the room. At that same moment, Terah arrived home. Hearing the commotion in the temple he went to investigate.

He met his son Abram inside the door. 'Abram. Is everything alright? I heard a commotion when I was outside, just as I was entering the house.'

Without saying a word, Abram brushed past him and sat outside under the night sky. Terah, seeing the frustration in Abram's eyes, rushed into the temple and was hit by the devastation. In all his days he had never witnessed anything like it. Scanning the room Terah could see the gods smashed to pieces. The room was littered with their remains. In the hands of the largest god, which was whole and free from damage, he could see the axe. Before the remaining idol was the dish of savoury meat offering. None of it had been eaten.

When Terah saw this destruction, he was so stunned that he was unable to move. Then his anger flared up within him and he realised that Abram must be responsible for this destruction. He ran through the house and eventually found Abram, sitting outside in the courtyard, looking up at the stars.

Approaching Abram he asked, 'What is this that you have done to my gods?'

'I have done nothing to your gods, my father.'

'You have smashed my gods and have broken them up into little pieces.'

'You're mistaken, my father. It wasn't me. I prepared a dish for them, a savoury meat offering, and I set it before them. As soon as I placed the dish before them, they all stretched out their hands together to eat the meat. But they all reached out before the Great One had reached out to take the meat.'

Terah, speechless, looked aghast at his son Abram.

'Because they were disrespectful of the great god, and reached out before him, his anger was kindled toward them and he went and took the axe that was in the house. He returned with the axe and he swung it and struck them all until they were reduced to little pieces. I quickly left the room for fear that he would strike me as well. I'm sure that the axe is still in his hands.'

Terah was furious upon hearing the words of his son Abram. In his anger he screamed, 'What kind of a tale is this that you tell me? How can you expect me to believe that? These gods are made of wood, stone, and clay. They have no life in them to do all that you accuse them of doing,' he paused for breath. 'The largest god smashed them all? No. No. It was you,' he pointed his accusing finger at Abram. 'You took the axe in your hand and smashed them all.'

'How then, can you serve these gods that have no life in them? You yourself had them made by the hand of man, you even fashioned some of them by your own hand. Can any of these idols that you trust, deliver you? Can they set you free from your enemies? Can they fight any of your battles for you? Can they hear your prayers at all, or give you advice? No. They can't. After all, they are just made from wood, stone, and clay and can neither see nor hear.'

'Before you made the wooden gods, what were they? Were they not tall trees rooted in the ground? The trees were tall and beautiful to behold with many branches and leaves and flowers and fruits, giving shelter to the birds of the air and the tiny insect creatures. They provided shade for the weary from the intense heat of the noonday sun. The roots of the trees spread far and wide under the earth, anchoring them in their place and aiding them in the search for moisture and goodness to sustain them.

'Then what did you do? You took an axe and with violence you cut down the trees and with your skill you cut out a shape and fashioned an image. You cut out a figure of a man with a body and head and you placed him on a pedestal in your temple. There, to this day, you bow down before this idol and you worship it. You worship this product of your own making. The life it had was in the sap of the tree. But when you cut down the tree the sap dried up and now there is no life left in it. It has dried up. It is dead.'

Terah was reeling and unable to speak.

'So why do you and the men of this land bother to worship these idols?' asked Abram. 'You have all been led astray. You are so foolish that you can't see the truth. Your eyes can't see the truth, your mind has been blinded with lies. There was a time when everyone knew of Elohim, the one true God. But the devil leads men astray. He tells lies and he tries to convince everyone that God is not real. And now you serve wood and stone. For this you have brought a great evil upon yourself and your family.'

'I've served these gods all of my life,' shouted Terah who was not used to being spoken to in this manner. 'My own father, Nahor, also served these gods.'

'This land was given to Arphachsad, the son of Shem, son of Noah,' answered Abram. 'And he worshipped the one true God.

Rightfully, this land is yours, you have inherited it from him. So why is this usurper, Nimrod, ruling your kingdom?' he paused for an answer but none came. 'I will tell you why. Your forefathers abandoned Yahweh Elohim, the one true God, and went astray, worshipping false gods. Because of this, Yahweh Elohim surrendered them to their own foolish desires and as a consequence of their sin, they lost their inheritance. In effect, you have given what is rightfully yours over to Nimrod, the son of Cush. Nimrod should be living in the land of Cush, not in the land of Shinar. You should be the king of this land.'

'Nimrod is a mighty warrior,' answered Terah. 'And this strength was bestowed upon him by the gods. His power came to him when he unlocked the power hidden by the Watchers. This secret knowledge was written down and preserved. The truth was carved on stone and it was Ham, the son of Noah, who discovered it. He has passed on this secret wisdom to all of his sons. This secret knowledge enables us to control the spirits, so that they will do as we ask them.'

'These spirits that you speak of,' answered Abram, 'they can't be controlled by you. It is you who are deceived and you are being controlled by them. These are the same wicked spirits that led our forefathers into sin. Our forefathers turned from Elohim the one true God and they sought the wisdom of the deceiver, the devil and his wicked angels. The wickedness of these people became so great that God decided to wipe them off the face of the earth. So he sent the flood. In order to save mankind, he chose one man and his family to preserve humanity. This man you know well. This man, Noah, has been walking in righteousness all the days of his life. For this reason, he and his family were rescued by God.'

'How can I stop worshipping the gods?' protested Terah. 'This is what I've known all the days of my life. I've inherited this faith from my own father, Nahor.'

'Father, I love you,' answered Abram. 'And I want to keep you safe and well and free from evil and error. I must do what I feel is right in my heart. Father Noah has been good to me, he has taught me the truth and I have grown up in his ways. If I neglect to do all that's in my power to save you then I will forfeit my own life.'

In saying this he sprang up onto his feet and rushed into the house. Entering his father's temple, he took the axe from the hands of the largest idol; with all of his might he swung the axe, destroying the idol, breaking it into little pieces.

Terah was too late to prevent him from carrying out this act of destruction. Abram quickly left the house and Terah fell down on his knees and wept. He was broken hearted, believing that Abram hated him and wanted to destroy him. Terah was mindful of all that he had done to rescue Abram from death at the time of his birth.

'Now look at what he has done,' he said to Amthelo. 'This son, who I rescued from the jaws of death, has destroyed the gods that I love and worship. How could he do such a thing to me?'

Terah went to bed that night with a heavy heart and tears in his eyes. He could not sleep. His mind went over the events of the day and his imagination explored what might transpire between himself and Abram in the morning. By dawn he had reached a decision and he knew what he would do. Abram had to pay.

CHAPTER 11

Betrayal

Terah went to Nimrod, the king. To the prince of idolatry, he revealed the course of events that had taken place in his own house. He told Nimrod that the child that he had slain fifty years ago was not his own son Abram, but a child born to one of his servants.

'Now, my lord and king,' said Terah, 'I appeal to you to pass judgement on my son, according to the law of the land. You are wise and know how to administer justice, for these crimes committed against me.'

As soon as he revealed the truth to Nimrod, he felt a pain in his heart, a regret at revealing what he should have kept secret. But his heart burned with anger toward his son, for the damage that had been done to his gods and for Abram's wicked behaviour toward his father.

So Nimrod sent three of his servants to the house of Terah, to arrest Abram and bring him before the king. The king's servants found Abram in his father's courtyard and presented him to the king as they were instructed. Nimrod sat in the company of some of his princes and wise men, who were there that day. The charges of the crime against his father and against his father's gods were put to Abram.

'Now,' asked Nimrod, 'how do you answer these charges?'

'It wasn't me who destroyed the gods,' answered Abram. 'When my father entered the room, he discovered the axe in the hand of the largest god. It was the largest god who destroyed the other gods. He did this because the lesser gods showed disrespect, by reaching out their hands for the savoury meat offering before him. In his anger he punished them, by destroying them with the axe. I broke the large god with the axe for the crime that he committed.'

The king said, 'And did they have the power to speak and eat and act, as you said?'

'If there's no power in them, why do you serve them and worship them at all? This worship of idols that you've imposed upon these people is foolishness. You've caused them to go astray. There's only one God and he is Yahweh Elohim, the one that must be worshipped. What you've given to these people is nothing more than a lie.'

'Who are you to pass judgement on me? I am the one who administers judgement in my kingdom.'

'I am not passing judgement on you,' said Abram. 'It is the one true God, Yahweh Elohim, who passes judgement—'

'Enough,' interrupted Nimrod. 'I've heard enough nonsense from you.' He motioned to his servants, 'Take him away and put him into prison.' Turning to Abram he said, 'I will make a decision concerning your fate. You will be punished, and you will be punished most severely. Perhaps you'll end up like your father's gods.' He smiled and Abram was taken away.

Meanwhile Nimrod ordered an assembly of all his kings, princes, judges, and governors. The sages, soothsayers, and magicians came also, at the command of the king. They came before Nimrod who sat on his throne. They listened intently to the story that the king conveyed to them, concerning Abram and his father Terah.

'I ordered Abram to be put into prison and he is there these past ten days. He spoke to me without respect, and he showed no humility before me. He is proud and haughty, and he did not flinch when I told him that he would be punished most severely for his conduct toward his father and his father's gods. He didn't listen to reason, assuming that only he is right and everyone else is wrong. So now I put it to you to pass judgement on him concerning the laws of our empire.'

'He has reviled the king,' spoke one.

'Anyone who reviles the king must be hanged upon a tree until he's dead,' said another.

'But because he has done all of these things, like you have said,' reasoned another. 'Because he despised our gods and destroyed them, and because he abused his own father in this manner, there is only one punishment that fits the crime.'

They all agreed and said, 'The law in this matter states that he must be burned to death.'

Nimrod nodded his head in agreement.

'Let us, your servants, kindle a fire in the brick furnace and let Abram be cast into it,' suggested one of the wise men.

'Let us be sure that the furnace is good and hot. It must burn for three days and three nights before he is thrown into it,' said another.

So the fire was kindled in the brick furnace in Casdim at Nimrod's command. It burned for three days and three nights as directed and the people gathered.

The magicians and wise men approached Nimrod and they declared, 'O great King Nimrod, is this man Abram not the same child, who at his birth was written in the stars? Is this not the same star, the new star that rose in the east and travelled across to the four corners of the heavens and swallowed up four stars in its path?'

'We warned you then of his evil rise to power. This happened fifty years ago.'

Listening to these men, Nimrod commanded that the written

records of fifty years ago should be found. So they were found and the record was written, how the same astronomers and astrologers had warned Nimrod of this same son born to Terah, the greatest of all the princes. The record stated that this child was killed and posed no further threat.

Nimrod was furious and ordered Terah to be brought before him. When Terah arrived, Nimrod told him what the astronomers and astrologers had said concerning the events of fifty years ago.

'Now tell me the truth about the events that took place,' Nimrod looked very stern.

Seeing how angry the king was, Terah trembled in fear.

'If you speak truly,' said Nimrod. 'I will acquit you of this crime.'

'Yes, my lord, what your sages and wise men tell you is the truth. I did transgress and I mocked you by exchanging my son for another child, born to one of my handmaids. You killed the wrong child. I hid my son from you, so that you might not know that he still lived.'

'How could you do such a thing, to disobey my orders and deceive me by giving me a child that was not your own? And you took the value for him in silver and gold.'

'It is because I was overcome with love for my own son and anything else was better than allowing him to be killed. That is why I deceived you, by giving you a different child.'

Nimrod came down from his throne and stood so close to Terah, forcing him to step back. 'You will tell me the truth. Now.'

Terah could feel the spittle from Nimrod's mouth on his face.

'Who advised you to do this? Do not hide the truth from me or you will die. Give me his name.'

Terah hesitated. He did not know what to say. He thought to himself, 'If I tell Nimrod that it was my own decision, then I will suffer the same fate as Abram. If I falsely accuse someone else, then that person will die for a crime they did not commit.'

'Tell me,' roared Nimrod, showering Terah's face with spit.

Terah was shaking with fear. 'It was my eldest son, Haran.' Immediately the regret of his own words fell heavily upon him. 'Why did I accuse my son Haran? Why did I not accuse one of my enemies?' he said to himself.

Haran had done no such thing. Terah's fear for his own life was far greater than his love for his son Haran. What was done could not be undone, unless he confessed his own guilt to Nimrod. Terah cowered before Nimrod who had such power over him. The words of Abram, spoken to him only a few days ago, kept rolling around in his mind.

'This land was given to Arphachsad, the son of Shem, son of Noah, and he worshipped the one true God. Rightfully this land is yours, you have inherited it from him … You have given what is yours over to Nimrod … You should be the king of this land.'

'What have I done?' he said to himself. 'I never should have listened to Nimrod, and followed his ways. But then, what else do I know? I followed in the steps of my own father, Nahor. If I change, if I follow Abram's God, will he deliver me from Nimrod? Will he rid this land of Nimrod and restore it to me? Abram is going to die in the fire. Not even his God can rescue him from that.'

'Your son, Haran,' said Nimrod. 'He must die through fire. He will be thrown into the brick furnace, along with Abram. The two will die together. Haran has rebelled against me, and he deserves to die for giving bad advice to you. Your life will be spared, because you have spoken the truth.'

'The truth,' exclaimed Terah to himself. 'The truth is far from me. All I have spoken is lies and the price for these lies is the death of my two sons.' His heart was pierced and he could not help himself, but he broke down before Nimrod. His knees buckled under him and he wept bitterly.

Haran was intrigued by Abram, his younger brother. The incident in the temple in his father's house had amused him. He was raging with himself that he had not witnessed the destruction of the gods. Abram was so full of life, talking about the one true God, and Haran had listened so intently to the stories that Abram told of Noah. Haran was half inclined to learn more about this one true God, but he needed more time to consider the matter. This he kept to himself.

He knew of Abram's arrest and he could not quite understand his father's motives. 'Why would my father surrender Abram to Nimrod? Does he love the gods, made of wood, stone, and clay, more than his own son, made of flesh and blood? If it happens to be true that Abram is right, then father loves nothing more than a lump of wood and no god at all. If the one true God is real, as Abram believes, and if Abram is rescued by his God then I will join Abram and follow his God. But if Abram should perish, at the hand of Nimrod, I will keep silent. Why should I stir up trouble for myself? I will continue to pretend to worship the gods.'

While he was deep in thought three men arrived, looking for Haran. 'We've been sent here to take you to King Nimrod. You must come with us immediately.'

'What's all this about?' he asked.

'You must present yourself to the king and answer to your crimes.'

'I've committed no crime. What have I done?'

'You've deceived the king, and for this crime you must pay.'

'I've committed no crime against the king. In my entire life, I've never even met the king.'

'Come with us. Now.'

He resisted, but they were stronger than him and they forced him to comply. They hauled him before Nimrod, who read out the accusation of rebellion to the commands of the king. Haran made protest to the charges because he knew that he had never rebelled against the king. He cried innocence, but his father, his accuser, was not present to hear his cry of innocence.

'It's not true,' said Haran repeatedly. 'I know nothing of this.'

'Sentence has been passed upon you, Haran, son of Terah. For your crime the punishment will be the same as that of your brother, Abram. For this crime, you will be thrown into the furnace that has been burning for three days and three nights.' With a gesture from Nimrod's hand, Haran was hauled away to the brick furnace in Casdim.

All the kings, princes, governors, magicians, and sages gathered with all the inhabitants of the land to see the execution by fire. About nine hundred thousand men were there. Women and children also gathered and every rooftop, wall, and tower was crowded with people who had come for the spectacle.

Abram and Haran were brought to the brick furnace and the citizens of Shinar observed them. The two brothers were stripped of their garments, except their under garments. Then their hands and feet were bound with linen cords. When they were bound, the servants of the king raised them up and cast them into the fiery furnace. The crowd roared with delight upon seeing them thrown into the furnace.

Twelve servants cast them into the brick furnace and the heat was so intense that they too were overcome by the flames and died. This was a delightful spectacle and the crowd roared with laughter. Never before had they been as entertained as they had this day.

Haran died immediately when they cast him into the brick furnace, because his heart was not right with God. His body was quickly reduced to a heap of ashes. To everyone's amazement, Abram could clearly be seen in the brick furnace. For those who were far back this could not be seen. But Yahweh Elohim, because he loved Abram, came down into the furnace with Abram and delivered him from the fire. Abram was not consumed by the heat.

The linen cords that had been used to bind his hands and his feet were burned by the flames. His under garments did not burn, nor did Abram. Not even a single hair upon his head was singed by the flames. Abram could be seen walking about in the flames, and he continued to walk about for three more days and three more nights.

The people were greatly amazed and some of the servants of the king went to Nimrod's palace and told him that Abram lived. The king considered them fools and he dismissed them, but more came, telling him the same news that Abram lived. Nimrod sent more of his servants to witness the scene. They returned with the same news.

'Abram lives. We have seen him, O king. With our own eyes we have seen Abram alive, walking about among the flames in the brick furnace in Casdim.'

'The linen cords that bound his hands and feet have been burned up,' said another. 'But his under garments have not been burned. He walks around freely in the flames.'

When King Nimrod heard these words, his heart sank and he would not believe them. 'I must see this for myself. I can't believe what you're telling me.'

So Nimrod rose up and travelled to the brick furnace in Casdim, to see for himself if what his servants had told him was true. Sure enough the king looked and there he saw with his own eyes, Abram walking to and fro in the brick furnace amidst the flames. Haran, he could not see, because he had been consumed by the fire.

Perplexed at this sight, Nimrod ordered his servants to remove Abram from the furnace. The king's servants approached the furnace to release Abram, but the heat was so intense that they were forced to back away. They ran away from the flames and Nimrod rebuked them.

'Take him out of the furnace,' he barked. 'Do it now, or you will die.'

Fearing Nimrod more than the flames from the brick furnace, they approached again to bring out Abram. The flames covered them, and the faces of eight men were so badly injured that they fell down dead. Nimrod came to his senses and realised that no one could remove Abram from the fire. So he called out to Abram instead. 'O servant of the God of heaven,' he called. 'Abram, come out of the fire and come here before me.'

Hearing the voice of the king, Abram climbed out of the brick furnace and presented himself before Nimrod. All were amazed upon seeing Abram climb out of the fire. There were no burn marks upon him. No scorching of the skin, no soot upon his garments. The only thing that was burned was the linen cord that bound his hands and his feet.

'Tell me,' asked Nimrod, nervously. 'How is it possible that you have not been consumed by the fire? This is impossible,' Nimrod's voice trembled. No one had ever witnessed him shaking like this before.

Abram answered, 'It was the God of heaven and earth, Yahweh Elohim, that saved me from the flames. He is the one true God, and only he has the power to save. Because I love him and place my trust in him, he decided to come down and rescue me, to save me from the fire into which you cast me. It was not because of anything that I have done, that I deserved to be saved, but because of his great love and mercy for me. That is why he saved me. I didn't die in this way, at this time, because God has a plan for my life and I have not yet fulfilled his plan.'

Haran was nowhere to be seen, since he had been consumed by the flames. All that remained of him was a heap of ashes. Haran was eighty-two years old when he died in the fire in Casdim. On the day that he died, Haran's children lost their father, his son Lot and his two daughters, Milca and Sarai. They mourned for their father.

King Nimrod knelt down, bowing his head to the ground before Abram. All the inhabitants of the land, seeing their king prostrate himself before Abram, did likewise. But Abram told them stop.

'Do not worship me, for I am only a servant of the God of heaven and earth. And do not worship your false gods, because they will always disappoint you. Worship Yahweh Elohim, the one true God, because he is the only one who deserves worship and praise. Serve him and give up your sinful ways. He is the one who has the power to deliver man from all his woes. He is the one who has created you and has given life to you. Trust in him.'

Nimrod was so overcome, he considered that Abram was a god and he showered many gifts upon him. The princes, governors, judges, sages, and magicians all gave gifts to Abram. He received silver, gold, and pearls, jewels of many kinds. He left that place and returned to his father's house in Ur. The king also gave Abram many servants, including the two head servants from the palace, Oni and Eliezer, of the city of Damascus. These went with Abram to his father's house and became his own servants. Abram increased in wealth, with cattle, sheep, donkeys, and camels. Three hundred men joined Abram that day. Abram turned the hearts of all who followed him, to love and serve the one true God, Yahweh Elohim.

Lot, Milca, and Sarai now had no father and Abram felt a responsibility to care for them. Milca married Abram's brother, Nahor, and Abram adopted Lot, his nephew. Abram married Sarai, his brother's daughter. Sarai was barren, she was unable to conceive and bear children.

Living in his own house was never the same for Terah. He lived in fear of Abram because he had never witnessed anyone leave the furnace unscathed. The twelve idols that had been destroyed by Abram were never replaced. Terah never entered the temple room again but Abram stripped the room from all the debris and used the room to pray to Yahweh Elohim. In this room he taught all of his followers about the one true God, according to the teaching that he had received from Noah.

The anger and frustration and the rage boiled up within Terah concerning the destruction that Abram had brought upon his twelve gods. At the same time he was overcome by the shame of his betrayal of his two sons to Nimrod. He never revealed his betrayal of Haran. He held his tongue regarding this truth. What was clear in his mind was that Abram's God was truly powerful, but Terah was not able to abandon the gods that he still loved. He had a lot of soul searching to do and the turmoil in his mind was fierce.

CHAPTER 12

Dream

Two years after Abram came out of the fire, Nimrod fell asleep whilst sitting upon the throne in Babel. In his dream, he was standing with his princes and army, opposite the brick furnace in Casdim. Looking up, he saw a man climbing out of the brick furnace. This man looked like Abram. He came and stood before the king with a drawn sword in his hand. He leaped forward, toward the king, to strike him dead. But the king ran as fast as he could because he was in great fear. The man threw an egg, which landed on the king's head. This egg turned into a great river.

All of the king's army was overcome by the tumult of the river and they sank in the water and drowned. The king barely escaped, with three of his men. As they were in flight, the king took note of the appearance of these men. They were clothed in princely garments, like they were three kings. So Nimrod and these three kings were still running, to escape drowning in the river. Suddenly the river turned back into an egg. Out of the egg then came a small bird which flew into the face of the king and pecked out the king's eyes.

The king woke up from his dream and he was greatly distressed. Terror had seized him and, after he woke up, he summoned his sages, wise men, and magicians to him. When they assembled before him, he told them of his dream during the night. He told them to give him an interpretation of the dream, to put his mind at rest.

The wise men considered the king's words and consulted each other for the true interpretation of the dream. One of these servants, whose name was Anuki, answered the king, giving the true meaning of the dream.

'My lord and king, this is the evil that we foretold to you fifty-two years ago. In the sky, we saw a new star rise up in the east, and quickly cross to the four corners of the heavens. This new star swallowed up four stars in its path. These four stars are the three kings with you in the dream. The star that swallows them up is none other than Abram. The evil of Abram and his seed will spring up against you in days to come. If Abram lives, then he and his children and all who follow him in his household will rise up against you and fall upon the king and his army. Your army will be destroyed, but you will escape with three kings of the earth.'

Anuki paused, allowing Nimrod to take in the severity of his words. 'But in time you will be in great peril. The river that turned back into an egg, and the young bird that came out of the egg, is none other than the seed of Abram. A young boy will strike and slay the king in days to come. This, my lord, is your dream and this is the true interpretation of it. To this interpretation do all of your servants present in this place agree.'

'So, my lord, listen to the advice that your servants have given you today. If Abram is allowed to live, then this will result in your downfall. Why, my lord, do you allow Abram to continue living? Rid yourself and the land of Shinar from this man. Live a long and prosperous life.'

Nimrod listened to the words of his servant Anuki and decided that, again, he must try and rid himself of this torment, Abram. He sent some of his servants, in secret, to go and abduct Abram and bring him before the king, so that the king could slay him.

Eliezer of Damascus, the servant of Abram, was in the palace in the presence of the king. He overheard the judgement passed on Abram. So, quickly, he returned to Abram and told him of the king's dream. He repeated the interpretation of Anuki and the king's decision, regarding the fate of Abram.

'Now you must rise up and flee,' said Eliezer. 'For the king is determined that you must die this time.'

'I'm so weary of this man,' cried Abram. 'Why does he torment me so much? Can I not live my life peacefully without fear of death?'

'Not today,' urged Eliezer. 'Hurry. You must run, before you are captured.'

So Abram left his father's house in Ur of the Chaldeans and fled as quickly and quietly as he could. Abram's faithful servant Eliezer accompanied him in flight, putting his own life at risk. Eliezer was wise enough to prepare for flight and brought a bag of silver pieces, in order to purchase food to sustain them. Abram avoided contact with people who might recognise him and possibly report his whereabouts under the duress of torture. He slept in the wilderness under the stars and prayed for God's help. His concern was not only for himself but for his family that he had left behind.

The king's servants were dispatched in haste to find and capture Abram. But they were too late. He had already left. Questioning the members of the family and the servants of Abram, the king's servants were unsure of where Abram was. They searched the immediate neighbourhood but without success. Returning to the palace, they mustered the help of more men and ventured further afield, searching all the cities in their path. No one had seen any sign of Abram.

After many moons, carefully avoiding contact with men, Abram arrived at the house of Noah. There he hid himself. 'I'm tired of all this running,' cried Abram. 'I can't rest. I'm always on edge, looking over my shoulder. Waiting for the next attack.' He paused. 'When will Nimrod leave me alone?'

'Praise God, Abram,' said Noah. 'Give thanks to him because you have been saved from the hand of Nimrod. This rebel of a man will not overcome you. He will try, but he will fail. Put your trust in Yahweh Elohim, because he is the most powerful God and Nimrod has lost his power.'

'I know that, Noah. But I have anxious thoughts about all that is happening.'

'Remember, Abram, that the thoughts in Nimrod's mind are far more anxious than yours. Since the fall of the Tower of Babel, he has lost a lot of control. Many people perished and more have left him. Kedorlaomer, the king of Elam, who was a prince under the authority of Nimrod, has turned his back on him. Soon there will be friction between them. There will be war.

'And Hayk, the king of Armaneak, has also left the company of Nimrod. You do know that Hayk is a powerful and courageous man, who was Nimrod's finest archer. But he could see the wickedness of the Babylonian Empire under Nimrod. The son of Nimrod was sent to Hayk, to secure his return to Nimrod. He died in battle at the hand of Hayk. Nimrod has not avenged his death. Believe me, he has lost his power.

'Soon you will be able to return home to your wife Sarai and your mother and father. Nimrod's eyes will be drawn elsewhere. But you are not to stay in the city of Ur, because I don't believe that it's the right place for you to remain. You must seek Yahweh Elohim and get his direction for your life. Listen to the voice of God. Trust in him and do what he tells you to do.'

'I can never return to Ur,' answered Abram. 'Because as soon as I do, I will be captured by Nimrod. He's so powerful. His eyes are everywhere. It's not just him that I fear, but all of those who are controlled by him. All those whose minds he has trapped, plundered, and deceived. Others will be watching my father's house, and waiting for me to reveal myself. No doubt Nimrod has promised a rich reward for any news leading to my capture,' he paused for thought. 'Noah, I'm not a powerful man. I haven't been trained for battle. I'm not equipped to wage war on him. I'm too weak to defend myself.'

Shem, the son of Noah, interrupted him. 'Who saved you from the fire, from the brick furnace in Casdim? Was it not Yahweh? Only a miracle could have prevented you from being reduced to ashes. You saw with your own eyes what happened to Haran your brother. May he be at peace with Yahweh. The servants of Nimrod also, were they not burned to death?

'Abram, you must put your trust in Yahweh, the Lord God. You say that you're weak, that you're not powerful and that you haven't been trained for war; well you don't need to be. Elohei Tzeva'ot, the God of Hosts, the God of Armies, is with you, wherever you go. He'll be the light to guide you. He's the rock on which you stand and you'll not falter nor fall if you walk in his ways. He is your defence. All you must do is go, in the little strength that you have. He will give to you whatever is lacking. So rejoice.'

So Abram remained, concealed in the house of Noah. After a month, his father Terah arrived, in secret, to visit him.

'How can you continue to serve that rebel of a man?' asked Abram of his father Terah. 'Look at all that he has plundered from you. Your son, Haran, he has killed and even now he is trying to kill me. He has taken the land given to our ancestors, and made himself king over us all. He has no right to be king, except in his own land of Cush.

'It's not for your benefit, but his own, that he has exalted you to the prince of his entire host. He has coaxed you and beguiled you to serve him. He has thrown out the bait and you have taken it, and he has hauled you in. Like the skilful hunter that he is, he has hunted you and trapped you, and flattered you by praising you and showering you with gifts, with wealth and with power. But a greater power belongs to you.

'A greater wealth is waiting for you, but to grasp it you must let go of what you hold in your hand. The greater gift, he can't supply. This greater gift is freedom. Freedom from fear, freedom from domination, freedom to live in happiness. What's better than freedom from Nimrod? So many have left his service because they have grown tired of his tyranny. Why do you still dally?

'I feel that God is working in you his salvation. He's drawing you away from the darkness of idolatry, into his own wonderful light. We must leave Ur of the Chaldeans. I feel that God is directing us to move far away from the grasp of Nimrod. God will direct us to find a land, where we can live in peace. This will be the land where God will create a people for himself. We must rise up and leave the land of the darkness of idolatry and go where God will create a land of salvation for the whole world to see.'

The Lord God opened the ears of Terah and he listened to the words of his son. Noah and Shem agreed with the decision in Abram's heart. They prayed together to seek the counsel of Yahweh Elohim. Terah remained with them for many days then he returned to Ur and made the arrangements to leave. When Nimrod was away and busy with his own affairs, Terah brought out his entire household. His wife Amthelo, Sarai the wife of Abram, Nahor the son of Terah and his wife Milca, and Lot, the son of Haran, gathered their possessions and loaded the camels. The servants of Terah and the servants of Abram left the city of Ur of the Chaldeans and travelled north, up the course of the Euphrates River with all their cattle, donkeys, and sheep.

They travelled as fast as they were able and it took many moons to reach the region of the upper Euphrates. There they settled near the city of Haran in the land of Paddan Aram. The land was lush and green and provided rich pasture for their cattle and sheep. So the city dwellers became nomads, they left their old lives and old ways behind them. Instead of living in houses they lived in tents, which could easily be dismantled and transported.

Haran was not Abram's final destination, but he remained there with the extended family and they were very happy in this new land. The people of the land were kind and welcoming and they became close friends with Abram. The people of Haran were influenced by the presence of God, who was in Abram, and he taught them the ways of Yahweh Elohim.

CHAPTER 13

Hedad

After three years, living in the land of Haran, God appeared to Abram and he spoke to him. 'Abram, I am Yahweh Elohim, I will bless you and transform you into a mighty nation. Your name will become great and you yourself will become a blessing. Those who bless you I will bless and those who curse you will be cursed by me. All the people living throughout the earth will be blessed through you.

'You must now rise up and leave the land of Haran. Take your wife Sarai and your servants, cattle, and sheep and all belonging to you, and go to the land of Canaan and remain there. I will be your God and your people will be my people. I will go before you and prepare the way.'

So, in obedience to God, Abram rose up and took his wife Sarai and all belonging to him, and he left behind the land of Haran. Bidding farewell to his father and mother and his brother Nahor, who all remained in Haran, Abram left and went to the land of Canaan, as Yahweh the Lord God had directed him. At the age of fifty-five, Abram came to the land of Canaan and there he pitched his tent in the midst of the children of Canaan, those who were already living in the land.

Again, Yahweh Elohim appeared to Abram. He said to him, 'This is the land which I have given to you and to your offspring forever.'

Abram built an altar there, where Yahweh Elohim had spoken to him. He offered sacrifice upon it and sang praise to the God of heaven.

Three years after Abram had settled in the land of Canaan, with his wife Sarai and all belonging to him, Noah died. He died at the age of nine hundred and fifty years. This was three hundred and fifty years after the flood. He was the father of all who were living upon the face of the earth. Abram grieved for Noah, because of his great love for him. Abram was fifty-eight years old when Noah died.

Two years after the death of Noah, while Abram was still living in the land of Canaan, the people living in the cities of the plain, including Sodom and Gomorrah, revolted from the control of Kedorlaomer, king of Elam. All of the kings of the cities of the plain had served Kedorlaomer for the past twelve years and were forced to pay him a tribute of tax every year. They decided to end this servitude to a foreign king. So they became free and refused to pay taxes to the king of Elam.

The people living in the cities of the plain were very sinful in their behaviour. These cities were Sodom, Gomorrah, Admah, and Zeboiim. They were all situated in the valley of Siddim, close to the shores of the Salt Sea. The inhabitants of these cities defied the God of heaven and earth and his ways and they lived according to their own desires. They behaved in an evil way toward their neighbour and treated strangers who came to their cities in a most abominable fashion.

The valley of Siddim was extensive and it was well watered and the land was rich in pasture. The inhabitants of these cities would go to this valley four times during the year. The men would go with their families, wives, children, servants, and slaves. Not one person would remain in the cities.

There in the valley, all of the inhabitants of these cities would play music, sing and dance, and drink wine until they were unable to stand up. During the time of revelry, men would take hold of the nearest woman and lay down and have sex with her. It did not matter if this woman was married to another man or not. Men would be in the arms of a strange woman and see their own wife in the arms of a strange man. Women would see their own husband in the arms of a strange woman and make no remark about it.

They all behaved in whatever way they liked. Their sons and daughters were encouraged to behave as their mothers and fathers. Men engaged in a sexual manner with other men and young boys. The women were also in the arms of other women and young girls. The cities were full of illegitimate children and no one knew who the true father was for most of them. Incest was rife. Brother and sister did not know if they were brother and sister, even if they did they had no concern about it. The behaviour of the inhabitants of these cities angered God.

Their behaviour toward strangers was atrocious. If a merchant arrived in one of these cities, hoping to sell his goods, the people would surround the man. Men, women, children, old and young would take the man's goods, leaving him with nothing. They would refuse to pay for what they had taken. If the man complained about their behaviour toward him, they would taunt him and make fun of him. Many a visitor was beaten and run out of the city, bleeding and distressed.

There came a time when a man was travelling through the Siddim Valley, in an easterly direction. He was sitting upon his donkey and he had a long journey of many moons ahead of him before reaching home. It was late in the evening and the sun was about to set. He entered the city of Sodom, with the intention of staying for the night.

He tried many places, but no one would offer him shelter for the night. Everywhere he went to enquire for lodging, the door was shut in his face. 'What will I do?' he said to himself. 'Am I to spend the night in the street? I can't continue my journey, because I'm tired and am about to fall asleep. My donkey is also tired and needs to rest. I can't continue in the dark because there's no full moon to light the path. The donkey, like me, is exhausted.'

While these thoughts were passing through his mind, a wicked man, known as Hedad, spied the stranger in the street. 'What's this?' said Hedad to his wife. 'There's a stranger outside looking for shelter for the night.'

'Aww. And no one will give him a bed for the night. Ha, ha, ha,' cackled his wife.

'This is a chance for us to make some mischief,' said Hedad.

'Never mind mischief,' answered his wife. 'Let's strip him of all his wealth,' they both laughed together.

Lifting the latch on the door, Hedad left the house and went out into the street. 'Stranger,' he called. 'Stranger. What are you doing out in the street so late at night?'

'I was on my journey to the east when the sun set. I was near to your city, so I came in, hoping to find some shelter for the night for myself and my donkey.'

'And why are you still wandering around? It's getting late. It's not safe to be on the streets so late at night.'

'I've been trying for the last few hours, ever since the sun set, to find a bed for the night, but no one would offer me shelter. I ask for nothing else because I have bread and water for myself and hay for my donkey.'

'Then you must come with me,' laughed Hedad. 'You're very welcome to eat and sleep in my house.' Putting his hand on the man's shoulder, he led him to his house.

Upon reaching Hedad's house, the stranger was asked to wait. 'I will go inside and fetch a lamp. Then we'll settle your donkey for the night. He'll have company of his own kind and there's plenty of hay and water to refresh him.'

Returning with the lamp, Hedad's eyes lit up when they fell upon the mantle which covered the donkey's back. It was a beautifully rich garment, embroidered in many colours. 'Oh you can't leave this beautiful mantle here for the night,' said Hedad, licking his lips.

'Surely it will be safe here,' answered the stranger.

'No. Not at all,' said Hedad, shaking his head. 'You are a stranger here. Believe me, you don't know the people of Sodom like I do.' Lifting up the mantle he said, 'I will hide this mantle in my house, so that no one will see it. There it will be safe, until you need it again in the morning, when you continue your journey.'

'Thank you. It's very kind of you. You're very gracious.'

'Don't mention it,' said Hedad, with a glint in his eye. Giving the man a friendly clap on the back, and with a hearty laugh, he said, 'Come inside. Eat and drink and rest yourself. You've had a long journey. After a good night's sleep, you will feel refreshed, then you may continue your journey in the morning.'

He was ushered inside Hedad's house, where he met Hedad's wife. She sat him down and prepared some food for him which he ate gratefully.

'Where are you from?' enquired Hedad.

'I'm from the land of Elam.'

'Elam!' exclaimed Hedad. 'Why that's a long way away. You certainly do need to rest up for the night.'

The mention of Elam raised the hairs on the back of Hedad's neck. The inhabitants of the city of Sodom hated Elam, since

Kedorlaomer, the king of Elam, imposed a yearly tax on them. Because of this, the people of Elam were hated by the inhabitants in the cities of the plain.

'I'll punish this man from the city of Elam,' said Hedad to himself.

So the man lay down and slept through the night. When the sun rose up he felt refreshed and he got up to leave. Hedad pressed him to stay for a while.

'Eat and drink with me. It'll set you up for the day's journey.'

'Thank you very much for your hospitality, but—'

'Don't mention it,' interrupted Hedad cheerfully.

'But I really must continue my journey. I do have a long way to travel.'

'Yes you do,' agreed Hedad. 'And it will take you many moons to get there.'

'All the more reason for me to leave.'

'All the more reason for you to stay. What is a few hours compared to many months? It'll give you a chance to rest and eat and drink with me. You don't know when you'll get your next meal. And you may not find the same hospitality in the next city you visit.'

Reluctantly, the man agreed to stay, and the day wore on until the late afternoon when he decided to rise up again and leave.

'Ah look,' said Hedad. 'The day is almost spent. It's the ninth hour already. It will be foolish for you to leave now at this hour. Nightfall will be upon us soon and you'll be looking for somewhere to sleep for the night. It'll be dark before you reach Gomorrah, and if you think that the people of Sodom are inhospitable, then wait until you reach Gomorrah. They're much worse.'

So he was persuaded, and he remained in the house of Hedad for a second night. In the morning the stranger rose up before the sun had risen.

'You're up and rearing to go, I see,' said Hedad.

'That's right. I've delayed long enough. I have a long way to go today.'

'You're right. It's good to leave early. You'll leave a good distance behind you. Now before you go, sit down and have a morsel of food with me.'

The stranger was about to protest, and Hedad could see the frustration in his expression. 'Then after you eat, I'll help you to prepare and get your donkey clad for the journey.' Placing a hand on his shoulder, Hedad said, 'Sit down and eat and drink with me,' he pushed the man down. 'It will sustain you for your journey,' he was very persuasive.

However, every time the man got up to leave, he was persuaded to sit down again. But in the afternoon, he rose up with a determination to leave. He left the house under protest and went to prepare his donkey for the journey. While he was outside he discovered that the mantle of many colours was nowhere to be seen. Then he remembered that Hedad had taken it into the house to keep it safe.

Meanwhile, Hedad's wife had plenty to say. She was fond of complaining. 'So he's leaving I see.'

'Indeed he is. He's gone to prepare his donkey'

'He's spent the last two days eating every morsel of food in the house. And now he's leaving. And no sign of payment for all the food and drink that he's consumed,' she capped her last statement. 'And not even a word of thanks.'

'Shush, woman,' said Hedad, peering through the gap in the door.

'Don't shush me,' she answered, standing defiantly before Hedad, with her hands on her hips.

'I have a plan,' he hissed, raising his hand. 'Shush. He's coming back. Now be quiet,' he looked her in the eye and raised his finger.

'Ah Hedad, I've just remembered. I need my mantle to place on my donkey's back before I go.'

'Mantle?' questioned Hedad. 'What mantle do you speak of?'

'The mantle of many colours, of course. The same one that you insisted on bringing into your house for safe keeping.'

'Oh,' laughed Hedad. 'Of course. The dream that you had of a mantle of many colours, and the length of cord with which to tie it. I will give you the interpretation of your dream.'

'Dream?' questioned the man. 'What dream? I had no such dream. When I took the mantle off my donkey you insisted upon bringing it into your house for safe keeping. You told me that if it was left in the stable it would be stolen.'

Ignoring the man, Hedad said, 'This is the interpretation of your dream. The cord which you did see in your dream means that your life will be long, like the cord which is long. And the mantle of many colours that you saw in your dream, means that you will have an orchard of many fruits, represented by all the embroidered colours of your mantle.'

'What is this nonsense?' the man was astounded. 'I had no dream about a mantle of many colours and I need no interpretation of a dream. All I want now, is the mantle that you hid in your house for safe keeping. Then I will saddle my donkey and continue my journey.'

'I have told you the true interpretation of your dream. It is a good dream and it will come true. The interpretation is not false. This is my profession. I'm an interpreter of dreams.'

The stranger stood open mouthed, not knowing what to say.

In the pause Hedad continued, 'Normally I charge four pieces of silver for the interpretation.' He paused. 'But for you, I'll be generous. I'll only charge you three pieces of silver.'

'I won't pay you for the interpretation of a dream that I never had.'

'Oh you won't, will you not?' exclaimed the wife of Hedad. 'But will you pay for the food you ate and the wine that you drank, and the shelter that was offered to you for two nights?'

'Yes. I will pay for food and shelter, but I will not pay for the interpretation of the dream, since I didn't have a dream.' Turning to Hedad's wife, he asked, 'How much do you want for food and shelter?'

'Let me see,' said Hedad's wife. 'Food and shelter for two nights. That's two pieces of silver. One for each night.'

'That's excessive!' exclaimed the stranger.

'And for your donkey, one piece of silver each night. That's two pieces of silver. So, altogether, four pieces of silver,' she finished with a sly grin.

'No,' he answered in frustration. 'You're robbing me.'

'Alright,' said she with her feet planted apart and her hands on her hips. 'Three pieces of silver. And I'm being very reasonable.'

'You didn't shelter me in a palace.'

'If you were sleeping in the street, you would have been beaten and robbed. Possibly even killed,' her smile broadened.

'Well, you are certainly robbing me. You want to charge me a fortune for bread and wine and fodder for my donkey?'

'And a bed for two nights,' she insisted.

'But I didn't even want to stay for the second night.'

'No. But you did,' said Hedad.

'I want my mantle back. And I will pay you one silver piece for the food and shelter. And no more.'

'We'll see about that,' said Hedad. 'Let us go, you and I, to Serak, the judge of Sodom.'

So they presented themselves to Serak, the judge of Sodom. They found him at the gate of the city. The man from Elam presented his case and Hedad and his wife presented theirs. Serak listened to them all.

When they had finished speaking, Serak turned to the stranger and said, 'Do you not know that this man, Hedad, is famous in Sodom for his most accurate interpretation of dreams. If he says that this is true, then believe him. It is. His price for interpreting your dream is four pieces of silver, but he has generously offered the interpretation for only three pieces of silver. I strongly advise you to accept his offer.'

'No,' responded the stranger. 'He has stolen my mantle, and I want it back. I had no dream and I won't pay.'

Hedad exploded, 'I take back my generous offer. I now demand the full price. Give me four pieces of silver.'

'That's reasonable,' announced the judge. Turning to the stranger, he said, 'You heard Hedad. I advised you to accept his generous offer but now you must pay him four pieces of silver for the interpretation of your dream. And you must pay his wife four pieces of silver for food and shelter for two nights, for yourself and your donkey.'

'No. You must search his house. You'll find my mantle of many colours there. I want it returned to me.'

By this time a crowd had gathered and they were listening intently to the commotion taking place at the gate of the city. Serak, the judge, ordered his servants to search the man from Elam. They found his purse, which contained all of his silver and gold.

'Count out four pieces of silver for Hedad,' said Serak. 'And four pieces of silver for his wife.' This was done. 'And now for my fee,' said Serak. 'I will charge you four pieces of silver for my judgement. You're also expected to pay taxes upon entering the city and taxes upon leaving the city. I will also tax you upon all of your purchases of food and shelter for you and your donkey, and taxes for the interpretation of your dream. And I will fine you for falsely accusing Hedad of stealing your donkey's mantle.'

The crowd roared with delight. The stranger's silver was taken and he was thrown out of the city, himself and his donkey. He continued his journey upon his donkey, weeping with frustration at the injustice done to him in the city of Sodom.

CHAPTER 14

Kedorlaomer

After a further five years of Abram living in the land of Canaan, war broke out between Nimrod, king of the land of Shinar, and Kedorlaomer, king of Elam. Nimrod, seeing that the cities of the plain had successfully removed themselves from Kedorlaomer's power for the past five years, decided that the king of Elam was weak and had no power. So he came to fight with Kedorlaomer, to subdue him.

Nimrod was puffed up with pride and was filled with anger. 'This man, Kedorlaomer, must be punished. He must be brought down. After all, was it not I, Nimrod, who elevated him to give him a position as one of my own princes? He served under me and for that he was well rewarded. And he dared to leave, without regard to his lord. I will bring him down. I will teach him a lesson in humility. I will show him who is lord and who is the greater.'

So Nimrod assembled his forces, with his princes and loyal servants and all under his influence, and he set out to subdue the king of Elam. Nimrod assembled with many thousands of men and they prepared for battle in the Valley of Babel, between Elam and Shinar.

Kedorlaomer went out to meet Nimrod with a much smaller force and they clashed in the Valley of Babel. They fought with each other and the battle was fierce. There in the valley, even with far superior forces, Nimrod was defeated. Nimrod's forces were overcome and about six hundred thousand of his men fell in battle. Mardon, the son of Nimrod, the cruellest of all men, fell in the battle and died.

Nimrod was utterly defeated, and he fled from the scene of the battle. He was disgraced and he returned to his home in shame. He was placed under subjection to Kedorlaomer, and remained under his control. Kedorlaomer returned a victorious king to his home in Elam. He sent the princes of his host to enforce his laws, to the kings living around him who were now subjected to him.

Kedorlaomer made a covenant agreement with Arioch, king of Elasar, and Tidal, king of Goiim. Two altars were constructed using large boulders. Kedorlaomer and Arioch took a heifer and slaughtered it by slitting its throat. The blood from the beast was collected in a basin. Then the creature was cut in half, with the left half on one side of the altar, facing the right half on the opposite side of the altar. A trail of blood was poured out on the earth leading to the right half of the beast and another trail of blood was poured out on the earth leading to the left half of the beast.

In order to ratify the covenant between them, Kedorlaomer had to walk along the trail of blood, barefoot, and stand beside his half of the beast upon the altar. Arioch also had to walk along the trail of blood to his half of the beast upon the altar opposite Kedorlaomer. There they each raised their right hand and swore allegiance to one another, bringing blessings for loyalty to each other and curses for breaking the covenant. This they swore before their god. Then the sacrifice was set alight on the altar, to be ratified by their god. This same covenant was repeated between Kedorlaomer and Tidal. They were no longer subjected to Nimrod, but now they were obedient to the commands of their new master, Kedorlaomer.

In the seventieth year of Abram, who had been living in the land of Canaan for fifteen years, the Lord God again appeared to him.

Abram and Sarai were still childless, because Sarai was barren.

God said to Abram, 'I am the Lord who brought you out of the land of Ur of the Chaldeans, to give you this land for an inheritance. Walk righteously before me and keep my commands and to you and your offspring, through all generations, I will give this land, from the River Mizraim, as far as the great River Euphrates, as an inheritance. You shall live a good and long life and go to your fathers in peace. For your people, there will be a time away but the fourth generation shall return here to this land. It is their inheritance forever.'

This news had to be shared and Abram was inclined to visit his mother and father again, so Abram, his wife Sarai, and all belonging to him returned to the house of his father Terah in Haran. Abram dwelt there for five years and in that period of time he observed that his father Terah was only lukewarm in his devotion to Yahweh, the one true God. In the house of Terah Abram encouraged his father to fully abandon idolatry and accompany Abram to the land of Canaan. But Terah refused, claiming that he was content in the city of Haran. It saddened Abram that he was unable to persuade his father to abandon idolatry. Still, Abram's wife Sarai was unable to bear a child.

CHAPTER 15

Rikayon

By lot the sons of Ham were given the land that is now known as Africa. One of the lands of Africa, called Mizraim, otherwise known as Egypt, was given to Mizraim, the son of Ham. He founded the nation and became the first king of Egypt. He built the city of Memphis. Mizraim was also known as Menes; many people were known by different names ever since God confused the language. Mizraim was killed by a hippopotamus when he was exploring the land and his son Anom became the next king. Oswiris, the son of Anom, succeeded his father and became the third king of Egypt.

At the same time when Abram escaped death at the hands of Nimrod and confined himself in the house of Noah, a man arrived in Egypt. He was seeking out King Oswiris, the son of Anom, to reveal his wisdom to the king. He was a handsome and wise man but he was very poor, living in the land of Shinar. He was unable to look after himself in his homeland, under Nimrod's regime. So he set off, determined that he would find favour in the eyes of the Egyptian king. He hoped to be raised to a position of power and wealth.

This man's name was Rikayon. He arrived in Egypt a very impoverished man. He asked the Egyptians about the customs of King Oswiris.

'The king lives in his palace and no one can go to him or speak to him.'

'How is it possible to speak to him at all?' he asked.

'One day, every year, the king leaves his palace and comes among his people. This is the only opportunity we have to speak to him. Many people want him to pass judgement on a dispute that they may have with their neighbour, but it's impossible for him to hear everybody in one day.'

'I've been waiting for three years now,' said another. 'I'm longing to speak with King Oswiris but I may not be fortunate to get an audience with him next year.'

'Next year,' cried Rikayon. 'It will be another year before King Oswiris will leave his royal palace and come among his people?'

'Yes,' they answered. 'This is his custom. We may be fortunate next year. We must wait and see.'

'And does the king ever leave the royal palace at any other time?'

'No. Never.'

Rikayon was disheartened and very sorrowful because he could not see the king. 'That's such a ridiculous custom. How can he rule his kingdom in isolation? How does he know what is happening in his land?'

Rikayon wondered then if he had done the right thing by leaving the land of Shinar. He remembered when he got sight of the River Sihor, his heart leaped and he was filled with expectant joy. He expected this land to be his salvation. But now he was not so sure.

In the evening, as the sun was setting, Rikayon wondered how he would survive. His empty stomach was gripped with pain and he felt dizzy with the hunger. Trembling with weakness, he found a ruined house in which he could take shelter. He was unable to sleep and he spent the night imagining different scenarios, of how he would establish himself in this land.

Begging was his only means to live. He was unknown in the city and he had no family to turn to for sustenance. 'What am I to do?' he asked himself. 'I'm too proud to beg. I won't be able to bear the shame. But these people don't know me,' he reasoned with himself. 'I'm a complete stranger. It's better to be a beggar and alive, instead of a wise man who's dead from starvation. Where's the wisdom in that?'

As the sun rose up over the horizon he ventured out of the shelter of the ruined house and into the streets. Noticing market vendors selling fruit and vegetables, he approached them and fell into conversation with them. 'I'm a stranger in this land.'

'Where are you from?'

'I'm from the land of Shinar,' he answered as his mouth drooled at the sight of the produce. 'What are you selling here?'

'Fruit and vegetables,' said the vendor, taken aback. 'Have you never seen these before?'

'No. Well, I've seen some of them before, but some are strange to me. Do they need to be cooked before you can eat them? Can they be eaten fresh, without cooking?'

The market trader looked at Rikayon and considered him a fool. 'Do you not eat fruit and vegetables in your own land?'

'Yes I do, but some of these, I've never tasted. May I taste some to see if I like them?'

'Do you wish to buy them?' asked the vendor with suspicion.

'Well, of course. But I don't want to buy something from you and then discover that I don't like it. I will only waste my silver.'

The vendor looked at Rikayon with a hardened expression. 'That's reasonable, I suppose,' he said. 'What would you like to try? I will cut some for you to taste,' reaching for his knife he began slicing his produce for Rikayon to taste.

So Rikayon sampled morsels of vegetables and fruit from different vendors to ease his hunger pangs. 'Perhaps I should consider trading in fruit and vegetables and grains and spices,' he said to himself.

So he begged a few vegetables and tried selling them. But the rabble, seeing that he was a stranger and totally out of his depth as a street vendor, made fun of him and took his vegetables, leaving him with nothing. Disappointed at his own failure to earn a living selling vegetables, he went back to the derelict house in which he had spent the previous night and tried to get some sleep. But sleep evaded him. He was so angry and frustrated and he despaired of ever making his way in Egypt.

'If only I could speak to the king,' he cried. 'If King Oswiris encountered my wisdom and listened to the words that I speak, he would marvel at my wisdom and elevate me to a position of influence and power.' With this thought, he devised a plan. 'I can do as I please for a whole year, because the king is hidden away in his royal palace, except for one day every year. Whatever I do will not and cannot be challenged, until the king shows his face.'

When dawn arrived, he rose up with a hopeful resolve to change his fortune forever. He went into the streets and, with feigned authority, he found thirty strong-looking men who were carrying weapons and he commanded them to follow him.

'King Oswiris of Egypt has commanded me to hire thirty strong men. I'm hiring you, in the king's name, to do as he commands. Follow me.'

The men followed Rikayon, with the promise of a good wage, and he led them up to the top of the Egyptian sepulchre; the burial ground of the dead. There he gave them their instructions. 'This day, King Oswiris has appointed you guardians over this sepulchre. You must be strong and valiant. You must stand your ground. No man, woman, or child is to be buried here from this day forward, unless they pay two hundred pieces of silver. Only then may they pass through into the sepulchre. Only then may their dead be entombed.'

These men then set themselves up as the guardians of the sepulchre and nobody passed through them into the sepulchre to bury their dead without paying the tax of two hundred pieces of silver. It was not long before Rikayon became a very wealthy man. Rikayon was a wise man and he ensured that the men that he had chosen were well paid. This ensured their loyalty to him. He went out and bought horses, giving them to his men as a reward. He also hired more men and paid them a good wage. All of his men were loyal to him and none of them ever betrayed or cheated him.

The only enemies he made were the citizens who were trying to bury their dead. They grumbled, 'The king exacts taxes from us and we have to pay it every year. Now our king makes us pay to bury our dead. Even in death, we can't avoid paying our taxes. The king is cruel to do this to us. No other nation on earth expects the dead to pay a tax.

The one day in the year arrived when the king left his royal palace and descended among the inhabitants of Egypt. The people gathered together and, in one voice, they fired their complaints to King Oswiris. They were very unhappy at having to pay tax in order to bury their dead. 'Of all the kings in the earth, you are the most cruel to impose such a tax on us. No other nation has done this to their citizens.'

King Oswiris was dumbfounded upon hearing this news. 'This is not from me,' he assured them. 'I had no hand in imposing such a tax. It's very unreasonable.'

Still they were angry and they pointed out, 'None of your family have allowed this tax in the past. And never has such a tax been imposed since the time that Adam walked on the earth.'

The king was most annoyed at this accusation that had been thrown at him. His anger burned within him. 'Who is responsible for this?' he asked. 'Bring this man before me, the one who has imposed this tax. Because it didn't come from me. Where is this wicked man, who has imposed this tax on us without my permission and without my knowledge? Get him and bring him here before me, so that he can explain himself and take punishment for his crime.'

Rikayon, being shrewd and full of wisdom, took a thousand children, both boys and girls, and had them clothed in rich silks and embroidered garments. Placing them on horses, he presented them to the king as a gift. He was ready and had anticipated this day. His men brought these children along with silver, gold, and precious jewels and presented them to King Oswiris as gifts from Rikayon.

These children were given promises and the parents were delighted to see their children in the service of the king. The finest horse that could be found was reserved as a personal gift to King Oswiris, and Rikayon himself led the horse into the presence of the king.

King Oswiris was overcome with joy upon receiving such wonderful gifts. He was amazed at the appearance of Rikayon, for he was a very handsome man and was dressed in the richest of garments. He presented himself well and he came in confidence. The king composed himself and asked Rikayon about all the works he had done in regard to the sepulchre. Rikayon, choosing his words wisely, spoke flattering words to the king, in the hearing of all the king's servants and all the inhabitants of the land of Egypt.

The words of Rikayon fell from his lips like a rich melody, like the most exquisite music, delighting the listening ears. This was truly the skill of Rikayon. He had been waiting a whole year to speak to the king and had all that time to rehearse what he would say. His words were not wasted. Soon the king, his servants, and all the inhabitants of the land were dancing to the melody. He was once the most hated man in Egypt, but now he was the most loved.

After Rikayon had turned the hearts and minds of all in his favour the king said, 'From this day forward, your name shall no longer be

Rikayon, but you shall be called Pharaoh. You shall now be known as the Lord of the Dead, because you are the one who caused the dead to pay taxes.'

Rikayon was greatly loved by the king, his servants, and wise men and all the inhabitants of Egypt. They assembled together and, after consultation, they agreed to make him Prefect of Egypt, under the king. This was then written into law. So Rikayon the Pharaoh was made prefect under King Oswiris and he governed over the kingdom, daily administering justice. Whereas, King Oswiris would appear one day a year, as was his custom, to administer justice.

In this manner, Rikayon became Pharaoh of Egypt and, with his cunning wisdom, he usurped the power of King Oswiris. A decree was made that all kings from this time forward would be called Pharaoh. So Rikayon became the first Pharaoh and thus began the second Egyptian dynasty.

CHAPTER 16

Pharaoh

While Abram was living in Haran, in his father's house, Yahweh appeared to him for the third time. God said, 'Leave your father's house and go to the land I've promised you. In this land, I will bless you and I will make your name great. I will make you a great nation. You'll be a blessing, and those who bless you I will bless and those who curse you, I will curse. And all the families of the earth will be blessed through you.

'Now, rise up and leave this place. You, your wife Sarai, and all the members of your household, your servants, and all the friends you have made in Haran who cling to you. Leave this place and go to the land that I have promised to give you, to the land called Canaan.'

Abram obeyed Yahweh, and, packing all of his belongings, he and his entire household departed. He bid farewell to his father and mother and all of his relations who remained in Haran. His nephew Lot decided to travel with Abram and he left with him for the land of Canaan. Abram at this time was aged seventy-five.

Abram entered the land of Canaan and travelled south through the land to the place of the great tree of Moreh at Shechem. The city of Shechem was built in the valley between the mountain of Gerizim to the south and the mountain of Ebal to the north. A deep sorrow and loneliness entered the soul of Abram. Where this sorrow came from he did not know but he fell down on his knees and wept. The tears fell copiously from his eyes.

Running up to embrace her husband, Sarai cried out, 'Abram. Abram. What is wrong? Why the sorrow in your heart?'

'You ask me why I'm in sorrow and the truth is, I don't know. As we entered this place I could sense, deep in my soul, a terrible loneliness. A separation, a pulling apart, division. A glimpse of things to come. Perhaps Yahweh is showing me of things to follow in this place. I'm sorrowful for things that have not yet happened.'

After he composed himself, Abram wiped his tears and stood up. 'Here in this place we must build an altar to Yahweh and offer a fragrant burnt offering to God upon it.'

There Yahweh appeared to Abram and said to him, 'I give this land to you and your seed forever.'

The reason for his sorrow was not made clear to him. Yahweh in his infinite wisdom kept this revelation from Abram. It was not for Abram to know. Abram trusted in Yahweh and surrendered completely to the love that God had for him. Advancing from Shechem he moved south into the hill country to the east of Luz, pitching his tent between Luz to the west and the city of Ai to the east. In that place he built an altar to Yahweh and there he called upon the name of Yahweh, praising his holy name.

When Abram travelled further south into the land of Canaan he pitched his tent and settled in the plain of Mamre with his entire household. Yahweh again appeared to Abram, and he promised, 'This land, I will give to your offspring.' And Abram carried large stones and he built an altar. There he offered sacrifice to God, giving him thanks and praise.

Within a short time after arriving and settling in the plain of Mamre, a famine fell upon the land of Canaan. Many people were forced to leave the land because they were unable to sustain themselves. So, along with the people of Canaan, Abram and his entire household struck camp and travelled south through the Negev, on their way to the land of Egypt.

At the River Mizraim, which was almost bone dry because of the drought, they halted. There they rested, for the journey was arduous on account of the shortage of food. While they were resting there, a fear gripped Abram. He beheld his wife Sarai and gazed upon her beauty. The wind blew gently and her beautiful long hair danced in the breeze, sending out shimmers of gold. Her sky blue eyes caught the glance of her husband Abram, 'He is daydreaming,' she said to herself. 'What thoughts do you have, Abram?' she asked.

'Sarai, these people in Egypt are not God-fearing men. If they see you, they will fall for your beauty. They will kill me and take you away. I am afraid that they will defile you. Be sure to cover your face with your veil. If they should see you, I'll tell them that you're my sister. It's true that you're the daughter of my brother Haran and the sister of my nephew, Lot.'

Abram spoke to his entire household, telling them that they must all insist that Sarai is his sister and not his wife. He explained the reasons why and they all agreed to do so. They all loved Abram and Sarai and wanted no harm to come to them at the hand of the Egyptians.

Crossing the border at the River Mizraim, they entered into the land of Egypt. At the city gates, Abram and his people were stopped by the guards. 'To enter this city, you must pay a tax from all of your possessions.' The people were examined and all had to pay to enter through the gates.

Abram, fearing the Egyptians, had asked Sarai to conceal herself in a chest. The guards approached Abram, saying, 'What have you in the chest? You must open it and pay the appropriate tax for the contents of the chest.'

Abram answered, 'I will not open the chest. But whatever tax you impose upon it, I will pay to Pharaoh.'

'Why will you not open it?' asked the guards.

'Look around and see what else I have and take more tax from me.'

The curiosity of the guards was now truly aroused. 'You must have priceless jewels in the chest.'

They surrounded Abram with weapons in their hands. Forcing him back they seized the chest and opened it. Looking inside, they were astonished to see a beautiful woman looking up at them. They drew her out of the chest and gazed upon her beauty. All those who witnessed the revelation of Sarai in the chest gathered around. This crowd drew more people. Word soon spread and people were amazed at her beauty. They all wondered what she was doing, hiding in the wooden chest.

Overcome with admiration of her beauty, the officers and servants of Pharaoh Rikayon quickly sent word to him, telling him of all that had happened and praising the beauty of Sarai. Upon hearing the news, Pharaoh Rikayon ordered his servants to bring Sarai to him.

When Pharaoh laid eyes on Sarai, he was overcome by her graceful beauty. His heart leaped for joy and he was determined that he would have her for himself. Gifts were given to the men who discovered Sarai, hidden away in the chest. Sarai was taken away, to the palace of Pharaoh Rikayon. There she was prepared to meet him. She was bathed and dressed in the finest of garments and adorned with beautiful jewels before being doused in perfumes and scents fit for a queen.

Abram was most anxious because his wife Sarai was taken away from him. He had hoped that this would not happen. He and his entire household prayed to God to preserve Sarai from defilement by Pharaoh Rikayon and to save her life from punishment and death.

Sarai prayed, 'O Yahweh remember the promise you made to your servants Abram and Sarai and remember our faithfulness to all of your commands. You told us to leave the land of Ur of the Chaldeans and we travelled to Haran. You told us to leave Haran and go to the land of Canaan and this we did. You promised that all would go well with us if we obeyed your commands, and this we have done. From the land of Canaan we came here to Egypt on account of the famine that fell on Canaan, and now I am separated from Abram and am contained in the presence of the Pharaoh of Egypt. O Yahweh be merciful unto me and deliver me from this defilement by Pharaoh Rikayon.'

Pharaoh Rikayon was determined to make Sarai his bride. As far as he was aware, Sarai was a free woman. She was not married to Abram. Because she was a sister of Abram, Pharaoh gave many riches to Abram in exchange for Sarai. Abram was given silver, gold, and precious stones, menservants and maidservants, sheep, cattle, donkeys and camels and as much grain as these animals could carry. All of these gifts were given to Abram in exchange for Sarai. Abram looked upon all that he had been given and it meant nothing to him. Without his wife Sarai, he considered himself to be the poorest man that ever lived.

Abram was highly exalted and was being entertained in the palace of the Pharaoh. At the same time, Pharaoh Rikayon came into the presence of Sarai and he sat down before her. Yahweh listened to the prayers of Abram and Sarai and he sent an angel, who appeared to Sarai to comfort her. The angel said to Sarai, 'Do not be afraid, Sarai, because Yahweh has heard your prayer. I'm here to deliver you.'

Rikayon reached out his hand to touch Sarai. As he did so the angel of Yahweh struck him and the hand of Pharaoh turned white with leprosy. This was a heavy blow to Pharaoh. Never before had he experienced a supernatural encounter such as this. Thinking that his eyes deceived him, he reached out his hand again to touch Sarai. The angel of Yahweh again struck him and his forearm, up to his elbow, turned white with leprosy.

Being struck with desire for Sarai was greater than Rikayon's fear of leprosy and so he reached out again to touch Sarai with his left hand. Before his hand could reach her, the angel of Yahweh came between them and again struck Rikayon. This time his left hand was stricken with leprosy. But Rikayon would not give up. His lust for Sarai was so great that he made so many attempts to touch her and each time the angel struck him white with leprosy. Soon his whole body was afflicted with the disease.

Screaming with frustration Rikayon cried, 'What kind of witchcraft is this? What power do you have over me? And why do you afflict me so?'

Rising up, he left her alone in the bedchamber. Then he discovered that not only himself, but his entire household was stricken down with the same disease, including his servants.

Calling his sages and wise men and the magicians to his palace, Rikayon consulted them regarding the events leading to the disease upon himself and his entire household. 'What has brought this upon me?' he asked. 'And how can I be cleansed from this disease?'

The magicians conjured up magic spells and potions to remedy the skin disease. The sages and wise men asked more questions about Abram and Sarai to determine the source of this affliction. 'My Lord Pharaoh, you must ask the woman about the man, her brother.'

'Why was the woman concealed in a wooden chest?' asked another. 'Perhaps she is skilled in sorcery. She must be a witch, and a very powerful one.'

'She may have been placed in the chest to conceal her power. Now she is released from the chest and is free to cast her evil spells. This brother of hers must know what she is capable of and how to control her. If she is capable of inflicting this disease upon you, she may be willing to remove it and cleanse your skin.'

Sarai was summoned before Pharaoh Rikayon in the presence of his wise men, because they were all eager to discover the source of her power.

'Who is this man, who brought you, concealed in a wooden chest, into our land of Egypt?' asked Rikayon.

Although Abram had forbidden Sarai to reveal the truth, that she was his wife, she was prompted by the angel, sent by God, to speak truthfully. 'This man who brought me here to Egypt, is my husband.'

'Why did he deceive me,' gasped Rikayon, 'by telling me that you were his sister?'

'He was afraid for his life,' she answered. 'He truly believed that if you discovered that I was his wife, you would have him killed in order to take me as your own wife. That is why I was concealed in the wooden chest, so that you would never lay your eyes on me.'

'This man has brought evil upon me and my entire household. He deserves to be punished.'

Sarai flinched at this remark. 'Please do not punish him, Pharaoh. He is a good and upright man. He hid me to protect me and save his own life. He means you no harm, nor do I.'

'You mean me no harm?' screamed Rikayon. 'Then who afflicted me with this disease?'

'I prayed to Yahweh Elohim, the God of heaven and earth, and he listened to my prayer, to keep me from defilement at your hand. He sent an angel who stood between you and me. It was this messenger of God who struck you each time you tried to touch me.'

'Then how am I to be set free from this disease?'

'Pharaoh,' she replied. 'You must let me return to my husband, unharmed. You must promise to cause no harm to my husband Abram. When you do this, the disease will be lifted from you and your household. Because you have inflicted no harm to us, God will honour your actions and you and your entire household will be released from this disease.'

'Call Abram, her husband,' said Pharaoh Rikayon to his servants. Abram came before Pharaoh Rikayon who expressed his anger to Abram concerning his wife Sarai. 'Why did you deceive me?'

'In truth, Sarai is the daughter of my father's household. I married her and she became my wife.'

'Take her now, and go from us. Leave this land before you cause any more trouble for us. To show that I feel no ill will toward you, I will give you more silver, gold, and precious gems; menservants and maidservants; sheep, cattle, donkeys, and camels. You may take enough grain to see you through the famine. Go back to your own land. My guards will escort you to the River Mizraim.'

So Abram, his wife Sarai, and his entire household were banished from the land of Egypt. Abram was a wealthy man considering all that Pharaoh Rikayon had given to him. They crossed over the border leaving Egypt behind and when they entered the land of Canaan the disease fell from Pharaoh Rikayon and his entire household was cleansed.

CHAPTER 17

Dispute

Abram went from Egypt to the Negev and he travelled from place to place, as he found grazing for his animals. He came to Luz, to the place where he had previously camped, and built an altar between Luz and Ai. There Abram offered sacrifice and prayed to God.

Between them, Abram and Lot had so much livestock, cattle, sheep, donkeys, and camels, that the land was not able to sustain them as long as they remained together. Lot allowed his livestock to enter the fields of the inhabitants of the land and graze upon their property. The inhabitants complained to Lot and his herdsmen, but Lot refused to listen to them. Finding no solution to the intrusion by Lot and his herdsmen, the inhabitants came to Abram.

'Why do you allow your livestock to graze on our land? The land has not long recovered from famine. If this continues, then we will not have enough food for our own animals and we will perish.'

'I don't allow my animals to graze in your fields,' answered Abram.

'Lot and his herdsmen do so. Is he not part of your household? Is he not under your authority?'

'I will speak to him,' said Abram. 'Forgive me for the intrusion on your property.'

The property owners met with Lot and Abram and they argued with each other. The herdsmen of Abram and Lot also argued. For days Lot continued to trespass in the fields of his neighbours and every day Abram and Lot would argue with each other.

'How long will this continue?' asked Abram. 'We can't continue like this because it will lead to fighting between us. I don't want to fight with you and I don't want to fight with our neighbours. We didn't come to this land to war with each other. The only solution that I can see is that we separate from each other.

'Find a place of your own, where you can live in peace and graze your cattle and sheep wherever you please. It's not right for us to fight with each other, because we are family. Keep a distance between us, so that there's no more quarrelling.

'Don't be afraid to go your own way,' said Abram. 'I'll never abandon you. And if you need help, come and find me. I'll assist you. Look at the land around us and decide where you would like to go. If you choose east, I'll go west, and if you choose west, then I'll go east.'

Lot's eyes fell upon the plain of Jordan and he could see that it was well watered and provided lush pasture land for his livestock. In the valley there grew many oak trees and the fields were divided into equal lots. The land suckled its children like breasts that were full. The land was rich, bearing trees of the vine, of figs, of the pomegranate, of nuts, of the almond, of the apple, and the peach. So Lot made his decision to go to the plain of Jordan in the east and he parted company with Abram. Lot pitched his tent in the cities of the plain near to Sodom. Abram lived in the plain of Mamre in Hebron and there was no more trouble between them.

Under the great trees of Mamre in Hebron, Abram built an altar to God. Yahweh appeared to him and said, 'Abram, look with your eyes to the north and south, now look to the east and west. I will give to you and your offspring all of this land and it will be yours forever. Like the grains of dust beneath your feet that can't be counted, so your offspring will be multiplied. Go and enjoy this land, because it's yours forever.'

CHAPTER 18

Rescue

Shortly after this time, Kedorlaomer, king of Elam, summoned all the kings that were subject to him. The kings that he summoned were Arioch, king of Elasar; Tidal, king of Goiim; and Amraphel, who is Nimrod of Shinar. He called on them to assist him to take control of the cities of the plain that had rebelled against him, after serving him for twelve years.

The kings assembled with about eight hundred thousand men and they went to war in the Valley of Siddim, by the Salt Sea. They warred against Bera, king of Sodom; Bersha, king of Gomorrah; Shinab, king of Admah; Shemeber, king of Zeboiim; and Bela, king of Zoar.

Kedorlaomer and his allies had already defeated the Rephaites in Ashteroth Karnaim; the Zuzites in Ham; the Emites in Shaveh Kiriathaim; and the Horites in the hill country of Seir, as far as El Paran. They turned to Kadesh, defeating the Amalekites, and to Hazezon Tamar, defeating the Amorites.

So the battle commenced in the Valley of Siddim and it did not go well for the kings of the cities of the valley. They were overcome by the weight of the forces of Kedorlaomer and they fled. The Valley of Siddim is full of lime pits and some of those who fled fell into these pits; some managed to avoid the lime pits and managed to escape to the mountains to avoid capture.

Kedorlaomer and his allies pursued the five kings who fled to Sodom and Gomorrah. The cities of the kings were seized and all their goods were plundered. Not a morsel of food was left behind. In the plundering of the city of Sodom, Lot and his entire household and all that he possessed, cattle, sheep, and servants, were taken into captivity.

A man called Unic managed to escape capture and witnessed the events that had taken place near Sodom. He travelled to Mamre, in Hebron, to seek Abram and report to him that Lot had been taken prisoner. Abram's heart sank when he received the news but he remembered his promise to help Lot if he ever got into trouble.

Abram was determined to rescue his nephew Lot and he had Amorite allies named Mamre, Eshcol, and Aner. These three men, combined with Abram and his men, numbered three hundred and eighteen. They assembled together and Abram prayed for a blessing from Elohei Tzeva'ot, the God of Hosts, who is the God of Armies. He beseeched him to give them power and strength, thus enabling them to overcome Kedorlaomer with his vast numbers. 'Elohei Tzeva'ot will increase our numbers,' said Abram. 'Because he is mighty and willing to save, we will step out in faith and put our trust in him.'

Rising up, they set off in pursuit of the kings to rescue Lot and all that belonged to him. They travelled as far as Dan, where on the fifth day in the depth of the night a messenger of Yahweh came before Abram. The angel who was tall and strong raised the shofar, the ram's horn, to his lips. He blew the horn and the air was filled with a deep bellowing noise. Like approaching thunder, an earth-trembling rumble grew louder, filling the air and hurting the ears of Abram and his men.

Waking from his slumber, Kedorlaomer was gripped with fear. The earth below the four kings, on which they had been lying deep in sleep, shook, causing the men to tremble violently. Coming to their senses they sprang to their feet and took hold of their weapons. They were taken completely by surprise. The four kings could hear the shrieks of terror rising from their own valiant men.

'Who is attacking us?' asked Kedorlaomer, the astounded king. 'Who is so great to make our men scream and run like cowards?'

'Stand your ground,' shouted Kedorlaomer. 'I command you to stand and fight.' His command was ignored and the men pushing past him, their eyes wide with fright, knocked him to the ground. They had no regard for their king, so great was their fear. Peering into the distance Kedorlaomer caught a glimpse in the darkness of a cloud of dust, quickly approaching his camp from the east. With his eyes wide with fright, he roared, 'Run.'

With haste the four kings took off as fast as their legs could carry them. Rising up from the east, Elohei Tzeva'ot sent Aleph the mighty and powerful ox, the leader, the one endowed with strength and authority. He led the heavenly herd of oxen on a stampede and they sped through the camp, goring with their horns and trampling Kedorlaomer's vast army underfoot.

Looking around him Amraphel was reminded of his dream which had tormented him so many years ago. Here running beside him were three kings and he remembered that there were three men with him in his dream, dressed in princely garments. Here they were now, in reality running for their lives. Amraphel, who is Nimrod, was haunted by the vision of Abram pursuing him in the depth of the night.

The words of Anuki, his most respected sage, rang in his ears: 'In the sky we saw a new star rise up in the east and quickly cross to the four corners of the heavens. This new star swallowed up four stars in its path. These four stars are the three kings with you in the dream. The star that swallowed them up is none other than Abram.'

In his dream, his army was engulfed by the flood waters and destroyed. Here in this place he could see his army being destroyed by the stampeding oxen and glancing at the terrified men fleeing beside him, he heard the words of Anuki: 'Your army will be destroyed, but you will escape with three kings of the earth.' Full of regret at his own failure in the past he was reminded: 'You must slay Abram before his evil rises up to destroy you.'

Abram pursued his enemies north of Damascus, as far as Hobah. Kedorlaomer and his kings fled and it is even rumoured that Kedorlaomer died in the conflict. Abram rescued his nephew Lot with all of the members of his household and his possessions. The people of Sodom and their belongings were also saved from the hands of their enemies. Abram gave up the pursuit of the four kings as soon as the rescue of Lot and the citizens of Sodom was accomplished.

Abram and his men with his allies were returning from the battle with all the rescued people and their possessions that they had snatched from the grip of Kedorlaomer. They were passing through the Valley of Shaveh, which is also known as the Valley of Melech and the Valley of Kings, where they were met by Bera, king of Sodom. He had fallen into the lime pits and, after managing to escape, travelled north following the path of Kedorlaomer.

Salem was close by and Melchizadek, the priest and king of Salem, came out of the city to meet Abram and his men. Upon encountering Melchizadek, Abram knelt down on his knees and with reverence declared, 'Gadol Melchizadek. Great is the King of Righteousness.' All of Abram's company knelt down with him and declared before Melchizadek, 'Beracha Melchizadek. Blessings O King of Righteousness.'

Melchizadek, the King of Righteousness, brought out bread and wine to refresh Abram and his men. Melchizadek, king and priest of God Most High, blessed Abram, 'May El-Elyon, God Most High, creator of heaven and earth, bless you, Abram; and praise be to El-Elyon who delivered your enemies into your hand.'

Abram was delighted to meet Melchizadek, for he was none other than Shem, the son of Noah. Shem, in his name, carried the character of God Most High. The two men embraced and shed tears for their hearts were one, their love for each other was great. Abram had known Shem from the early age of ten years, when Terah brought Abram out of the cave to live in the house of Noah. Shem had always followed God in his own father's footsteps and his faith never wavered. Abram grew up under the influence of these two great men, Noah and Shem. It was by their example that he loved Yahweh and walked in God's ways.

Abram divided the spoils of the battle and gave to Melchizadek a tenth of all that he had as a tithe. Bera the king of Sodom approached Abram and requested of him, 'Return to me my inhabitants who were taken captive by Kedorlaomer and his allies, but you may keep all of their possessions and goods, as payment for rescuing them.'

'I lift up my hands to God,' answered Abram. 'To El-Elyon, God Most High, creator of heaven and earth, I have sworn an oath. He is the one who has redeemed my soul and has delivered me from all my enemies and placed them into my hands. I will accept nothing from you, not even a thread from your garment or a strap from your sandal. This way you can't say that you made me rich. It is God who has promised that I'll lack nothing. It is he that will provide for all my needs and he will bless the work of my hands. Here are your people, Bera, king of Sodom. They may keep all of their possessions. You may, however, give payment of food to these men, my allies who accompanied me and went in pursuit of your people to rescue them. To Mamre, Eshcol, and Aner you may give reward.'

This the king of Sodom did. Before parting company and returning to his city, Bera again pressed Abram to take a reward for his victory over Kedorlaomer. But Abram refused, 'Elohei Tzeva'ot, the God of Hosts, is the victor. He is my reward.'

Lot was distanced from his uncle Abram and felt ashamed and very uncomfortable in his presence. He was unable to look Abram in the eye for he was influenced by the sinful city in which he lived. However, Ado, the wife of Lot, was overcome with emotion and she fell down at the feet of Abram and shed copious tears of gratitude for her rescue. Taking her by the hand, Abram raised her up and comforted her. Bera, the king of Sodom, departed, along with all of the inhabitants of Sodom and all of their possessions and turning south they travelled home. Lot with his wife and children and all of his servants and goods returned with Bera to Sodom.

Abram and his men camped out in the Valley of Shaveh and spent the night with Shem, the same Melchizadek, the king and high priest of Salem, the City of Peace. In the morning Abram and Shem blessed each other and after embracing they parted company. Shem returned as king and high priest to his city, Salem. Abram and his company returned to the Oaks of Mamre which is in Hebron.

Weary after the rescue of his nephew Lot and the long distance that he had travelled over the last few days, Abram lay down to rest for the night. As tired as he was, he found himself unable to sleep. The blessing of Melchizadek that he had received from Shem kept rolling around in his mind. 'May El-Elyon, God Most High, creator of heaven and earth, bless you, Abram; and praise be to El-Elyon who delivered your enemies into your hand.'

After spending forty years in the house of Noah, Abram was very familiar with the words and pictorial imagery of the Hebrew language. He knew that El-Elyon meant God Most High but he was also aware that there was a much deeper meaning to the name. Considering the letters Aleph and Lamed for El; Aleph was the image of an ox and Lamed was the image of a shepherd's staff. 'El means power and did God not send a herd of powerful oxen to destroy Kedorlaomer's mighty army?' considered Abram.

'Elyon comprises the letters Ayin, Lamed, Yod, Waw, and Nun,' he said to himself. 'Ayin pictorially is the eye and can also mean watch, see, experience, and know. Lamed is the shepherd's staff, meaning shepherd, staff, teach, lead, yoke, and bind. Yod is arm, hand, work, and deed. Waw is nail, hook, secure, and add. Nun is seed, fish, life, and continue.'

Pondering this for a long time he came to the following conclusion: 'El-Elyon must mean, "By the power of God, you will see how, like a shepherd, he leads you and by the power of his arm will add to your seed." That's a most wonderful blessing. I praise you, El-Elyon, God Most High, above all gods and I thank you for all of your blessings.' With this prayer he fell asleep.

CHAPTER 19

Covenant

Abram woke up from his sleep, for Yahweh again appeared to him. Rising up from his slumber he fell down on his knees when he heard the voice of Yahweh speaking to him. Yahweh said, 'Abram, have no fear for I am your shield and will protect you. Your reward will be great.'

Abram was bold enough to answer, 'O my sovereign Lord, what reward can be so great, since I have no children? The only one to inherit from me is my faithful servant Eliezer of Damascus, who saved me from death at the hands of Nimrod.'

'This man Eliezer,' answered Yahweh, 'though he is faithful and upright and has remained loyal to you, will not be your heir. I will give you a child from your own flesh and blood and from your wife Sarai.' Yahweh led Abram out of his tent. 'Look up at the stars.' Abram gazed up at their beauty in the night sky. 'Is it possible to count them?' asked Yahweh. 'So vast shall your offspring be.'

'Adonai Yahweh, my Lord God. I believe in you and all of your words are truth.'

'Abram, you stand before me and behave in the right manner toward me. You believe in me, you trust in me, and you are obedient to my commands. You are truly my friend. So because of this I give to you the recognition that you deserve. Your faithfulness is your great strength. You have a righteous relationship with me, the Lord God. Remember, Abram, that I am the one who brought you out of the land of the Chaldeans, out of the city of Ur, and I have given this land to you, so that you may take possession of it.'

'How can I know, Adonai Yahweh, my Lord God, that I can take possession of this land that you have sent me to?'

'Bring me a heifer, a goat, and a ram, each of them three years old. Bring also a young pigeon and a dove.'

The sun rose up in the sky and the darkness was gone. Abram quickly carried out the instructions of Yahweh, the Lord God. He cut the animals in half, according to the custom of cutting a covenant, and arranged the pieces opposite each other on the altar, but he left the birds whole. In the heat of the day, the smell of the flesh attracted birds of prey but Abram drove them away. He was weary all day long, keeping the flesh of the sacrifice free from carrion. The sun began to set and the terror of darkness fell upon Abram. Exhaustion suddenly came over him and, though he tried to fight it, he could not. He fell into a deep and fearful sleep.

'Be sure of this,' said Adonai Yahweh. 'The time will come when your descendants will be enslaved in a country that I have not given to them. For a period of four hundred years they will be ill-treated and used as slaves by the rulers of the land. But when the time is ripe, I will rescue them and punish their slave masters. They will be released and come out with many possessions. In the fourth generation your descendants will return to this land that I have promised to you and they will take possession of it. At this time the sin of the Amorites will have reached its peak and I will displace them. You will live to a good age and go to your fathers in peace.'

Abram awoke suddenly to pitch darkness. Before him he observed a smoking fire and a blazing torch which appeared. This smoking fire and blazing torch passed through the pieces of the sacrificial offering and set the pieces ablaze. It was Yahweh who passed through the two halves of the sacrifice and it was Yahweh who set the sacrifice ablaze.

'I cut a covenant with you this day, Abram. To you and your offspring I give you this land from the River of Mizraim in Egypt to the great River Euphrates in the east. I give you the land of the Kenites, Kenizzites, Kadmonites, Hittites, Perizzites, Rephaites, Amorites, Canaanites, Girgashites, and Jebusites.'

CHAPTER 20

Paltith

Not long after his abduction by Kedorlaomer and his rescue by his uncle Abram, Lot settled back into his house in the city of Sodom. His wife, Ado, became pregnant and when her time came she gave birth to a daughter. They gave her the name Paltith, because Yahweh had rescued him and his family from the hands of the king of Elam and his allies.

Paltith grew up and she was taken by one of the men of Sodom and she became his wife. For all of her life, Paltith walked in the way of God. The day arrived when a poor man came into the city of Sodom, begging for food. As was the custom of Sodom, the inhabitants taunted this poor man. They gave him bags of silver and gold and his eyes opened wide in wonder.

'How blessed I am now,' he said, 'Blessed be the men of Sodom, for they have taken pity on me. Look how generous they are to give me such wealth, when all I need is bread to take away my hunger. Now I have plenty. I can buy as much bread as I need.'

This poor man tried to buy bread but no one would sell him any. He could buy neither bread nor flour and no one would even offer him a cup of water. 'What kind of people are the men of Sodom?' he asked himself. 'Why do they give me silver and gold and then refuse to sell me any food? Their money is no good to me. I can't eat silver and gold. I will leave this place and beg somewhere else.'

When he tried to leave the city he was prevented by armed men. They pushed him away from the city gates back into the city. 'Strangers are not allowed to leave.'

'Here,' he offered. 'I will return your silver and gold.'

'We don't want your silver and gold.'

'I just want to leave, so that I might beg for food elsewhere.'

'Once you enter the city of Sodom, you're not permitted to leave. This silver and gold is from our city and you can't leave with it. You must spend it here.'

'I can't spend it. No one will take it in exchange for food.'

'That's not my problem.'

'Will you sell me some food, please?'

'I have no food to sell you and I can't leave my post to buy you any food. I must guard the gate.'

'Then I will die from hunger,' sighed the poor man. 'Why do you punish me?'

'If a man of Sodom gives you food or water, then he shall be punished. He will be put to death. This is the law of the city of Sodom and Serak, the judge has decreed it. Now go away.'

The man wandered the streets, hoping to find scraps of food thrown to the dogs but he found nothing. He was starving and, reaching the point of exhaustion, the poor man lay down in the city square to die. People passed him on the street, stepping over him and examining him to see if he was dead or alive. The inhabitants placed bets with each other to see who would accurately predict the point of his death.

Paltith, the daughter of Lot, saw this poor man lying in the street at the point of death and she was moved with compassion for him. 'Yahweh Elohim, God of heaven and earth,' she prayed, 'have mercy upon this poor man. Save him from death. What can I do to help him?'

Several times each day, Paltith would go out into the square to fetch water from the well. She devised a plan where she managed to secretly feed the man. Each time she went out to fetch water she concealed some bread inside her water pitcher. Whenever she passed him by, she dropped the bread beside him. In this way she sustained him and kept him from death.

Every day she fed him in the same manner and the people of Sodom could not understand how the man was able to live so long without any food.

'This can't be true. No one can live this long without food. He must be getting food from somewhere.'

'But he hasn't moved from this place and no one has offered him any food.'

'Well if he hasn't been fed, it must be witchcraft.'

'No. Someone is secretly feeding him.'

'Who would do this? It's forbidden to feed poor beggars who come to Sodom and Gomorrah. Who would risk their own life to feed him?'

'We must watch him at all times of the day and night. Why don't we hide somewhere? A place where he can't see us, but we can see him. From this place of concealment we will be able to discover who is providing food for him to eat.'

The men concealed themselves and took it in turn to watch the man, to see if they could discover who was feeding him. In the morning Paltith went out of her house, as she would normally do, to fetch a pitcher of water. She concealed some bread inside the pitcher and as she passed the poor man on her way to the well, she tossed the morsel of bread to him. He quickly reached for the bread and concealed it in his tunic.

Filling her pitcher with water at the well, Paltith was approached by the man who had observed her feeding the poor man. 'You are the one who has been feeding this poor man bread. I saw you pass it to him on your way to the well.'

The poor man was also seized and the morsel of bread was found concealed inside his tunic. 'Now we have proof. Here is the bread. It's hidden in his tunic.'

'Why have you done this?' Paltith was asked. 'You know the law of this city. You know that it's forbidden to feed beggars.'

'Yes I know the law. I know that it's forbidden to feed the poor.'

'Then why have you fed him? Why have you disobeyed the decree?'

'I couldn't help myself. I saw the poor man, lying in the street, at the point of death and my heart was moved with compassion for him. I couldn't watch him die. It's cruel. It's evil. It's not right.'

'Who appointed you judge of Sodom? We have one judge, and he is Serak. Take her to him. Serak must decide her fate, for she has clearly broken the law.'

Paltith was dragged by the hair to meet with Serak. On her way there, she was slapped, kicked, and spat upon by the inhabitants of Sodom. The account was given to Serak of the course of events and witnesses gave testimony.

'Now Serak, what will your judgement be?'

'She must be put to death,' he answered. Turning to Sharkad, the judge of Gomorrah, who happened to be visiting the city of Sodom, he enquired, 'What is your judgement in this matter?'

'Yes I agree that she must die.'

'How will she die?' cried the crowd.

'Why don't you burn her in the fire,' suggested Sharkad.

'That's excellent,' agreed Serak.

So a large fire was lit in the city square and Paltith was bound and thrown into the fire, where she was burned to death. This was done as a punishment and as an example to all, for transgressing the laws of Sodom and Gomorrah.

During the burning of Paltith, Serak sat down with Sharkad to witness the event and they began to talk together. 'This burning is good,' said Sharkad, the judge of Gomorrah.

'Yes. It keeps order in our cities,' agreed Serak.

'I was speaking with Menon, the judge of Zeboiim, a few days ago. He was telling me that he was in Admah on one occasion, when a public execution took place.'

'What happened there?' asked Serak with interest.

'An event, quite similar to this burning, took place in Admah. Menon told me that he was visiting the city, when Zabnac, the judge of Admah, had to pass sentence on a young woman, similar to this one here in Sodom.

'A man travelling by, stopped in the city just as the sun was setting. He intended to rest for the night and then leave in the morning to continue his journey. He sat down in the street, facing the door of the house of this young woman's father. The young woman was entering the house when this stranger asked her if she would fetch some water to quench his thirst.

"Who are you?" she asked.

"I'm a stranger and while I was making my journey the sun went down. I came into your city of Admah for safety, hoping to find shelter for the night. All I want to do is rest here for the night and in the morning after I'm rested I'll leave."

So the young woman went into the house and brought out some bread and water which he ate and drank. The people of Admah soon found out what had happened and they took the woman from her home and brought her to Zabnac, the judge of Admah. Zabnac, upon hearing the case presented before him, passed sentence on the woman.'

'What was his judgement?' asked Serak, eager to know.

'The woman was given the death sentence for breaking the law.'

'But how did she die? That's what I'm interested in.'

'They brought her out and stripped her naked. She was raped repeatedly by the men who stripped her. They spread honey over her body, so that all of her flesh was covered. Then they tied her to a tree under a bee hive that had swarmed.'

'Oh that's good. I never would have considered such a sentence,' smiled Serak.

'Well, the bees landed upon her and her body was stung so many times that she almost swelled up twice her size.'

'I'd say she screamed.'

'Certainly, she did. She cried out, begging to be released, but no one took any heed of her. They laughed and jeered and rejoiced when she died from the stings.'

'That's a bit like the crowd here,' said Serak as he observed the revellers. 'The rejoicing will go on through the night.'

'The smell of her flesh is strong,' observed Sharkad.

'Enough to make your mouth water. I'm feeling really hungry now. Come to my house. We'll eat.'

'It's a shame to miss all the fun,' said Sharkad, as he dragged himself away.

On their way to the house of Serak, they passed by the beggar on the street. Sharkad could not help himself and he reached into his purse, taking out a piece of silver. He tossed the piece of silver to the beggar and taunted him, 'Take this piece of silver and buy some bread for yourself. Eat well and live a long life.'

Serak and Sharkad moved off, laughing at their own humour.

This kind of conduct provoked Yahweh Elohim and his patience with these cities was reaching its limit. The cities of Sodom, Gomorrah, Zeboiim, and Admah were well placed in a plain that was well watered, enjoying lush pasture. The inhabitants lacked nothing and were extremely wealthy, compared to other cities in the land. It was not for want that they would not feed the hungry, it was out of spite. Their nature was cruel and their evil ways increased over time. They were filled with pride and they rejoiced in doing evil. Their behaviour flew in the face of God. But their days were numbered.

CHAPTER 21

Hagar

After the death of Reu, the great, great grandfather of Abram, Sarai came to her husband and said, 'For many years now the Lord God has promised you many descendants. You are aware that I am barren and am unable to bear you any children. God must not want me to bear you any children. So how then can you be a father to a nation? God must want you to have children with another woman.'

But Abram tarried. For seven years Sarai pestered him in the same way. 'I will give you my maidservant Hagar, as a concubine; this same woman that the Pharaoh Rikayon gave to me as a maidservant when we left Egypt. I will give her to you and you will lie down with her and she will bear a son for you and a child that I can hold on my lap.'

This time Abram listened to his wife Sarai and he agreed with her. Taking Hagar, the handmaid of Sarai, Abram lay down with her in the tent and had sex with her. Hagar conceived and she was delighted. She expressed her delight in front of Sarai. Hagar scorned her mistress Sarai.

'I am better in the eyes of Yahweh than you, because your womb is dry and in all these years you have never conceived a child. But I have been favoured by Yahweh, since I have conceived in such a short time.'

Sarai was downcast. Her soul grieved. 'What have I done?' she cried. 'I have given my handmaid to my husband Abram and now she carries his child. This child will never be mine but will always be his. This child will be a stumbling block between us. Hagar, who has always been a good and faithful handmaid to me, has now turned against me and despises me. She has placed herself between Abram and me.'

Sarai found Abram, 'When I speak to you, if Hagar is present, she mocks me. She makes fun of me and she looks down upon me as if I am her servant. She treats me like a servant who has wronged her.'

Sarai and Hagar quarrelled with each other every day. Sarai spoke with Abram, 'Why will you say nothing? Can you see how she speaks to me? She never used to behave like this before. It's all your fault. You made her pregnant and now she despises me. Yahweh may judge between you and me.'

'She is still your servant,' answered Abram. 'And she is still under your authority. I haven't elevated her position in my household. You're my wife and she's not greater than you. You do with her as you wish.'

On hearing this, Sarai weighed down heavily upon Hagar with her authority and she ill-treated her. Every day they would argue and fight with each other and the conditions were so bad that Hagar fled. She ran away from her mistress Sarai because she could no longer bear to live under the same roof.

Hagar ran into the wilderness and she lay down weary and thirsty. The messenger of Yahweh, taking pity on Hagar, came and found her beside the spring in the desert, the one that is beside the road to Shur. In her haste to flee, she never considered water to drink. She had no jar to draw water from the well. She cried, expecting to die very soon from thirst.

'Hagar,' called the messenger of Yahweh. 'Servant of Sarai, where have you come from and what are you doing here? You are beside the well but you have no jar to draw water.'

'O Adonai, my Lord,' said Hagar, bowing to the ground. She knew the messenger of Yahweh and followed in the ways of Sarai and Abram. 'I have fled from my mistress Sarai, because she has mistreated me, on account that I've conceived and am pregnant with the child of Abram, her husband. She has turned against me in her jealousy and I can no longer bear her company.'

'Remember, Hagar,' said the messenger of Yahweh, 'when you knew that you were pregnant, you looked down upon your mistress Sarai, scornfully. You mocked her because you were able to conceive and she was not. This behaviour brought bitterness between you and your mistress Sarai, because you were puffed up with pride.'

Hagar knew that the angel of the Lord spoke the words of truth and she was ashamed of herself. 'Adonai Yahweh, my Lord and God, what must I do?'

'You must return to your mistress Sarai. You must humble yourself and submit to her authority. This conduct will soften Sarai's attitude toward you. Know this, Hagar, you are going to give birth to a son. You must name him Ishmael because I, the messenger of Yahweh, have heard your cry. I know of your sorrow. I will increase his descendants and they will be too numerous to count. He will be like a wild donkey and he will battle with everyone, and everyone with him. There will be hostility between him and his brothers.'

At this point the messenger of Yahweh left her. There beside her she found a jar and a rope tied to it. She let down the jar into the well and drew water to refresh herself and quench her thirst.

'Yahweh Elohim, the God of heaven and earth, has seen me,' she said to herself. 'He shall be called the God who sees me. And I have seen God. This well today shall now be called Beer Lahai Roi, because this is the well of the living one who sees me.' So she named the well and it is situated on the road between Kadesh and the wilderness of Bered.

Hagar, obeying the word of Yahweh Elohim, returned to her mistress Sarai. She returned in humility and there she submitted to the authority of Sarai. As God promised, the heart of Sarai was softened toward her. When her time came, Hagar gave birth to a son and Abram gave him the name Ishmael, which means God hears. At this time Abram was eighty-six years old.

CHAPTER 22

Eliezer

The incident concerning the man of Elam, who visited the city of Sodom with a mantle of many colours, is very sorrowful. But at least he left the city of Sodom with breath in his body. As time went by, the cities of the plain became more sinful, especially Sodom and Gomorrah.

Each of the cities had a judge appointed to it. The judge of Sodom was called Serak; for Gomorrah, Sharkad was the judge; Zabnac judged Admah; and Menon judged Zeboiim. Each city had a bed placed in the city street and if a stranger entered any of these cities, he would be forced to lie on the bed. They measured the height of the man according to the length of the bed. If the man was too short, he would be stretched by three men at his head and three men at his feet. But if the man was too long for the bed they would crush him until he lost his life.

They made a decree stating that this is how it shall be for any stranger entering their cities. If a poor man came to any of these cities and survived the testing on the bed, they would give him silver and gold. The decree was made that even though he had the means to pay for food, it was forbidden for the inhabitants to sell him food or water. When the man died from hunger, the silver and gold was retrieved by those that gave it to him. His clothes were taken from him and people fought over them. His corpse was then removed and dumped in the desert.

After Hagar gave birth to Ishmael, the son of Abram, Sarai felt very lonely and wanted comforting news of her brother Lot, who had settled to live in the city of Sodom, many years ago. Calling Eliezer of Damascus, the most faithful servant of Abram, she said, 'Eliezer, I haven't seen my brother Lot for many years and I wonder how he is. I want you to go to the city of Sodom and seek him out. I hope he is well. Come back with news of him.'

Eliezer assembled twelve strong and trustworthy men among the servants of Abram and he departed from their home. He travelled east to the Valley of Siddim and to the city of Sodom.

'I expect mischief in the city of Sodom,' announced Eliezer. 'When we come in sight of the city, we will break up into smaller groups and wait a distance from the city. If we approach as one group, we'll only draw attention to ourselves.'

So Eliezer split up his number into four groups, each numbering three men. Three men accompanied Eliezer to the city gates and the other groups rested in the plain, in sight of each other and in sight of the city gates. All of his men were armed with swords and some were equipped with bow and arrow. They were expecting trouble because of all the rumours about the cities of the plain and they were all ready to fight.

Eliezer asked his three companions to wait outside the city gates with his donkey. 'Be ready to flee if necessary. We don't know what kind of trouble we'll encounter. The people of this place are extremely wicked. Keep watch.'

Leaving his donkey in the care of his companions, he entered the city to search for Lot. Fortunately, he did not have to search for long, before finding Lot in the square. Looking up, Lot immediately recognized Eliezer, even though they had not seen each other for many years.

'Come inside the house, quickly,' said Lot. 'Strangers always encounter trouble here,' he ushered Eliezer into the house and quickly closed the door.

After the customary greeting, Eliezer said, 'Your sister Sarai sent me to enquire about you. She hasn't seen you in many years and has heard many reports about the wickedness of this place.'

'I'm well,' answered Lot. 'I had one daughter, who died many years ago, and another who is married to a man of Sodom and my wife Ado is well. Sit down with us. Eat and drink and refresh yourself. I'll fetch water and you can wash your feet after the long journey.'

'I'll eat a small morsel of food with you. I half expect trouble here and I'm afraid I'll have to fight my way out.'

'The people here have grown worse,' admitted Lot.

'Why do you remain?' asked Eliezer. Then he regretted asking. 'Forgive me, Lot. It's not my place to question you, since I'm only a servant. But I ask on behalf of your sister Sarai. She is worried about your welfare.'

'The city of Sodom was not so bad when we first came here. But over the years, the nature of the people here has become worse. Wickedness has certainly grown.'

'Then why do you remain? Why don't you leave? Things will only become worse.'

'I can't really leave. Everything I have is here. I've invested a lot of silver and gold, purchasing my possessions, and I can't walk away and leave my property behind. This is our home. Our daughter is now married and she lives here with her husband and he is a man from Sodom. She will have her own children here and Ado and I can't abandon them.'

'Take your daughter and her husband with you and come back to Abram and Sarai. They will be glad to see you.'

'No,' answered Lot, casting his eyes down and shaking his head. 'I've caused a lot of trouble for them in the past. I don't want to burden them again. Tell them that I am well and settled here in Sodom. I can't see the people here getting any worse than they already are.'

Eliezer was unable to persuade Lot to leave. They parted company, blessing each other on the threshold of the house. Returning on his way to the gates of the city, Eliezer came upon a confrontation in the street. A man of Sodom was fighting with a stranger. The stranger was stripped of his clothes. Upon seeing Eliezer approaching, the stranger cried out to Eliezer for help.

'What are you doing to this man?' questioned Eliezer.

'What business is it of yours?' replied the man of Sodom. 'And what business have you in our city?'

'You must not mistreat this man.'

'Is this man your brother that you care so much about him? And have you been appointed judge that you may question me? We have our customs and laws and you must abide by them.'

Eliezer reached forward to retrieve the poor man's clothes but the man of Sodom quickly avoided him. 'Give back this man's clothes,' said Eliezer.

Reaching down to the ground, the man of Sodom picked up a rock and swung it into Eliezer's forehead. The incident happened so fast that Eliezer was caught off guard. He was not expecting it and, staggering, he fell to the ground. The blood was gushing from his wound.

Grasping hold of Eliezer, the man of Sodom dragged him to his feet. 'Now pay me what you owe me, for releasing this bad blood from you. You owe me a day's hire, for releasing you from this bad blood.'

Eliezer was dazed and his head was throbbing in pain from the blow. 'What do you mean?' he asked. 'You expect me to pay you for striking me on the head and making me bleed?'

'Yes. This is the custom here in Sodom.'

'Well it's not my custom.'

'Nevertheless, you'll pay me a day's hire.'

'I will not.'

'Yes you will,' said the man from Sodom. He dragged Eliezer, who had not yet recovered, up onto his feet. He led him, stumbling, to meet Serak, the judge of Sodom. At the city gate Serak listened to the account of what had taken place. The man of Sodom insisted upon payment from Eliezer for having bad blood drawn from his head.

'This is ridiculous,' said Eliezer. 'This man assaulted me and wounded me, drawing blood from my head. Now he expects me to pay him for doing so.'

'That's correct,' replied Serak. 'This is the law of Sodom. A decree has been made and it will not be broken. You must now pay this man a day's hire, for ridding you of this bad blood.'

'Is that so?' asked Eliezer, stooping down to reach for a large stone. 'So because he hit me with a stone like this, I must pay him for a day's hire?'

'Yes,' confirmed Serak.

'Now pay me,' demanded the man of Sodom.

'I will pay you,' said Eliezer. Turning to the judge, he struck Serak a heavy blow with the stone on his head. Immediately, Serak staggered backward and fell to the ground. Blood spilled from the wound. 'If this is the custom in the city of Sodom, then you can give to this man what I owe him, because you now owe me. This is your decision and this is your decree.'

Eliezer walked out of Sodom through the gates and leaped upon the donkey that his men were holding ready for him. They could see the blood on his forehead and had their hands on their swords.

'Go. Quickly,' urged Eliezer. The donkeys raised the dust with their hooves. A tumult followed them out of the city gate. The men of Sodom were anxious to capture Eliezer and make him pay. They followed him in haste out of the city. But out in the plain, the men of Sodom were not expecting to be ambushed.

The men of Sodom were afraid when they came upon Eliezer's armed men. Several arrows were pointing at them. The men of Sodom ran out of the city in such haste that they never thought of bringing weapons with them. They did not expect to find Eliezer's men, lying in hiding, waiting for them in the plain.

The men of Sodom hurled the only weapon they had, a lot of angry words, 'If we ever see you again, near the city of Sodom, we'll kill you and your men.'

Eliezer and his men turned and continued on their journey home. They were cautious on their return journey, making sure that they were not being followed. It was important that they did not attract trouble for Abram and his household. At least they had found Lot and they had news for his sister Sarai.

CHAPTER 23

Circumcision

Abram was taken by surprise when God appeared to him. Abram was ninety-nine years old and God said to him, 'I am El-Shaddai, the Breasts of God, the all-sustaining one, the all-nurturing one. I am the one who cares for you and comforts you. As a mother feeds her baby at the breast, so do I feed you and enable you to grow to maturity. All of your security and comfort can be found in me. Come to me and look upon my face and you will not die in the light of my glory. Live a righteous and upright life and I will cut a covenant agreement between us and I will multiply your descendants.'

Abram fell face down to the earth before El-Shaddai.

'This will be my covenant with you,' said El-Shaddai. 'You will father many nations. I will now change your name. Because of your obedience to me, leaving your father's house at my bidding, forsaking all of his wealth and your promised inheritance, I now change your name. You will no longer be called Abram, meaning exalted father. You abandoned the wealth of your father's house and have accepted me as your father. Today I breathe my spirit into you and you are lifted up by my spirit. You are now called Abraham, meaning the father of many nations and it is through you that I will be revealed to the world.

'You will be fruitful and many nations will spring forth from you and many kings shall rise up from you. My covenant with you will last forever. It will never come to an end. In this covenant, I will be Elohim, your God, and I will be Elohim, the God of all your descendants. You are now a stranger in this land of Canaan, but I give you this land to be your possession, for yourself and for all of your descendants for all time. Forever I will be Elohim, their God.

'For your part, you must safeguard my covenant agreement and so must all of your descendants for all time to come. Every male in your household, and all males over eight days old, must be circumcised for all generations to come. This will be the sign in your body of the agreement made in the covenant between us. Any male who is not circumcised in the flesh will be cut off from your people, for he has broken my covenant.

'Now for your wife Sarai, her name will be changed from this very day. From this day forward, she will no longer be known as Sarai, meaning princess, but she shall be known as Sarah, this means princess of the nations, for I have breathed my spirit into her. I now bless her and I open her womb. She will become pregnant and will give birth to your son. She will be the mother of many nations and many kings will come from these nations.'

On hearing this, Abraham could not help himself. He laughed. Thinking to himself he said, 'Is it possible for a son to be born to a man as old as one hundred years? And how will Sarah give birth to a son at the age of ninety?' Not forgetting his firstborn son, Abraham asked El-Shaddai, 'Will my son Ishmael also receive your blessing?'

'Yes,' answered El-Shaddai. 'I'll bless your firstborn son, Ishmael. He'll be fruitful and his numbers will increase. I'll make of him a great nation and twelve rulers of nations will descend from him. But my covenant will not be with Ishmael. Your wife Sarah will bear a son and he will be called Isaac, which means he laughs. My covenant with him will be an everlasting covenant, for all of his descendants.

By this time next year, your wife Sarah will bear your son, Isaac, to you.' El-Shaddai finished speaking to Abraham and he ascended to heaven.

With haste Abraham rose up and gathered all the males in his household to be circumcised. Not one of them refused and they all agreed to have their foreskin removed. Abraham and Ishmael were the first to receive the circumcision. Ishmael was aged thirteen at the time. So the covenant agreement between Abraham and his people and El-Shaddai was fulfilled that same day. This day was the fifteenth day of Nisan, the month of redemption, the month of miracles when the barley and wheat grains ripen.

Three days after the circumcision, when Abraham was still in pain, he was sitting at the entrance of his tent, under the oak trees of Mamre. He was resting in the shade of the trees in the heat of the day, when Yahweh appeared to him. Lifting up his eyes he saw three men approaching from a distance. Rising up carefully, because he was still in pain, he ran out to greet them. As he met them, he bowed down low to the ground and he welcomed them to his tent.

'If I find favour in your eyes, Adonai, my Lord, please do not pass me by, but come into my tent and rest for a while. I will fetch water that you may bathe your feet and I will prepare food that you may eat. Then, when you are refreshed and rested, you may continue your journey.'

'As you wish,' they answered. 'We will rest awhile.'

So Abraham brought them water and they bathed their feet. They rested in the shade of the oak tree at the entrance to Abraham's tent. Running into the tent Abraham found Sarah and he said to her, 'Sarah, we have guests. We must welcome them to rest and eat because they are weary from their journey. Quickly, get three measures of fine wheat and kneed it and prepare some bread. I'll go to the herd and select the finest, the most tender and unblemished animal for their meat.'

Selecting the finest calf, he gave instructions to his servants to slaughter it and prepare it and cook it for his three guests. This they did with haste and when the meat was ready he presented the food to them. He gave them the meat, the bread, curds, and some milk. His guests gave thanks and began to eat the food. While they were eating their food, Abraham stood nearby under the shade of the tree.

'Abraham,' they asked. 'Where is your wife Sarah?'

'She is inside the tent, my Lord.'

'We will return to you this time next year and your wife Sarah will have a son of her own.'

Now Sarah was at the entrance of the tent and the man speaking had his back toward her. When she heard these words, she laughed quietly to herself. She could not help herself. 'Can it possibly be true?' she said to herself. 'If only this man had spoken these words fifty or sixty years ago. Now I'm ninety years old and I'm worn out. I don't have the energy to look after a child. And how would I endure childbirth at my age? It would probably be the end of me. At this age I won't be able to bear a child. This is a joke.'

Yahweh then asked Abraham, 'Why does Sarah laugh? Why does she doubt that she will have a child, even at her age? Does she not know, that nothing is impossible for Yahweh?' he paused to let the words sink in. 'I will say it again. This time next year, I will return and Sarah will give birth to a son.'

Sarah, in a state of anxiety, ran out of the tent and presented herself to Adonai, the Lord Yahweh. Falling down on her knees in fear she said, 'Adonai, my Lord, I did not laugh.'

Then Yahweh looked upon her and answered, 'Sarah, you did laugh.'

CHAPTER 24

Intercession

The time arrived and Abraham's three visitors put on their sandals and picked up their staffs. They were ready to leave and continue their journey. They bid Sarah farewell and gave her a blessing, thanking her for her hospitality. They made a promise to Sarah that they would return and she would give birth to a child. They asked Abraham to accompany them on the road leading to the cities of the plain; the cities of Sodom, Gomorrah, Zeboiim, and Admah.

The three men spoke quietly together and Yahweh said, 'Must I hide from Abraham the plans that I intend to carry out? Abraham himself will surely become a great and mighty nation and all the nations of the earth will receive a blessing through him. He has been chosen by me and he will teach his children and all descendants that come through him to keep the statutes of Yahweh and to walk in the way of the Lord God. And surely in doing so, I will bring about all that I have promised him.'

When they came in sight of the plain with the cities clearly visible, they all stopped. Looking toward the cities Yahweh said, 'I hear the outcry against Sodom and Gomorrah. Their sin is so great, it has reached my ears. Now I must leave you, Abraham, and go down to

"

these cities and see for myself if this wickedness is true. When I stand in their midst, then I will know the truth, because I will hear what they say and see what they do.'

The two who were with Yahweh pressed on and headed for the cities of the plain. It was in the afternoon and it would be dark by the time they arrived in the plain. Yahweh remained and he was facing the city of Sodom. Abraham came and stood before Yahweh, between God and the cities of the plain. 'Are you going to destroy the righteous along with the wicked?' asked Abraham.

Yahweh looked at Abraham but remained silent.

'What if there are fifty people who are righteous, living in the city?' asked Abraham. 'Will they perish when the city is swept away? Will you not destroy the city, for the sake of the fifty who are not wicked? You could not possibly do such a thing, to destroy the righteous along with the wicked. Why should the righteous pay for the sins of the wicked? Will the judge of the earth not make a fair judgement, unlike the wicked judges of the cities of the plain?'

'Don't worry, Abraham. If I find fifty righteous people living in Sodom, I will spare the entire city for the sake of the fifty righteous people.'

'Who am I to question you, Adonai, my Lord?' said Abraham. 'I am only a created being, formed from ashes and dust. But supposing, my Lord, that there are not fifty righteous people living in Sodom. Maybe there are only forty-five righteous people living in Sodom. Would they still perish with the wicked? Would you spare the entire city for the sake of the forty-five people who are righteous?'

'If I find forty-five righteous people living there, I will not destroy the city,' answered Yahweh.

'Perhaps there are only forty righteous people there?'

'For the sake of the forty, I will not sweep away the city.'

'Please, let Yahweh not be angry with me for my persistence. But what if there are only thirty good people there?'

'If I find thirty good people living there, I will not destroy the city.'

'My Lord Yahweh, indeed I am very bold to ask. What if you go down to the city of Sodom and you only find twenty good people living there?'

'For the sake of the twenty good people, I will not destroy the city.'

'May Yahweh not be angry with me; I am your humble servant. This is my last question to you. If you find only ten righteous people living in Sodom, will you still destroy the city?'

'No. If I find ten righteous people living in Sodom, I will not destroy the city.'

'Thank you, Yahweh,' said Abraham, bowing to the ground, touching his forehead to the dust. When he raised up his eyes, he discovered that Yahweh had departed. Abraham, with a heavy heart for his nephew Lot and his family, turned and went home.

CHAPTER 25

Brimstone

It was evening time when the two messengers of Yahweh arrived at the gate of Sodom. Lot was sitting at the gate along with the elders of the city. When he saw the two angels approaching, he stood up and ran out to greet them.

Bowing down with his face to the ground, he cried out, 'Adonai, my Lords, please look favourably upon your servant and come home to my house with me. There you may wash your feet, after your journey. Then you must sit down and eat and drink with me and my family. You may rest for the night and then continue your journey in the morning.'

'No,' was their answer. 'We will not stay for the night in your house. Instead we will spend the night in the square.'

'Please, Adonai, my Lords,' answered Lot. 'Don't spend the night in the square, it's not safe.'

'We will spend the night in the square. We're here to discover what the people of Sodom are like.'

'My Lords, you'll discover that the people of Sodom are extremely wicked. Please come to my house, where you may eat and rest.'

'No. We must see and hear for ourselves what the people are like.'

Lot persisted and eventually he managed to persuade them to go with him to his house. There at his house, Lot's visitors washed their feet after their journey. Then they washed their hands and faces before sitting down to a lovely meal, prepared for them by Lot's wife, Ado.

After their meal and before they had settled into bed for the night, an angry mob of men assembled outside Lot's door. All of the men, both young and old, had gathered there. 'Lot. Lot. Send out the two men who you are sheltering in your house.'

Lot was afraid and did not know what to do.

'Send out the strangers who came to your house today,' they pounded their fists on the door. The house shook.

'I can't send them out to you. I've invited them into my house and they're under my protection.'

'You send them out to us now. You know the law in this city regarding strangers. There's a decree and you have broken it.'

'Send out the men,' shouted another. 'We're going to rape them.'

'We'll defile them. We'll give them a Sodomite welcome.'

'Ha, ha, ha. It'll be a night to remember.'

'Send them out. Now.'

Opening the door, Lot stepped outside to reason with them. 'My friends,' he said, closing the door behind him. 'Please don't defile these men. That's a wicked thing to do.'

'We want them. You know the law. You must keep the law.'

'Look, I have two virgin daughters. I'll send them out to you. You can do whatever you want to with them.'

'We don't want your daughters. We have a duty to defile these men.'

'We always enjoy performing our duty,' roared another. The whole company of men broke into laughter.

'We're going to enjoy performing our duty tonight. Now, send them out.'

'Please don't do anything to harm these men. They've come under the protection of my house.'

'Who are you? You're nothing but a stranger who settled here in our city many years ago. Now you're pretending to be our judge.'

'We'll teach you a lesson,' they shouted. 'Because you have defied the decree of this city, regarding the abuse of strangers, we're going to treat you worse than any stranger.'

'Strip him,' they chanted. 'Rape him until he's dead.'

The crowd pushed forward and were ready to beat down the door of Lot's house. At that moment the door opened and the two angels brought Lot back inside the house, shutting the door behind him. The angels struck the men outside blind, so that they could not see and were prevented from finding the door.

'Who else lives in this city belonging to you?' asked the angels. 'Sons, daughters, or their spouses or betrothed?'

'We have a daughter and her husband and two men who are betrothed to these two daughters of mine,' answered Lot.

'Then you must go now and warn them. Tell them that they must get out of this city, because Yahweh is going to destroy this place. Nothing will be left of it. In the morning it will be completely swept away.'

'But,' trembled Lot. 'The men outside. You heard what they'll do to me.'

'No they won't. They're blinded and will not find you.'

'But they might hear me.'

'No, they will not see you. Neither will they hear you nor feel your presence. All of their senses have been dulled.'

Going outside, Lot could see that the men had no perception of reality. He ran to the home of the first man who was to marry his daughter. He explained to the young man what was about to happen but the man did not believe Lot. He thought that Lot was joking. Lot ran to the home of the second man, who was to marry his youngest daughter and he likewise laughed at Lot, believing that he had lost his mind. Lot then came to his daughter's house. It was the furthest away from his own dwelling. Lot begged his daughter to come with him, to save herself and her children, but she also laughed at him and said, 'Ah, you're doting in your old age. There are no angels and there is no God.'

'The victims of Sodom and Gomorrah have cried out to Yahweh,' he pleaded. 'There are two angels, the messengers of Yahweh, standing in my house now. They have been sent by Yahweh to destroy this city. Please come with me.' He paused but his daughter made no reply. 'I'll get the children,' he said, going toward them.

'You leave them alone,' she said. 'They're asleep in bed and you're not to wake them. Go home and leave me alone. You've obviously had too much wine. Go home,' she guided him to the door. 'I'll speak to you tomorrow, when you're sober.' She closed the door, leaving him outside.

Back home, the messengers of Yahweh said, 'Lot, hurry. Take your wife and your two daughters, who are here with you, and leave the house. It'll soon be dawn and then the city will be punished. Everything will be swept away.'

Lot hesitated. He looked around at all of his possessions that he would have to leave behind. The messengers of Yahweh, knowing the need for haste, grasped the hands of Lot, his wife, and his two daughters and led them quickly out of the city.

'Now you must run,' said the angels. 'Run for your lives. Run to the safety of the mountains or you'll be swept away. Don't stop anywhere and don't look back or you'll be destroyed. Every living thing in the cities and in the plain will perish. Not even a blade of grass will escape.'

'No. No my Lords,' wept Lot. 'I'm too old. I'll never make it to the mountains in time. The sun is nearly up. Let us flee to that city in the south. It's only a little city. Can you spare it, the city of Zoar? I'll be able to run there in time. Will you let us escape there? Then our lives will be saved.'

'I'll grant your request. You may flee to the city of Zoar. Because it is a small city, I will not destroy it. You will find refuge there. But you must go quickly, because the disaster can't fall upon the cities and the plain until you reach safety.'

Lot and his wife with their two daughters ran as fast as they could. Lot's wife, Ado, was filled with grief, because her daughter and grandchildren would not leave with them. All of her wealth was invested in the city of Sodom and all of her possessions were behind in her house.

'How I long for the comforts of home,' she said to herself. 'Here I am now, a refugee. No more clothes to wear, no bed to lie on, no roof over my head. No daughter and no grandchildren. My heart is broken. I must take one last look upon my home and children.'

Lot saw her turn around. 'Ado,' he shrieked. 'No. Don't turn around. The angels warned us not to look back.'

His warning came too late. Ado's heart was still behind in the city of Sodom and as she looked back longingly for her comforts, the sun rose up over the horizon. At the dawn of the new day Yahweh rained down fire and brimstone upon the cities of the plain. As soon as she turned around, Ado, the wife of Lot, was turned into a pillar of salt.

The four cities were destroyed, Sodom, Gomorrah, Zeboiim, and Admah. Every living soul died. The animals grazing in the plain perished and every blade of grass was burned up. The valley filled up with the Salt Sea which extended to the south, filling the plain where the cities had once been. Now, they were no more. They were gone forever from the face of the earth.

Abraham woke from his sleep early, before the sun had begun to rise. Leaving his tent, he returned to the place where he had pleaded with Yahweh for the safety of the righteous in the city of Sodom. He trembled at the devastation that lay before him. Balls of fire were falling from the heavens. Elohim cast them down. Down they fell, crashing on the earth below. Flaming sparks exploded upon impact on the earth and billows of smoke filled the sky.

The cities were rent asunder. 'How can anyone survive such devastation of fire and brimstone?' he asked himself. 'I hope that Lot has been rescued. Yahweh promised to save him. I put my trust in God. My help comes from him. Elohim,' prayed Abraham. 'You are righteous and just and you are all mighty and powerful. There is none like you. The wicked you punish for their sins, but the righteous, you hold safe. You rescue the just from all harm. Blessed be Yahweh. Praise your holy name.'

Abraham's household rose from their sleep when they heard the explosions and felt the impact of God's devastation upon the cities of the plain. Seeing the clouds of smoke rising from the earth and the fiery balls falling from the sky, they ran to the place where Abraham was standing. All of them trembled with fear and gave praise to Elohim.

Lot and his two remaining daughters did not remain in the city of Zoar for long. The people of Zoar looked upon them in fear. They were banished from the city because the inhabitants feared that the destruction of Sodom would follow Lot to Zoar. Although Lot and his daughters were banished from Zoar at least the inhabitants were merciful enough to give them some unleavened bread and a skin of wine to sustain them.

Remembering the words of the angels, the messengers of Yahweh, to flee to the mountains, Lot and his daughters left the city of Zoar behind them and travelled toward the mountains. They feared that Zoar and other cities, even the entire world, would be destroyed like Sodom and Gomorrah. So they climbed high up to escape the wrath of God. They found the cave of Adullam, where they dwelt for some time.

Lot and his two daughters were overcome with grief. Lot had lost his wife Ado, who became a pillar of salt. His eldest daughter, who refused to escape with him, perished in the destruction of Sodom along with her children. His herd of cattle, his flock of sheep, his donkeys and camels were all gone, along with his house and all of his worldly possessions. In fleeing from Sodom, he also left behind all of his silver and gold. All of his wealth had gone up in a cloud of smoke and he would never see his wealth again. He was now destitute.

The only consolation he had now was the wine in which he overindulged. Completely drunk and out of his mind most of the time, his daughters devised a plan for themselves. 'There's no hope for us now,' said the eldest girl to her sister. 'The men we were to marry are now dead and the whole world is under the judgement of God. There is no one left on the face of the earth but the three of us.'

'What do you intend to do?' asked her sister.

'While our father is drunk, we can lay down with him and have sex with him so that we can bear children and the life of man may continue upon the face of the earth.'

'O no, that's not the right thing to do.'

'How else will life continue? Look around. There are no other men,' she paused, waiting for her words to sink in. 'I will lie down with him tonight and he will make me pregnant and you can lie down with him tomorrow night and he'll make you pregnant.'

So this is what happened. The eldest daughter lay down with Lot and he was so drunk that he thought he was lying down with his wife Ado. The eldest daughter conceived from her father's seed. The following night the youngest daughter did the same and lay down with her father and she also conceived.

When her time came, the eldest daughter gave birth to a son and she named him Moab, because she said, 'This means that he is from my father.'

The youngest daughter also gave birth to a son when her time came and she gave him the name Ben-Ammi which means, son of my people. Moab became the father of the Moabites and Ben-Ammi became the father of the Ammonites.

CHAPTER 26

Abimelech

Abraham had spent twenty-five years in the land of Canaan and he was now one hundred years old. Abraham travelled further south from Mamre, in Hebron, to the Negev and he dwelt in the territory between Kadesh and Shur. For a short time he dwelt in Gerar, which lies north of the Negev, in the land of the Philistines.

Mizraim fathered the Casluchim and the Pathrusim. These families traded their wives with each other at the bazaar. It was through this immoral behaviour that the Pelishtim came into being. The Pelishtim were also known in some tongues as the Philistines. They migrated to the island of Crete in the Great Sea and from there they arrived in the coastal area of Canaan. They became known as the Sea People.

Upon entering the land of the Philistines, Abraham was gripped with fear. He feared because of the beauty of his wife Sarah and he knew that the Philistines had no fear of God. He feared that Sarah would be taken from him, that she would be defiled and he would be killed.

Like the time when he entered Egypt, at the time of the famine that befell Canaan, Abraham drew his wife Sarah to him and said to her, 'When they ask of you in Gerar, tell them that you're my sister.'

'Oh please, don't do that to me again,' pleaded Sarah. 'It was very unpleasant having to hide in a chest.'

'I won't put you in a chest this time, I promise. But there's no fear of God among these people—'

'Yes, and you're afraid that they'll kill you and take me to be someone else's wife.' Looking at Abraham she could see the anxiety in his eyes. She softened toward him. 'Alright. Alright. I'll do it. Don't be afraid.' There was a moment of silence between them. 'I thought you trusted in Yahweh? Didn't you defeat the king of Elam with just a handful of men? Was Yahweh not fighting for you?'

'Yes. That's true. At that time Elohei Tzeva'ot, the God of Hosts, filled me up with a supernatural courage. A courage not of my own.'

'Well why don't you pray for that now?'

'I have prayed. But instead of courage, I am still filled with fear. I am brought low. I am going into the land of the Philistines in a state of humility. It must be for a reason that I don't understand. Yahweh must have a plan that he hasn't revealed to me. This must be for the greater good.'

'We must trust in Yahweh,' said Sarah, 'and place all our hope in him.'

While they were living in the land of the Philistines, the servants of Abimelech, the king of Gerar, saw Sarah and noticed that she was very beautiful. They asked Abraham about her and he told them that she was his sister.

These servants returned to King Abimelech and they told him, 'A man has come from the land of Canaan and he is dwelling in our land. He has a sister with him and she is exceedingly beautiful.'

Being taken by the enthusiasm of his servants, regarding Sarah's beauty, Abimelech instructed them, 'Find this man who has come from the land of Canaan and ask for his sister. I would like to meet her.'

So Sarah was brought to the house of Abimelech. When he laid eyes upon her, he was immediately stricken by her beauty. The sight of her beauty gladdened his heart and he felt love for her.

'Who is this man that has brought you to this land?' he asked.

'He is my brother,' answered Sarah, remembering the conversation that she had with Abraham earlier.

'And why are you here in Gerar, the land of Philistia?'

'We are nomads,' answered Sarah. 'We came here from the land of Canaan with our cattle and sheep. We go wherever there happens to be pasture for our animals.'

'You and your brother are welcome to stay in our land. You may place him anywhere that he pleases. He may settle wherever he likes. He'll be protected and well cared for in this land and I will exalt him above all others because he is your brother. I will send for your brother, so that I may speak to him.'

Abimelech dispatched his servants who found Abraham and brought him before the king. Abimelech stood up when Abraham entered into his presence. The king embraced Abraham, 'Welcome Abraham. Come wash your feet and sit down and eat with me. It's good that you've come to my land.'

'Many thanks to you, King Abimelech, for your kind welcome.'

'I'm really taken by your sister Sarah. She's very beautiful. And because of her beauty I will honour you, above all others in my kingdom. All of this, on account of your beautiful sister Sarah.'

Abraham departed after feasting with the king of Gerar. Abimelech showered him with gifts and told him, 'This land, my land, is laid out before you. You may choose to live wherever you desire. No harm will come to you. I have placed you under my protection.'

In the evening, after the meal but before retiring to his bed, King Abimelech was sitting on his throne when a heavy tiredness came upon him. He fell asleep upon his throne and it was a deep sleep. During his sleep, he had a dream. The angel, the messenger of Yahweh, appeared to him, holding a drawn sword in his hand. The angel stood over Abimelech and raised the sword, about to strike him dead.

'You Abimelech are a dead man,' declared Elohim. 'The woman that you have taken into your house is a married woman.'

The king was terrified and cried out to the messenger of Yahweh, 'O Elohim. What have I done to deserve death?'

'The woman Sarah that you've taken into your house is a married woman. You must not defile her. She is the wife of the man from the land of Canaan, called Abraham. If you touch Sarah, I will certainly kill you with the sword.'

'Adonai Elohim,' pleaded Abimelech. 'How was I to know that she is a married woman? Abraham told me that Sarah was his sister and Sarah told me that Abraham was her brother. I have been deceived, I have not sinned.'

'Know this,' answered Elohim. 'It was because of the fearfulness of Abraham that you have been deceived. But if you should fail to return Sarah to her husband Abraham, you will surely die. And not only you, but your entire household will perish along with all the inhabitants of the land.'

On that night throughout the land of the Philistines, a great terror seized them all. They saw the angel, the messenger of Yahweh, standing over them with a drawn sword in his hand. Elohim struck the Philistines with the sword and they fell, screaming in fear. Though they ran, they could not escape the sword in the hand of Elohim. He continued to strike them down.

All night long the messenger of Yahweh struck down the inhabitants of the land. Not one escaped the wrath of Elohim. The messenger of Yahweh closed up the bowels of every citizen living in the land, freeman and slave alike, so that none could relieve their pain. All of this was done to them on account of Sarah, the wife of Abraham.

Abimelech, the king of Gerar, woke up from his dream and he was drenched in sweat. He was seized with terror and he trembled at what he had seen in his dream. Calling on his wise men, he related to them the dream that he had during the night. The wise men were afraid of the punishment that would fall upon them because of the king taking Sarah into his house.

'My Lord and King,' responded one of his wise men. 'It was Elohim who put you into a deep sleep while you were sitting on your throne. He did this to prevent you from touching this woman. He has given you a warning and you must return her to her husband. If you don't return her, if you do touch her, then you and your family and all the inhabitants of the land of Philistia will perish.'

Another wise man spoke, 'My Lord and King, this reminds me of an incident that I heard of in the land of Egypt. It was during the famine that took place about twenty-five years ago. A similar thing happened there. A man and his entire household arrived in Egypt, from the land of Canaan. The famine in Canaan had driven them to the land of Egypt in search of wheat, because it was plentiful there.

'The men of Pharaoh Rikayon, of the second dynasty, discovered a beautiful woman hidden in a wooden chest. They had opened it to exact taxes from the man when he entered the land. The servants told Pharaoh of this woman. He was told that she was a sister of the man who had hidden her in the chest.

'So Pharaoh Rikayon took her into his house to become his wife. In the bedchamber, when he came to her, he was stricken with leprosy, which turned his hand white. He tried many times to touch her but the angel, the messenger of Yahweh, stood between them and struck another part of his body with leprosy. This continued until every part of his body was covered with the disease.

'Then he discovered that she was already married to the man who brought her to Egypt. Pharaoh returned the woman to her husband the next day and he gave many gifts to the man before sending him on his way.'

'What became of Pharaoh Rikayon?' asked Abimelech.

'Well Pharaoh Rikayon was not the only one afflicted with the disease. His entire household, including all his servants, were stricken with the disease. When the woman and her husband left the land of Egypt, they prayed to Elohim and Pharaoh Rikayon and all his household were healed. The leprosy fell from them.'

'My Lord and King, this woman that you've taken into your house must be the same woman that was taken in by the pharaoh of Egypt.'

There was a stunned silence. It was broken by one of the wise men, 'My Lord and King, last night we were all woken from our sleep in terror. We were all stricken by the sword of the messenger of Yahweh and even now stand before you in considerable pain. We'll all perish if this woman is not returned to her husband.'

'Go and fetch the woman Sarah and bring her here before me,' commanded the king. 'And go and find Abraham and bring him here before me.' The servants left to get them.

Abraham and Sarah were brought before the king and he asked them, 'What is this that you've done to me? Why would you deceive me about your relationship?'

'It was out of fear that I told you that Sarah was my sister,' answered Abraham.

'But why the deception? If she is your wife, why say that she is your sister?'

'Because I was afraid. I entered this land knowing that the one true God is not known here. If there's no fear of God, then, because of the beauty of my wife Sarah, you would kill me and take her for yourself.'

'This is a cruel deception,' stated Abimelech.

'It's not a deception, for Sarah is from my own father's household. She's both my sister and my wife.'

Remembering the account of Pharaoh Rikayon of Egypt, Abimelech showered many gifts on Abraham. He gave him a herd of cattle, flocks of sheep, menservants, maidservants, and a thousand pieces of silver.

'Take your wife,' said Abimelech, passing Sarah over to Abraham. 'You're welcome to spend time in my land. You're free to settle wherever you please and no harm will fall upon you, because you are under my protection. The wrong done to you, Sarah, has now been put right.'

The Philistines were still in pain from the terrors of the night, when the messenger of Yahweh had struck them down. Abimelech asked Abraham, 'Pray for me to your God, Elohim, so that the punishment on me and my people might be lifted.'

Abraham prayed and Yahweh listened to his prayer. Elohim healed Abimelech, his family, servants, and all the inhabitants of the land. The bowels of the Philistines were released and they lived. Abraham departed with Sarah his wife and they lived among the Philistines in peace.

CHAPTER 27

Isaac

Yahweh remembered his promise to Sarah and he came to visit her. Later she conceived a child of Abraham. Her waters broke at the time when the rain and the melting snow caused the River Jordan to swell and she gave birth to a son. He was born at the time when the ripening of the barley and wheat grain takes place, during the month of miracles. His birth took place on the fifteenth day of Nisan, exactly one year after the covenant of circumcision. This son they named Isaac.

Sarah was overjoyed and she said, 'Here now is my reason to laugh. I laugh with joy and everyone who hears that I've given birth to a son at the age of ninety will laugh with me. Who else but Yahweh would have promised Abraham that I would nurse a son and hold him on my lap? It's a miracle. Here I am feeding my son at the breast, at the age of ninety, and Abraham a father at the age of one hundred.'

Abraham, according to the covenant that he agreed with the Lord God, took his son Isaac and on the eighth day he circumcised him. Isaac became the first boy to be circumcised at the age of eight days.

The boy Isaac grew and was weaned and on the day that he was weaned Abraham gave a great feast, a banquet, a celebration.

Abraham's menservants and maidservants were very busy preparing for this feast. The most unblemished beasts were put aside for the banquet. Abraham selected beef, lamb, venison, and chicken. These were slaughtered and roasted and the choicest cuts of meat were presented to his guests. Abraham offered his guests many varieties of vegetables, fruits, and spices that he had purchased specially for the feast. He bought wine from the city of Salem and from the city of Hebron. Beer was purchased from as far away as the land of Egypt.

Many people came to the feast to rejoice with Abraham and Sarah. Shem, also known as Melchizadek, the king and high priest of Salem, arrived with his great-grandson Eber. Abimelech of Gerar, the king of the Philistines, came with his servants and with Phicol, the prince of his host. Mamre, Eshcol, and Aner, the close friends of Abraham, arrived from the land of Hebron with their families.

Terah, the father of Abraham, and Amthelo, the mother of Abraham, came along with Abraham's brother Nahor and his family. They travelled from Haran, the city in Paddan Aram, where they were still living. There was great rejoicing at the feast. Musicians played their instruments and the people sang and danced well into the night. Terah and Nahor and their families remained for many days with Abraham and Sarah in the land of the Philistines, before returning home to Haran.

A year after the birth of Isaac, the great-grandson of Eber died. His name was Serug and he was the son of Reu and the great-grandfather of Abraham and the grandfather of Terah. When Serug died he was two hundred and thirty-nine years old.

CHAPTER 28

Tyranny

In the city of Babel, Nimrod still ruled as king of the land of Shinar, which is Babylon. But Nimrod was not a happy man. He had been disgraced by the king of Elam, Kedorlaomer, when he was defeated in battle by a much smaller force. Nimrod was then forced to serve Kedorlaomer who had once served Nimrod. At the command of Kedorlaomer Nimrod was forced to go into battle against the Hamites living in the four cities of the plain, Sodom, Gomorrah, Admah, and Zeboiim. It irritated him that he had to fight against his own people.

Nimrod also had to swallow his pride when he was defeated by Abram. Even though the alliance of kings under Kedorlaomer had a far superior army and had conquered and pillaged all the cities in their path, it was Abram with a much smaller body of men who overthrew them near the city of Damascus. The embarrassment irritated him and he craved for power, he longed for control, it was his desire to dominate the world. So he appealed to the gods for their favour.

Women were an easy target for Nimrod and he made a decree that every bride, on her wedding night, had to spend the night in his bedchamber. This gave his lust for sex some satisfaction. In this way every marriage was defiled by him and every firstborn child belonged to Nimrod. Many tried to defy Nimrod but they paid the price for their disobedience. The husband was put to death and his bride became the slave of Nimrod and she was often treated in a most brutal way.

If this was not bad enough, Nimrod claimed ownership over these children and they had to be given over to the palace. The babies were never seen again by their mothers. These sons and daughters of Nimrod were then sacrificed as burnt offerings on the altar to the gods. His belief was that in offering his own seed to the gods, they would look more favourably upon him and grant his desire for more power and give him domination over his enemies.

A man and his bride defied the decree of Nimrod and on their wedding night they took it upon themselves to flee, secretly under the cover of darkness. They revealed their plans to no one. Not even their closest friends nor family members knew of their plans. Before the palace guards arrived the couple slipped away. When their disappearance was discovered there was uproar as the palace guards wrecked the house searching for the fugitives.

Nimrod flew into a rage. The palace guards who failed to present the bride to the bedchamber of Nimrod were thrown into prison. 'You will never see the light of day again,' declared Nimrod. 'I will search for and find these people myself. They will pay severely for their disobedience. I will kill the groom and I will enslave his bride. She will suffer most severely under my hand.' Turning to the imprisoned men he warned them, 'When I return after the hunt, you can be sure that you will suffer the most cruel and painful torture. It will be so bad that you will beg me to kill you.' Shrugging his shoulders he said, 'And so, you will die. But first I will have my fun.'

Nothing excites the hunter like the pursuit of his prey and Nimrod left the palace with a determination that the fugitives would be captured. The house where the wedding celebrations had taken place was the first place to be investigated. All of the guests had been detained so that Nimrod could interrogate them. He used torture and brutality to extract information from them. No one was able to tell him of the married couple's plans to escape.

'I want to know how they left this house,' he roared. 'Did they leave on foot or did they ride away on horse or camel? Count the animals and tell me if any of them are missing.'

After the count, it was discovered that one of the horses was missing. This news was pleasing to Nimrod, 'At last, we can now follow their tracks. It will not be long now before I find them.' Turning to the parents of the bride and groom Nimrod said, 'Believe me, I will take great delight in finding them. You will never see them again. I can assure you of this.'

At this remark the families burst into tears and fell down before Nimrod, begging him for mercy. Nimrod was gone, he did not wait to hear their supplications. 'Mercy. There will be no mercy from me. If I grant them mercy they will think that I am weak. They will know that I am not weak; I am strong. They will know of my strength. The only way to govern these people is through tyranny. What else do they know; I am Nimrod.'

Following the tracks of the horse was not a difficult task for Nimrod. It was not long before he found the whereabouts of the horse. A man was holding the beast by the bridle and showing off the horse to a group of men. They were stroking the horse and were clearly in admiration of it.

'Where is the owner of this horse?' demanded Nimrod.

The group of men, recognizing Nimrod, fell to the ground in fear.

Nimrod dragged the man holding the bridle to his feet. He knew that this man was not the one that he was pursuing. 'Where did you get this horse?' he roared.

'I bought it for a fair price from a man, this very day.' The man trembled.

'Was this man alone or was there someone with him?' asked Nimrod.

'When he sold me his horse he was alone but I noticed him return to join his wife, after the transaction was made.'

A smile of satisfaction crossed the lips of Nimrod. 'Ah that's good. Describe the man's appearance to me. What did he look like and what was he wearing?'

The man tried his best to describe the bridegroom and the bride but his descriptions were vague.

'Tell me, what became of them and where did they go?'

'They went down to the harbour by the river to board a ship, I think.'

'You think?' sneered Nimrod. 'Where are they going to on this ship?'

'My Lord, I truly don't know. They didn't confide in me. I got the impression that they were leaving the land of Shinar and wanted to cross over the River Tigris to enter the land to the east.'

Mounting his horse, Nimrod announced, 'Get up on your horse. You will come with me and help me to find these people, for they are fugitives. They must be captured and they must pay for their crime.'

'But my Lord,' protested the man. 'I have just purchased this animal and I am not used to riding a horse—'

'Well now is the time to learn,' interrupted Nimrod. 'Mount upon your horse now.'

The man could not refuse. He climbed up onto the horse's back and clung on for his life's sake, as the group of horses sped away toward the harbour. It was not long before they arrived at the harbour. The man begged Nimrod to allow him to dismount because he felt sick in his stomach with fear.

'No. You will find these people first. Then you can dismount.'

There was no sign of them at the harbour. 'I can't see them here. They must have already sailed.'

'Round up all the women and children and assemble them here before me,' commanded Nimrod to his servants.

With haste all of the women and children were forced to gather together before Nimrod. They were crying and screaming because they were in great fear. The husbands and fathers, seeing what was happening and being powerless to prevent it, were also greatly distressed.

'You men here present,' announced Nimrod, 'listen to me. Your women and children belong to me. I will remove every one of them from this place and will enslave them in the city of Babel. However, I will release them to you if you do as I command.'

'We will obey you,' answered the men. 'We will do all that you ask of us, if you will release the women and children without harming them.'

'I will not release them until you do what I ask of you.'

'Ask and we will obey you. Only do not harm them.'

'I am hunting a man and his wife. They have fled from me but they have to pay their debts to me. They are strangers to this district and you must have seen them and you must know where they have gone to. Tell me where they have gone or you will lose sight of your women and children forever.'

Out of fear one of the men said, 'We saw them earlier today. They came in on a horse and they boarded a trading vessel. They have sailed down the river.'

'Good,' said Nimrod with satisfaction. 'Now I will wait here and you will go and capture them. When you do this, you will bring them back here. Then and only then will I release your women and children.'

'But, my Lord Nimrod, they are long gone. We may not be able to find them.'

'That is true,' answered Nimrod. 'But consider this, if you fail to find them, then you must say farewell to the women and children,' he paused for a moment. 'I suggest that you go quickly.'

With this the men boarded their ships and pushed out from the bank. Raising their sails they sped off down the Tigris River as quickly as the wind and current could carry them.

Turning to the women with satisfaction, Nimrod laughed. 'Feed me,' he roared.

Nimrod's servants roused him from the bed of some other man's wife. 'The fugitives, my Lord.'

'What?' answered Nimrod, slowly climbing out of a deep sleep.

'They have been found, my Lord. The fugitives. They are here now.'

'Ah, that is good,' said Nimrod, coming to his senses. Rising up from the bed he announced, 'Now is the time to show these people what becomes of those who choose to disobey me.' Stopping to fill his mouth with water, he followed his servant out through the door.

The couple were a sorry sight to behold. Sailing through the water of the Tigris River they were congratulating themselves on escaping the tyranny of Nimrod. 'We are too far gone now to be captured. Soon we will be safe in the land of Elam. Nimrod will never pursue us there because he has been subdued by Kedorlaomer.'

No sooner had he spoken the words when many ships were spied in the distance quickly approaching them. The sailors dropped the sail because their neighbours were wildly waving at them to stop.

'What is happening?' asked the bridegroom, leaping to his feet.

'I don't know,' was the man's answer. 'But we will soon discover what this is all about.'

'No. Please. We must not stop. We paid you well, to take us to the land of Elam.'

'These men are my neighbours. I trust them.' Neither the supplications nor the tears of the couple were able to make the man continue his journey. 'I fear there is something wrong. I sense it.'

They were doomed. The couple knew it. Together they threw themselves from the ship and began to swim toward the eastern bank of the river. They did not get far and were hauled aboard like a great catch of fish. With their hands and feet bound, there was no escape. Fear had gripped the traders and with no words exchanged the fugitives were delivered into the hands of Nimrod.

Nimrod took great delight in raping the bride before her husband and the whole community. Nimrod had no shame at his own nakedness. 'Let this be a lesson to you all,' he announced, gasping for breath. 'I have made a decree and you will all obey it. Remember this day.'

Returning to the city of Babel, he made a public spectacle of the married couple. Again the bride was publicly raped and her husband was speared through the mouth and out through the bowel. His body was raised up high, like a beast on a spit waiting to be roasted. The carrion feasted on his flesh. Nimrod was the most feared and hated man on the face of the earth.

CHAPTER 29

Ishmael

When Isaac was five years old, he was sitting at the door of the tent and Ishmael came along. Seeing his younger brother Isaac sitting on the ground, he came over and sat down opposite him. Ishmael looked upon Isaac silently for a while and Sarah noticed him. Ishmael then slipped an arrow into the string of his bow and pulled back on the string, with the arrow pointing at Isaac.

Rushing forward with a scream of terror in her throat, Sarah snatched the weapon from the hands of Ishmael. 'Get out. Get out of here,' she screamed at Ishmael, striking him across the head and his back with the bow that she had taken from his hand. 'Abraham. Abraham,' she shrieked. 'Come quickly.'

The servants, hearing her cry, came forward to see what was happening and why she was in such distress. 'What is wrong?' they asked.

'Go and find Abraham. Quickly,' she panted. She passed the bow into the hands of the servants. 'Keep this away from Ishmael. He tried to kill Isaac with it.'

With tears flooding her face, she reached down and picked up Isaac. Holding him close, she brought him inside the tent for safety. Abraham was quickly found and he went into the tent to Sarah, to see what all the commotion was about. He listened to her account of what had happened and he was greatly distressed.

Abraham was furious at the conduct of his son Ishmael. He went in search of him and they argued into the night. 'Why did you aim your arrow at Isaac, your brother?'

'I'm fed up with Isaac. I see the fuss that is made of him. I'm your firstborn son but you have quickly forgotten me. All of your attention is now given to him. Since he was born, I have been cast out from your mind.'

'Yes, you are the firstborn son and you should have more sense. Isaac is only aged five years. Of course I'm going to make a fuss of him. He's my delight and was born in my old age, and he was promised to me by Yahweh.' A long pause followed. 'Why are you so jealous? Have I not loved you all the days of your life? Do I not care for you, that you should be so angry with me and take out your anger on your brother?'

'That woman. That wife of yours, she has always been jealous of me. What have I ever done to her? She hates me.'

'She has never tried to kill you,' shouted Abraham.

'I hate her. And I hate him, because he has come between you and me.'

'I love you, Ishmael. I have always loved you and I always will. But look at yourself. You're now nineteen years of age and you must not be consumed with hatred and jealousy.' A long period of silence followed. Emotions were high and hearts were thumping. 'I'll speak to you again, after the sun has risen,' said Abraham. 'Go to your tent now.'

'No. I'll not go to my tent.'

Calling his servants, Abraham had Ishmael forcefully escorted to his tent, where they kept watch over him, to ensure that he got up to no mischief during the night.

In the morning Abraham called Ishmael and Hagar to him. Taking twelve loaves of bread and some water he sent them away, because they could no longer be trusted around Isaac and Sarah. So Hagar and her son Ishmael went into the wilderness, where Ishmael became an expert with the bow. They lived in the wilderness of Paran for many years.

Abraham was heartbroken at the departure of his son Ishmael and he wept bitterly for many days. 'If only Ishmael had looked favourably upon his brother Isaac, he would not have been sent away,' said Abraham to himself. 'O Yahweh,' cried Abraham. 'I had to dismiss Ishmael from my household on account of his threatening behaviour toward Isaac and Sarah. But I do still love him and care for him. Adonai, Lord, take care of my firstborn son Ishmael. Protect him and may he prosper in the land, wherever he goes.'

Yahweh said, 'Abraham, do not be anxious because Sarah insisted that Ishmael be banished from your household. I will make of Ishmael a great nation, because he is your son. For all of his life, I will remain with him and guide him and I will also care for his mother Hagar.'

To Hagar the slave girl and mother of Ishmael, Yahweh said, 'Hagar do not be afraid. Though you have been banished from the house of Abraham, you have not been abandoned. I am with you and your son and I will not forsake you. I will never leave you. Submit to my will and I will prosper you wherever you go. Give over your son to me and I will soften his heart. Give yourself to me in humility. I will remove your anger and frustration and I will give you peace. Rest in the knowledge that I have a plan for you and Ishmael and it is good for you. Surrender into my loving care and all will be well.'

Ishmael and his mother Hagar travelled to Egypt and remained there for some time and there, Hagar found a wife for her son. Ishmael married Meribah, who was also known as Ribah, and she conceived and over a period of time gave Ishmael four sons and two daughters. Ishmael and his family with his mother returned to the wilderness and there they lived. They lived as nomads in tents and travelled through the wilderness. Ishmael had flocks of sheep and herds of cattle and he prospered in the wilderness as God had promised.

Abraham missed his son Ishmael. The heartache remained and the years passed by and Abraham always enquired of him whenever a stranger from the lands to the south came by. 'Sarah,' he announced one morning. 'I haven't seen Ishmael, my son, in years and although I've heard word about him, I would like to travel and seek him out for myself.' Mounting his camel he told her, 'I will return in a few days. It may take some time to find him but the latest news is that he is living in the wilderness of Paran.'

Off went Abraham and he travelled over a long distance. He was a few days away from home when he came upon a tent. Approaching the tent he saw a young woman sitting inside the door of the tent, taking shelter from the heat of the noonday sun.

'Shalom,' greeted Abraham. The woman glanced up but made no remark. 'I greet you, good woman,' he said. There followed a moment of silence. 'May I have a drink of water please?' asked Abraham. 'I have travelled a long way and I am weary in the heat of the noonday sun.'

'I have no water, nor do I have any bread.'

'I don't need bread,' he answered. 'Only a little water to quench my thirst.'

'I told you already. I have no water.'

She lied because Abraham could see that the water jar was full inside the tent.

'Is this the house of Ishmael, son of Abraham?'

'It is,' was her response.

'I would like to speak to him,' said Abraham. 'Is he at home?'

'Does it look like it?' she sneered, without looking at him. 'He's not here.'

'When will he be back, do you know?'

'No. I don't know and I care less. He's gone off hunting with his bow and he could be gone for days.'

The children inside the tent were restless and were crying and creating a fuss. The mother turned around screaming and shouting at the children, cursing them. This pierced Abraham's heart with sorrow because she began beating them harshly. She also cursed Ishmael, her husband. Abraham was very hurt and it angered him.

'Woman. Come out to me,' shouted Abraham.

Stepping out of her tent, she stood before him in defiance.

'When Ishmael your husband comes home, give him a message from me.'

'I might forget,' she answered scornfully.

'Well make sure that you don't forget, because this message affects you as well as him.'

'Give me the message then,' she said, half interested.

'Tell him that a very old man from the land of the Philistines came by to visit him today. Tell him that you didn't ask me my name, but you can describe my appearance to him. My message is this, he must remove this tent peg,' he pointed it out to her, 'because this is unsuitable, he must throw it away and place a better tent peg here instead. Will you give him this message?'

She paused, 'I will. But what does it mean? It makes no sense to me.'

'Ishmael will understand. He'll explain it to you when he comes home after hunting.'

'How will I benefit?' she was eager to know.

'You'll receive your just reward,' he answered. 'Now I must leave. I have a long journey to make before I reach home.' Turning his camel, he journeyed north in the direction of home.

At nightfall Ishmael had finished hunting and he returned home. Meribah, his wife, said, 'An old man came here today. He was looking for you.'

'Who is this old man that was looking for me?'

'I don't know his name.'

'Did you not ask?'

'No. He left when he knew that you were not at home. He didn't even get off his camel.'

'Did he not even eat bread and drink water with you?'

'No. I wasn't going to give him my bread and my water. He could easily stop at a well and draw water.'

'It's common decency to show hospitality to a stranger. You could at least have given him a cup of water. Now he will think that I am mean hearted and have no respect for others.'

'I'm the one who has to go and get the water from the well. Why should I waste my efforts on a passing stranger? I get tired carrying the water in this heat.'

'Where was he from?' asked Ishmael, frustrated with Meribah's attitude.

'He told me that he came from the land of the Philistines,' and she described his appearance.

Ishmael's heart leaped inside his chest, 'Did he say anything else?'

'He had a message for you. He told me to tell you that a very old man from the land of the Philistines came here to visit you today. And he said that you were to pull up this tent peg,' she pointed to it, 'because it is totally unsuitable. You're to throw it away and replace it with a new tent peg. That's it. I told him that it didn't make any sense, but he told me that you would understand what it means.'

Ishmael's jaw dropped. Listening to the words of his wife Meribah, he immediately knew the identity of the visitor. 'It was none other than my own father, Abraham the son of Terah, who came here today. You didn't greet him. You didn't honour him. You never offered him bread to take away his hunger, nor water to quench his thirst,' Ishmael's eyes filled with tears. 'You're a cold hearted and selfish woman.'

'What?' she roared.

'You're the unsuitable tent peg and you need to be discarded and thrown away. I know now that you were mistreating the children in the presence of my father, and I know that you must have cursed them and me while he was here. He must have witnessed your bad behaviour.'

Ishmael was furious with his wife Meribah and he burned with anger toward her. He cast her away from him and forbade her to remain in his tent. She left him and returned to her father's house in Egypt in disgrace. Then Ishmael travelled to the land of Canaan and found another woman to be his wife. He returned to the wilderness of Paran and she lived the life of a nomad in his tent.

Three years later, the wife of Ishmael was sitting at the door of her tent, sheltering from the heat of the noonday sun, when a stranger arrived. He was a very old man sitting on a camel and he came travelling from the lands to the north. The sun was roasting hot and it was blinding his eyes.

'Young woman,' said the stranger. 'Shalom. Peace to you and your house. Is this the house of Ishmael?'

Noticing the man she ran out of her tent and returned the greeting with a smile, 'Shalom stranger. Yes. This is the house of Ishmael. You're welcome here. Climb down off your camel and rest for a while. I'll pour water and you can bathe your feet and eat bread with me and quench your thirst. There's plenty of water and even some wine.'

This is what Abraham did. He noticed that she was courteous and kind and had a generous spirit.

'Please tell me your name, stranger, so that I may tell my husband Ishmael who called upon him this day while he was out hunting.'

'I will not reveal my name to you,' answered Abraham. 'But your husband will reveal it to you when he returns.'

'How will he know, since I show hospitality to so many strangers who pass by my tent?'

'If you repeat to him the message that I will give to you, then he will know who I am and he will tell you all about me.'

'You must know him well so?'

'Indeed, my daughter, I do. But first, blessings upon Yahweh Elohim for this food and drink and blessings upon you for your hospitality and for welcoming me into your home.'

'It's only the right thing to do, sir.'

'Nevertheless, you deserve to be blessed because Elohim is with you.'

'Thank you for your blessing.'

'Now the message that I would like you to pass on to Ishmael when he returns.'

'Yes. Tell me and when he returns I'll tell him.'

'This tent peg,' said Abraham, 'which you see holding this rope, is a very good tent peg. You must not pull up this tent peg and cast it away, because it is a very good tent peg and you must keep it.'

She repeated it several times to be sure that she would not forget it and she laughed heartily. 'That's a very unusual message, stranger. It's like a riddle. Do you think that he will understand what it means? It's a complete mystery to me.'

'He will understand what it means and he will reveal to you who I am.' Abraham sat upon his camel and the beast rose up onto its legs. 'Now I must be on my way. I'm pleased to have met you and thank you for your hospitality. Ishmael is blessed with you.'

'Where do you travel to now, sir?'

'I must travel home to the land of the Philistines.'

'Oh that's a long way to go,' she said. 'Please wait,' running into the tent, she wrapped some bread in a cloth and gave it to Abraham, she also gave him some water. 'Here, this will sustain you on your journey home. May Elohim be with you.'

They parted company and Abraham's heart was singing in his breast. 'This is a good woman for Ishmael. Praise Yahweh Elohim, God of heaven and earth.' He turned his camel to the north and headed for home.

Only a couple of hours after Abraham's departure did Ishmael arrive home from the hunt. After greeting each other his wife said, 'Ishmael, a stranger called here today.'

'Where does he come from and what is his name?' he asked.

'He didn't tell me his name, even though I asked, and he came from the land of the Philistines.'

'What was his appearance?' asked Ishmael.

She described him the best way she could. 'I welcomed him and gave him some bread and water and wine, which he ate and drank. He was very pleasant. He kept thanking me for my generosity and hospitality, as if what I did was unusual. He is travelling in the direction of his home tonight, so I gave him food and drink for the long journey.'

'Did he have any other news?' asked Ishmael. 'It's unusual that he didn't reveal his name.'

'It is very unusual and I said so to him. But he told me that you'd know who he is, after I give you a message.'

'Well,' asked Ishmael, 'what's the message?'

'It's most unusual,' she answered with a smile on her lips. 'You might laugh at it. I did. He said that this tent peg, which you see holding this rope, is a very good tent peg. You must not pull it up nor cast it away. You must keep it, because it's a very good tent peg.'

A beaming smile crossed Ishmael's lips. 'That's none other than my father, Abraham, son of Terah. He approves of you because you have shown welcome to a stranger. You've honoured him with your generosity and you've honoured me with your kindness.'

Abraham lit a fire after dark because he was going to spend the night in the wilderness of Paran. He was looking at the dancing flames and his heart was still dancing after meeting Ishmael's wife. Hearing a noise he turned and he could see a stranger come out of the darkness into the light of his fire. He was riding on a camel. Abraham stood up to greet him while the beast knelt down for the man to dismount.

'Ishmael,' said Abraham, with delight. He ran to his son and flung his arms around him. 'I'm so delighted to see you.'

'My father,' cried Ishmael, with the tears rolling down his face. 'My heart is full of happiness.'

Sitting beside the fire, they talked for many hours, well into the night. They spoke of many things and Ishmael was very remorseful for his behaviour toward Sarah and Isaac many years ago. 'In my youth I was foolish,' he admitted. 'Isaac came along and it was like I had been forgotten by you. All of your time was devoted to him and this provoked a deep jealousy within me. I lost my reason. It was wrong of me.'

'You're forgiven, Ishmael,' said Abraham. 'Why don't you come home and visit me in the land of the Philistines? You'll be very welcome.'

'I fear that I will not be welcome by Sarah or Isaac.'

'I will explain to Sarah and Isaac that you are now settled and have children of your own. If you're remorseful and you tell them so, then they'll accept you back.'

'Then I will do that. I will visit with my wife and children, but I will only stay for a short while because I live the life of a nomad in the wilderness of Paran. This now is my home.'

When the morning came they parted company and some days later Abraham reached home. Ishmael rose up with his wife Malchuth and his children and leaving his servants to care for the cattle and sheep, he travelled to the land of the Philistines to meet his father. They all spent a few months together and a reconciliation took place between Sarah, Isaac, and Ishmael. The two brother's embraced each other and there was peace between them.

CHAPTER 30

Beersheba

Abraham had lived in the land of the Philistines for twenty-six years and after that period of time Abraham and his entire household, with all of his sheep and cattle, left that land. They went to the land near Hebron and lived there. In the area where they moved about, feeding their animals, they dug wells to provide enough water for them all to drink because the flock of sheep and herd of cattle was vast.

The servants of Abimelech, king of the Philistines, heard that Abraham had dug new wells on the borders of the land of the Philistines. These men came and argued with the servants of Abraham. They overpowered the servants of Abraham and took possession of these wells. Abraham and his household was forbidden access to the great well to drink for themselves or to provide for their animals.

Abimelech heard what had happened and he came with Phicol, the prince of his host, and twenty men and he met with Abraham. 'El, the great God is with you and behind all that you do,' said Abimelech. 'Promise me that you will not deal falsely with me or my household. I've always dealt fairly with you and have given you the freedom to travel and settle anywhere you choose in my land.'

'I swear,' answered Abraham. 'I will speak truthfully to you.'

'Why did my servants have to seize this well? Have you forbidden them to use it and to draw water from it?'

'No, Abimelech. It's not I nor my men who have done wrong, regarding this well. It was my servants, with their own hands, who dug this well. We did so with no help from you or your men. Now we are prevented from drawing any water from this well by your men. We can't water our cattle and sheep nor can we take a sip of water from the well to quench our own thirst.'

Abimelech was astounded, 'Abraham, I swear to El, the God of heaven and earth, that I wasn't fully aware of what had happened here until this moment. I beg you to forgive me for the conduct of these, my servants, because I didn't command it.'

Abraham took sheep and cattle and presented them to Abimelech and they made a covenant together. Abraham also put aside seven ewe lambs from his flock.

'What's the significance of these seven ewe lambs?' asked Abimelech.

'I'm giving you these seven ewe lambs so that you may take them from my hands as a witness for me that I dug this well that is beside you.'

So Abimelech accepted the seven ewe lambs and swore an oath with Abraham. Abimelech agreed that Abraham had dug the well and that it belonged to him. From that day the well was called Beersheba, because it means the well of seven and also the well of the oath. The covenant was completed after they each walked the path of blood to their own half of the sacrificial victim on the altar. After the cutting of the covenant, Abimelech, along with Phicol and his men, rose up and returned to the land of the Philistines. It was there in Beersheba that Abraham planted a tamarisk tree and there he called upon the name of El-Olam, the Everlasting God.

CHAPTER 31

Nahor

It was in the thirty-fifth year of Isaac that his grandfather Terah died. Terah, the son of Nahor, lived to the age of two hundred and five years and he died in the city of Haran, in the land of Paddan Aram and there he is buried.

Nahor, the brother of Abraham, lived in Haran along with his father Terah. He did not move to Canaan with Abraham. Nahor settled in Haran with his wife Milca, the daughter of his brother Haran and the sister of Sarah, the wife of Abraham. Milca had many children and these are the eight sons, Uz, Buz, Kemuel, Kesed, Chazo, Pildash, Tidlaf, and Bethuel. Nahor also had a concubine named Reumah and she bore four sons to him. These are Zebach, Gachash, Tachash, and Maacha. Altogether, Nahor had twelve sons and he also had many daughters.

Uz, the firstborn son of Nahor, had four sons, Abi, Cheref, Gadin, and Melus, he also had a daughter, Deborah. Buz had four sons and these were Berachel, Naamath, Sheva, and Madonii. Two sons were born to Kemuel and these were called Aram and Rechob. Kesed had four sons; Anamlech, Meshai, Benon, and Yifi. Three sons were born to Chazo and these were called Pildash, Mechi, and Opher. Pildash had four sons called Arud, Chamum, Mered, and Moloch. The sons of

Tildaf were Mushan, Cushan, and Mutzi. Bethuel had two sons called Sechar and Laban and a daughter called Rebecca.

Aram and Rechob, the sons of Kemuel, left Haran and they settled in a valley by the River Euphrates. There they established a city named after Aram's son Pethor and it is known as Aram Naherayim to this day.

The children of Kesed also left the city of Haran and they founded a city which they named Kesed, after their father's name. The city of Kesed is opposite the land of Shinar. There they were fruitful and their families grew in number.

Terah, in his old age, after the death of Amthelo, took another wife. Her name was Pelilah and she bore a son to him and they named him Zoba. Terah lived another twenty-five years after Zoba was born. At the age of thirty-five Zoba had a son born to him, called Aram. He later had two more sons called Achlis and Merik.

Aram took three wives and had twelve sons and three daughters and he was blessed with wealth and had herds and flocks that were so great in number that the land of Haran could not sustain them. So he left there to find a place of his own. Aram left with his entire household, servants, and beasts. His brothers Achlis and Merik, with their own families, went with him. They lived in a valley in the eastern country and there they built a city called Aram, after the eldest of the brothers, and it became known as Aram Zoba.

CHAPTER 32

Departure

The day came when the sons of God, that is the angels, came and presented themselves before Yahweh, the Lord God. When they arrived, the Accuser, that is Satan, came among them. Yahweh, the Lord God, said to Satan, 'What are you doing here and where have you come from?'

'I've been wandering upon the face of the earth, going here and there, wherever I please.'

'And in your wandering upon the face of the earth, what have you seen of the sons of Adam?'

'I've seen all the children of the earth who come from Adam,' said Satan. 'And they are all foolish. They have all sinned, as I have encouraged them. Most of them have abandoned you, the living God. They serve their own desires.'

'Have all truly abandoned me?' asked Yahweh.

'They all remember you when they are in need. They pray to you for whatever they want and they continue to serve you until they get what they desire. Then when their prayers are answered and they are no longer in need, they forget all about you because they are in comfort. There's no love for you. They think only of themselves.'

'Surely you've seen Abraham, the son of Terah? He has served me all of his life. His love for me is great.'

'Yes. I've been watching Abraham. When you directed him, he followed your instructions and he built altars and offered up burnt offerings to you. And he never failed to give you praise. But then you answered his prayer and gave him a son, to a barren wife Sarah, causing the impossible to happen. After that, things changed.'

'What do you mean?' asked Yahweh. 'What changed after the birth of Isaac?'

'When you gave him Isaac, you gave Abraham what he wanted. You gave him a son. You gave him an heir. Both Abraham and Sarah had their prayer answered. Then when the child was weaned there was a great celebration. Abraham invited many to the feast. Shem, the son of Noah, arrived with his great-grandson Eber. The Philistine king, Abimelech, arrived with his servants and Phicol, the prince of his host. Mamre, Eshcol, and Aner came from the land of Hebron. Abraham's father Terah and his mother Amthelo came with Abraham's brother Nahor and his family.'

'Was it not right to celebrate?' said Yahweh.

'It's all very good to celebrate, but since then there hasn't been an altar built for sacrifice, no burnt offering has been made to you.'

'What of it? Hasn't Abraham remained faithful to me all these years? Not once has he faltered.'

'But since then, in thirty-seven years, there has been no burnt offering or peace offering. He has brought nothing to the altar for you; he hasn't sacrificed a heifer, sheep, goat, nor turtledove. Can't you see that since you gave him Isaac, the child that he craved for, he has forgotten you? He has completely forsaken you for all these years.'

'Not so, Satan. That's not true. There's none other than Abraham to be found upon all the face of the earth. He is faithful. He listens to me and walks in my ways. Abraham is truly a holy and upright man, he walks in the path of righteousness. When I give him a command to go, he goes. Whenever I give him a command to stay, he stays. He listens to my word.'

'Not a burnt offering has he made to you in all these years.'

'If I asked Abraham to present a burnt offering from his flock or his herd he would do it. Even if I asked him to offer up his son Isaac on the altar as a sacrifice to me, he wouldn't withhold him from me.'

'Speak to Abraham now,' suggested Satan. 'You'll see for yourself. He will transgress this day. He will turn his back on you and he will run from your word.'

'Ha. You speak falsely, Satan,' replied Yahweh. 'Abraham, my servant, will hold back nothing from me. Not even his son Isaac.'

'Put him to the test so,' mocked Satan.

Abraham heard the word of God. The word came clearly to him when Yahweh called out his name, 'Abraham. Abraham.'

'Yes, Yahweh. Hineni Adonai, here I am, Lord, I'm listening.'

'I want you now to take your son Isaac, the son that you love, and go to the land of Moriah. There upon one of the mountains that I will point out to you, I want you to offer up your son Isaac as a burnt offering to me.'

'Yes, Yahweh,' answered Abraham. 'I will make preparations and leave early at first light.'

'Now,' said God to Satan. 'Did you hear Abraham? He answered yes. He'll do as I ask. He won't hold back.'

'He said yes,' answered Satan. 'But he hasn't done it yet. After he sleeps on the matter he will change his mind. Wait until dawn.'

'Abraham will not falter,' declared Yahweh.

'Don't you know that Sarah will be his downfall?' said Satan. 'She'll be his stumbling block. Wait and see.'

'How will I convince Sarah?' Abraham asked himself. 'She'll never allow me to offer Isaac as a burnt offering before God,' he paused to think. 'I know what I'll do.'

Abraham sat down with Sarah and said to her, 'Many years ago I went to the house of Noah and I learned the ways of Yahweh, the Lord God. Our son Isaac is now in his thirty-seventh year and he needs clear instruction to lead a holy and blameless life. I am of a mind to take him to the house of Shem and Eber, to the city of Salem. There they will teach him the path of righteousness and how to learn to pray continuously before Yahweh.'

'This pleases me greatly,' answered Sarah. 'Go with my blessing, but don't keep him away from me for too long. You know how close Isaac is to me. In my old age I dote upon him and I can't be separated from him, for I pine for him. Pray to Yahweh so that all will go well with him and he'll return safe and soon.'

That night Sarah did not sleep. Her mind was full of concern for Isaac. Her mind conjured up fearful scenarios for her to consider. In all of his years, Isaac had never been separated from his mother Sarah for more than a couple of days at a time. Now he would be gone for a few years. 'How can I bear it, if Isaac is gone for many years?' she asked herself. 'Abraham was in the house of Noah for forty years. If Isaac is gone for forty years, I will be dead by the time he returns.'

Isaac lay asleep. He was sleeping soundly when Sarah entered silently into the tent. She sat down beside him and looked tenderly upon her son, reminding herself of all the events that had taken place in his life over the years. 'All of his thirty-seven years have passed by so fast, like the speed of a fierce wind or the flash of a lightning bolt,' she said to herself. 'Tomorrow he'll be gone from me,' she wept. 'When will I ever see him again?'

Early after sunrise, Abraham had the donkey saddled and was ready to go. He asked two of his servants to go with him and Isaac.

The servants set about collecting wood for the altar fire and heaped it on the donkey, tying it fast. They also assembled enough provisions for the journey there and back.

Sarah fussed over Isaac like she had never done before. She picked out the finest garment for him to wear. It was a garment given by Abimelech, the king of the Philistines, many years ago. She insisted that Isaac should wear it and he did so to please her. The tears. Anything like the tears. She nearly drowned him in tears that day, when he left his home in Beersheba.

Accompanying them on the road, Sarah found it so difficult to pull herself away from Isaac. 'It breaks my heart to say farewell. I will continue with you a little more.' The tears rolled down her face and fell to the ground like raindrops.

'You'll wear yourself out,' said Isaac. 'I'll come back soon. You can always visit the city of Salem and stay for a few days in the house of Shem. Both you and father.'

'Yes we can do that,' said Abraham.

'I will not be gone forever,' consoled Isaac. 'Don't fret for me.'

But Sarah's tears were plentiful and they were very infectious. It wasn't long before everyone in the small company was crying. Flinging her arms around Isaac, Sarah embraced him tightly. So tight that Isaac struggled to take in breath. 'I love you, Isaac. I love you, my son. You're all the treasure in the world to me. Look after yourself. Be careful while you're away. And come back safe to me. Your mother loves you.'

Here she stopped, she went no further with him. But there she remained, watching him travel further away from her. She watched as her beloved son diminished in size, until she completely lost sight of him. It was only then that she turned to go home. Her maidservants accompanied her and supported her over the rough terrain. They all wept together on the journey home.

CHAPTER 33

Satan

'Let us see how strong this man Abraham is,' Satan boasted to Yahweh. 'I will turn him from this task. I will make him defy you.'

While Abraham and Isaac and the two servants were travelling along the road, they met a very old man. Their path was blocked and they stopped when they reached the old man. 'What is this foolishness?' said he, directly to Abraham.

'Foolishness?' asked Abraham. 'What do you mean?'

'You must be a fool or maybe you're a fiend, to do this to your son.'

'You don't know what you're talking about,' answered Abraham.

'This is your son Isaac. The only son of your wife Sarah. The son that Yahweh gave you in your old age. Now you're going to give him up as a burnt offering before Yahweh. What kind of a God is he, that he should tell you to slaughter your son? Who then will inherit? Who will be your heir?'

'Yahweh gives and he takes away,' answered Abraham. 'He is able to restore the life of Isaac. Blessed be Yahweh, God of heaven and earth.'

'This instruction can't be from Yahweh. He'd never insist that you should slaughter your own son.'

'I know the voice of Yahweh,' said Abraham. 'Nothing is impossible to God. When I was thrown into the brick furnace in Casdim by Nimrod, the king of Shinar, did Yahweh not rescue me from the jaws of death? I was in the midst of the fire for three days and three nights and I came out of the fire with no burns to my skin. I know the voice of Yahweh. I've listened to him all the days of my life. But you,' Abraham paused, carefully observing the old man who blocked the path before him. 'I don't know your voice. You're not familiar to me.' Recognizing Satan, Abraham said, 'I rebuke you, Satan, go away from me now.' Satan vanished from the path before him.

After they had finished their evening meal, Abraham, Isaac, and the two servants sat around the fire for warmth and a young man approached them. He sat by Isaac and he was well dressed and good mannered. Leaning over to Isaac he said quietly, 'Do you know that your doting father here, is bringing you to the slaughter?'

'What do you mean?' answered Isaac, alarmed. 'Am I not going to the house of Shem and Eber, in the city of Salem?'

'Ha, ha, ha. Don't be silly. He's deceiving you. Because you are going to be sacrificed as a burnt offering to Yahweh.'

Isaac looked dumbfounded at the young man.

'That fool of a father of yours, believes that God called him yesterday and told him to offer up you, Isaac,' he pointed his finger at Isaac. 'You're to be offered up instead of a bull or a sheep on an altar, as a burnt offering before God.'

Isaac's jaw dropped, but the young man pointed to the huge stack of firewood, 'What do you think that's for?'

Isaac looked and there before him was the firewood, but there was no beast for the sacrifice. This young man's story was beginning to ring true. 'But we're going to the house of Shem,' said a mystified Isaac.

'No. You're not. That story was made up for the sake of your mother, who right now is weeping for you. She's waiting for your return. If your father had told her the truth, she never would have let you out of her sight. That stupid man, that foolish father of yours is going to kill you, and you'll go up in a puff of smoke.'

Isaac rose up and staggered across to his father Abraham. Sitting down beside his father, Isaac told him what the young man had said to him.

'Let me tell you who that young man is,' said Abraham. 'He's none other than Satan and he's here to prevent us from fulfilling the will of Yahweh.' Abraham revealed the truth to Isaac and Isaac believed his father. Isaac accepted Yahweh's plan for himself.

'I freely offer myself to Yahweh. God is good. He knows what is right.'

Turning directly to the young man, Abraham said, 'Satan, I rebuke you in the name of El-Elyon, God Most High. I command you to leave.' Satan immediately disappeared.

'Ha. I told you,' said Yahweh, the Lord God. 'Abraham is a man of faith. He has faith in me, not faith in his circumstances. He has faith in his creator, who loves him and cares for him. He knows that nothing is impossible for me. I am El-Elyon, God Most High, and I can bring the dead back to life. He knows that even if he surrenders his son to death, I am the one who can restore him to life. So Abraham is not afraid. Isaac is not afraid. Abraham will not falter. He will do all that I ask him to do.'

'I'll prove you wrong,' spat Satan to El-Elyon.

When the sun appeared over the horizon Abraham, Isaac, and the servants rose up and after praising Yahweh and giving thanks they ate some of the bread and drank some water. Then they loaded the wood and provisions on the donkeys and continued upon their journey.

Frustrated at his lack of progress in persuading Abraham to turn aside from the will of God, Satan secretly went ahead of Abraham on the road to Moriah. As they travelled along the road, Abraham could hear the sound of running water. The further they travelled the louder the sound of the running water became.

Upon reaching the bank of the river Abraham, Isaac, and the servants stopped. They looked at the strength of the river, wondering where would be the best place to cross. Linking their arms together and holding onto their donkeys, they entered the river as one body. At first the water reached above their knees and the going was good. Further in the river became much deeper and reached over their waist. They began to struggle but they continued cautiously.

A few steps more and the water was suddenly up to their necks. Their feet were still touching the river bed but the current was so strong that they were lifted and spun around in all directions. They were in danger of being swept away by the current and fear struck them.

Now they were forced to swim in order to keep their faces above the water. They had not even reached half way across the river. One of the servants cried out, 'Abraham, I fear that we're going to drown.'

'We must turn back or we'll perish,' said the other

'What river is this, that it will end our lives?' asked Isaac.

'I don't know this river,' said Abraham, splashing to keep his face above the surface. 'I've never seen this river before.'

'But you've often travelled this path before, haven't you?' asked Isaac.

'I've passed by on this path before and I don't ever remember having to cross this river.'

'Have we taken a wrong turn?' asked Isaac. 'Have we gone astray?'

'No. We haven't strayed from the right path. This is the right way. This is none other than the work of Satan,' said Abraham. 'He has put this river across our path to prevent us from fulfilling the will of

Yahweh.'

'Help,' screamed one of the servants, who became separated from the group. Splashing wildly as he tried to keep afloat, he drifted away and then he sank beneath the torrent.

'May El-Elyon rebuke you Satan,' said Abraham. 'Leave us alone now, because we're here to do the will of God.'

Immediately the river dried up. It stopped flowing and Abraham, Isaac, the two servants, and their donkeys fell to the ground, exhausted. Their clothes were saturated but the ground on which the river flowed was bone dry. Not a trace of water remained, except the pool of water forming under the men.

Satan left that place screaming. He was terrified at the God-given authority in Abraham's voice. Thwarted again he left the presence of Yahweh, frustrated that all of his efforts had failed. Abraham's company of men rejoiced. They had not perished. They were still alive.

'Satan almost killed us,' said one servant to the other.

'Thank Yahweh Elohim, the Lord God, that he failed.'

'Did you see how Satan is afraid of Abraham?'

'It's amazing. I've never seen anything like this before. Abraham even has authority over Satan. Where does he get that power?'

'It must come from Yahweh. He trusts in Yahweh and he hears his voice. He always walks in God's ways.'

'Well he saved my life today. Praise Yahweh.'

'Praise Yahweh indeed.'

That is exactly what they all did. There and then, they offered praise to Yahweh for saving them from the works of the devil. They sang songs of praise and danced and clapped, rejoicing in the works of El-Shaddai, the all-sustaining, all-nurturing, and all-providing God.

CHAPTER 34

Moriah

They went on from this place and, on the third day of their journey, Yahweh revealed the mountain of Moriah to them. Coming down from heaven to the earth was a pillar of fire and smoke, it settled upon Moriah, surrounding it with a cloud of glory.

Isaac gripped his father's arm, 'Look. In the distance. Do you see that?'

'Yes, I see it, son.'

'It's a pillar of fire and smoke, reaching up into heaven. It's wonderful.'

The two servants looked in the direction that Isaac was pointing out but they could see nothing, other than the land and the sky. Nothing unusual or noteworthy about it.

'Can you see it?' asked Isaac of them.

'We can see the hills and the sky, and the sun is shining bright. What else is there to see?'

'The pillar of fire and smoke. Look,' Isaac pointed his finger.

'I don't see it.'

'I see nothing like that.'

'God has revealed it to you, Isaac,' said Abraham. 'He has opened your eyes to see his glory.'

'What does it mean?' asked Isaac.

'It means that this must be the mountain upon which we must sacrifice the burnt offering. We must make haste.'

On they travelled until they reached the foot of the mountain. The pillar of fire and smoke remained until they reached it. Asking the servants to wait with the donkeys, Abraham loaded the wood upon the back of his son Isaac. Abraham carried the flint and the kindling to start the fire and the knife to slaughter the sacrificial victim.

'Abraham,' observed one of the servants, 'You have the wood, the flint and the kindling, and the knife. But where is the sacrifice? Where is the creature for the burnt offering?'

'Yahweh Yireh,' answered Abraham. 'God will provide.'

Climbing up the hill was hard going, especially for Isaac who was carrying the heavy burden of firewood. Abraham said, 'Isaac, my son, Yahweh has chosen you to be the perfect burnt offering this day.'

'Yes. I willingly offer myself to Yahweh.' Isaac slipped and fell down under the weight of his burden.

Assembling the firewood and tying it into a bundle again, Abraham lifted it onto Isaac's back. 'Have you any thought or doubt in your heart concerning this sacrifice, Isaac?'

'No. I love Yahweh Elohim, the Lord God, with all my heart and I love you, my father. I will do whatever is asked of me, providing it is you or Elohim who is asking it of me,' he continued climbing.

Stumbling again, Isaac fell down and cut himself on a sharp stone. Abraham lifted Isaac up, 'You have wounded yourself, my son. Is your heart troubling you at all?'

'My limbs ache and the wood is piercing my flesh. But I am willing to endure all of this to please my God, Elohim. We'll be at the top in a short while.'

The sun beat down upon them and Isaac was dripping in sweat. His clothes were stuck to him and the sweat ran through his eyebrows, stinging his eyes. 'O my father, I need to stop for a moment. I'm weary.'

'Let me mop your brow,' said Abraham, wiping the sweat away from his face. 'My son Isaac, is there any sorrow in your heart?'

'No, my father. Nothing can turn me aside, either to the left or to the right, from the path that Elohim has chosen for me.'

Abraham loved Isaac and he wondered at his son's faith. They still had a distance to go, so on they went. Catching his foot on a boulder, Isaac stumbled again but he managed to right himself. However, the burden of firewood shifted on his back and he fell down on the ground for the third time.

'I wonder how many people have fallen three times on this mountain of Moriah,' pondered Isaac.

'I'd say that you're the first. But you won't be the last.'

'I'm certainly the first to carry firewood up this hill to place on an altar for a burnt offering.'

'We're nearly there, Isaac,' said Abraham, lifting the firewood onto his son's back again. 'I will hold the firewood and help you up the last distance to the top. Are you reconciled, my son, to this offering to Elohim?'

'Weary as I am carrying this burden, I am joyful. My heart is singing because Elohim has chosen me this day to be a perfect sacrifice, to be a fragrant burnt offering to Elohim.'

They reached the top and Abraham and Isaac rested for a moment before gathering many stones, some large and some small. There on the top of Moriah, they placed the stones together, until a sizeable altar was formed. While the altar was being built the tears flowed from Abraham's eyes and all of the stones were covered in tears.

The stone altar was now complete and Abraham and Isaac spread out the firewood on top of the altar. When they were satisfied with the construction of the firewood, Abraham placed the kindling into the wood at the best place to receive the spark from his flint.

Then taking his son Isaac he stripped off his outer garments but left his under garments in place. They embraced each other and they wept many tears. They were both afraid but their trust in Elohim was greater than their fear. Abraham helped Isaac to climb up onto the altar and lie down on the pile of firewood. Then he bound the hands and feet of Isaac to the wood as the offering from the flock would be bound.

Abraham was choked up with grief and unable to speak but Isaac said to him, 'Promise me when the sacrifice is complete, that you will take my bones or ashes or whatever remains of me and that you will gather together my remains. Take them home to my mother. Say to her that this is the fragrant burnt offering of Isaac, your son. He has gone to Elohim.'

Hearing these words of Isaac was enough to break the heart of Abraham. He bent over his son, who lay prostrate on the altar, and he wept bitterly. The tears fell down upon Isaac, who, seeing his father so forlorn, weeping like he had never seen before, became very distressed. Isaac could not help himself, but he began wailing uncontrollably.

'This is the last time I'll ever see you, my father, and my last memory of my mother is to see her crying, on the road leading out of our home in Beersheba. I will miss you both dearly, but at the same time I'm pleased to offer myself to Elohim.' Offering his throat to Abraham, he stretched out his neck. 'Strike now, my father. Take your knife and slit my throat. Let my blood flow and present your offering to Elohim. Strike while my heart is ready to do the will of Elohim.'

Full of admiration at his son's courage, Abraham reached out for the knife. Grasping the knife in his right hand he placed his left hand on Isaac's head to hold him still. 'I love you, Isaac,' spoke Abraham with a faltering voice. He brought the knife to Isaac's throat.

CHAPTER 35

Deception

Meanwhile, back in Beersheba, in the tent of Sarah, she was overcome with the most dreadful anguish. This dread came upon her at the same time that her son Isaac lay prostrate on the altar, ready to become a fragrant burnt offering to Elohim, the Lord God.

'Sarah. Sarah,' called a voice.

Rising quickly, because she could hear the urgency in the calling of her name, she rushed out of her tent where she encountered an old man standing before her.

'Yes. I'm Sarah,' she answered. 'Who are you and from where do you come?'

'I'm Mastema and I come from all of the earth.' He had a comely appearance and a humble nature. 'Have you heard all that has happened concerning your husband Abraham?'

'You have news of Abraham?' she asked with her heart thumping wildly. 'Is all well with him? And what of Isaac, my son? What news have you?'

'It's well you ask,' he said. 'They have gone to the mountains of Moriah and there they built an altar to Elohim. Your son Isaac was presented as a fragrant burnt offering to Elohim. Your husband slit the throat of Isaac upon the altar and sprinkled his blood. Isaac, the son that you love, your only son, is dead.'

'Dead! Dead! No,' she wailed. 'It can't be so. Abraham loves Isaac, his son.'

'Do you not know that Abraham bound his son Isaac and forced him onto the altar? Isaac was unwilling and he resisted his father but he was overcome.' Mastema observed Sarah melting before him. 'Isaac your beloved son cried out. He screamed for mercy but Abraham wouldn't listen to him. He slew your only son on the altar and even though Isaac cried out, Abraham showed him no mercy. He had no compassion for him.'

Sarah fell to her knees, wailing uncontrollably.

'What kind of love is this?' he asked her. 'That a father should sacrifice his son. That he should offer up his son to Elohim. What kind of God demands a human life? Why is your son so special to Elohim?' With these words he left her.

Sarah wept bitterly, for these words cut through to her soul. At the news she tore her garments and with her hands she scooped up the dust of the earth and threw it on top of her head. Her handmaidens and menservants, on hearing her cries, came running to her aid.

'O my son Isaac. O Isaac. Why did you have to die? My one and only son. If only you had never left me. If only you remained here, safe with your mother. Why are you dead, my son? You are so young. If only I had died in your place, so that you might live. O my son, you brought joy into my life. You filled me with laughter. But now my joy has turned to sorrow. My laughter has turned to tears.

'I was barren for ninety years of my life. All I ever longed for was a son like you. For all those years I prayed to Yahweh. I pleaded with the Almighty to open my womb so that I might conceive. El-Shaddai listened to me. He heard my prayer. He performed a miracle. He turned what was impossible into a reality. When I was beyond the age of bearing a child he gave me you, Isaac. Yahweh, the Lord God has given,' she sighed. 'But now he has taken away.' Through gritted teeth she said, 'Blessed be Yahweh, the Lord God.'

'Sarah,' said one of her handmaids, placing her hand on Sarah's shoulder, 'who told you that Isaac is dead?'

Looking at her handmaid Sarah said, 'Did you not see him?'

'See who, Sarah?'

'The old man who came to me this day. He was here only a moment ago. Can you not see him?' she looked in all directions but he was nowhere to be seen.

'Who is this old man?' asked her handmaid. 'And where did he come from?'

'I've never seen him before. He told me that his name was Mastema and he said that he lives in all the earth. Send someone to find him.' The menservants went in different directions to search for this stranger. But they all returned to Sarah with no sight of him.

Sarah was very distressed at hearing the news of the death of Isaac. She found it hard to believe that Abraham would behave in such a callous manner toward his son. Because she knew her husband and she knew of his love for Isaac. In her heart she knew that the words spoken to her by the stranger could not be true. But still, the words did cause her to doubt.

'Yahweh, Lord God,' she prayed. 'I know that whatever has happened, has been done to your glory. Abraham and I have followed you devoutly all of our days. Abraham's ear listens to your voice. I know that if you demanded our son Isaac, then Abraham would not hesitate to give him to you. But Abraham would never act brutally toward Isaac. He has always been tender and compassionate to him.

'Isaac too has followed you faithfully and he would willingly submit himself to you. He would not hesitate in allowing Abraham to carry out your will. He would never transgress your commands, O Yahweh. He knows that his very life is in your hands.

'I give thanks to you Yahweh, my God, because you are good and righteous and holy. There is no other like you. None can compare to you.' Placing her hands over her eyes, she wept. 'Though I am broken inside and weep bitterly at the death of my son, my heart and my soul rejoices at your word.' With this she hung her head and fell into the arms of her handmaid, who held Sarah to her breast. She became as still as stone and some wondered if she still lived.

CHAPTER 36

Sacrifice

The blade of the knife touched Isaac's skin but before Abraham could lean into the cut the angel of Yahweh gripped his hand, pulling it away from the throat of Isaac.

'Abraham. Abraham,' called out the voice of Yahweh from heaven.

'Yes, Yahweh, my Lord God, I'm here,' answered Abraham as he trembled with shock.

'Don't lay your hand upon Isaac your son. Do not harm him at all. Now I see how much you love me. Now I see how far you'll go to obey me, your Lord and God. Your love for me is so great that you would not falter, even in offering up Isaac, your dearly beloved son to me. Your son Isaac for his part has proven to me that his faith is strong like yours. You've both endured much suffering but neither of you flinched, nor have you turned aside from the request of Elohim, the Lord your God.

'Unbind your son and know that this offering of yours to me this day has been accepted by me, as if Isaac had been sacrificed on this altar as a fragrant burnt offering before me. Take this ram, Abraham. This one that you see with his head caught in the thorn bush. This shall be the victim in the place of your son. This ram, like your son Isaac, is without blemish and is an acceptable offering in Isaac's place.'

With trembling hands Abraham untied his son's ankles and wrists and helped him down from the altar. Releasing the ram from the thicket in which his horns were caught, Abraham and Isaac bound the ram, laid it on the altar, and performed the sacrifice, spilling its blood and then lighting the fire.

Abraham sprinkled the blood of the ram upon the altar and he thanked God, 'Yahweh Yireh, the Lord God has provided. Let this blood which I sprinkle on the altar become an acceptable offering in place of my son Isaac, the intended victim.' Abraham completed the sacrifice and it was accepted by Yahweh. He accepted the offering of the ram in place of Isaac the son of Abraham. Yahweh blessed Abraham and his son Isaac that day.

'By my own name I swear,' declared Yahweh, 'because you have not withheld your son Isaac but have obeyed me, because you have willingly offered up your own son to me, I will certainly bless you. Your descendants will be as vast as the stars in the heavens and as numerous as the grains of sand on the seashore. The cities of your enemies shall be overcome by your descendants and they will take them as their own. All the nations of the earth shall be blessed through your offspring, simply because you have been obedient to me.'

Here in this place Elohim opened the eyes of Abraham and he showed him a glimpse of the temple. Abraham marvelled at the sight of it. Before him stood the temple of the Lord God, glorious in its splendour. The messenger of Yahweh led Abraham through the Gate of Thanksgiving and Abraham beheld the Altar of Sacrifice in the Outer Court of Praise, where a priest offered Olah, a burnt offering, where the victim was completely consumed by the flames. He watched the priest as he washed himself clean in the laver of water, held in the great bronze basin. The priest then climbed the steps and entered through the door into another chamber.

'What is the name of this place?' asked Abraham.

The messenger of Yahweh told him, 'Come, follow me. I will reveal to you the Holy Place.'

Abraham followed close behind the messenger of Yahweh and he beheld the Holy Place which was completely panelled in gold. The Holy Place was lit by the menorah, the golden lampstand upon which were seven oil lamps burning. The menorah was standing over to the south against the left wall and against the wall to the right stood a golden table. Abraham watched the priest present and consecrate the twelve pieces of shewbread in two rows of six at the table. The priest then sprinkled frankincense on the burning charcoal at the golden Altar of Incense and the smoke from the incense rose up to heaven.

'What is the priest doing here?' asked Abraham.

'This offering takes place in the morning and the evening. This incense represents the prayers offered up to Elohim by his people,' answered the messenger of Yahweh.

'I see a veil beyond the golden Altar of Incense,' observed Abraham. 'What lies beyond the veil?'

The messenger of Yahweh said, 'Beyond the veil lies the Kodesh HaKodashim, the Holy of Holies, the most holy place in the temple. It is here that the presence of Elohim resides always among his people. The priest may only enter here through the veil one day in the whole year.'

The messenger of Yahweh reached out his hand and parted the veil to reveal the golden Ark of the Covenant and Abraham beheld the glory of God. Yahweh sat upon his throne and the Seraphim, the angels with three pairs of wings, lifted him up and sang praise to God, 'Kadosh. Kadosh. Kadosh, ki malach Elohei Tzeva'ot. Holy. Holy. Holy, the Lord God of Hosts reigns.' The Seraphim encouraged the whole company of angels in heaven and they all burst into song. The melody was beautiful and was beyond anything that Abraham had ever heard or imagined. The light of the glory of

Yahweh shone with brilliant light and Abraham fell down on his face, trembling with fear.

'How can I behold the glory of Yahweh and still live, for none can look upon the glory of God and survive?'

'Yahweh has placed a veil across your face to protect you in his presence. Have no fear. You will not die.'

Abraham listened and he heard the voice of Yahweh speaking to him. 'This temple has been chosen by me and I have consecrated it. In this temple my name will remain forever. In the temple I will live among my people. This people are your descendants, Abraham; they will always be my people and I will always be their God.'

A terrible scene of a suffering people, held in captivity, appeared before the eyes of Abraham. 'What is happening here, Adonai?'

'Your people will, for a time, be in bondage in a land that is not their own, and will suffer under the hand of their oppressor. I will rescue them from slavery and lead them back to this land that I have given to you. In this place on which you stand, this beautiful temple will be built and your people will worship me here.'

The vision changed and Abraham beheld his own people praising and worshipping God in the temple. It gladdened Abraham's heart to see this. Then Abraham witnessed division among his own people. Another temple was constructed on the top of Mount Gerizim, overlooking the city of Shechem and burnt offerings were sacrificed there. Two kingdoms were created and Abraham's heart was filled with sorrow.

Then he beheld the abomination. In both kingdoms he saw his own people turning away from Yahweh, the one true God, and worshipping false gods and sacrificing their own children to the demons. The beautiful temple was destroyed and the altars were smashed. The gold panelling was stripped from the temple and the golden menorah, the bronze basin, and all the holy vessels were removed and taken as plunder. The entire land became desolate, because the presence of God had departed.

Abraham trembled and the tears flowed from his eyes because what he saw before him was shameful and terrible to behold. 'Adonai Yahweh,' he cried. 'What is to become of my people? Must this happen? Can it be prevented from taking place? If my people remain faithful to you, then this will never happen to them. You will always prosper those who remain faithful to you. You will always protect them.'

Yahweh answered him, 'The northern kingdom will be scattered across the face of the earth by the Assyrians and the southern kingdom will be invaded by the Babylonians. My people will be held captive in the land of Babylon. At the appointed time, when the period of chastisement is over, I will release them and a remnant will return. They will return to me with all their heart and never again will they worship false gods.'

'O thank you Adonai. Thank you for always showing your love. I pray that you will always love them.'

'I will always love my people and, at the right time, I will send my son who will come in the flesh and live among them as their Redeemer.'

Yahweh opened the eyes of Abraham and he beheld another scene. A man rode upon a donkey and the people waved their garments and branches of the palm. As he passed by they chanted with one voice, 'Baruch haba b'shem Adonai. Baruch haba b'shem Adonai. Blessed is he who comes in the name of the Lord.'

Later, this same man was seized and bound. He was falsely accused and was scourged at a pillar to the point of death; his flesh hung from his back. The men twisted a crown of thorns and placed it on his head. His tormentors then covered him with a king's robe and, after blindfolding him, they spat in his face and slapped him, saying,

'Who hit you? Speak prophet. Who slapped you?' After making fun of him they sent him to his death and bound to a wooden cross with nails through his hands and his feet, Abraham watched him die.

'My people cry out to me for help,' said Yahweh. 'And I desire to comfort them. Because I remain faithful to my covenant I will provide a holy and perfect sacrifice in this very place. Just as you offered your son Isaac I will send my own son and he shall become an acceptable and a fragrant offering, paying the penalty for the sins of my people. Because of my son's sacrifice, I will forgive my people their scarlet sins and will wash them clean, making them as white as snow.

'This will set them free from bondage to everlasting death and in exchange I will give them everlasting life. Their perishable bodies will be exchanged for imperishable bodies which will never experience pain nor decay. I myself will be the eternal temple and I will come down from heaven and live among them forever. For all time they will be my chosen people and I will be their God.'

Abraham's eyes were closed by the messenger of Yahweh and he could no longer see the vision of Yahweh in his holy place. When he opened his eyes Abraham could see that he was returned to Mount Moriah. The sacrifice was still burning upon the altar before him and Isaac was sitting by his side.

The strength of Abraham was sapped from his body and he trembled after witnessing the vision. 'Gadol Adonai Yahweh. Halleluiah. Halleluiah. Great is the Lord Yahweh. Praise God. Praise God.' Turning to Isaac, Abraham asked, 'Was I gone for a long time?'

'Gone where, my father?' enquired Isaac with a puzzled expression. 'To where did you go for a long time and when did this happen?'

'Yahweh appeared before me,' cried Abraham as he wiped his brow. The tears rolled down his face and his body shook violently. 'Yahweh revealed the future to me,' he gasped for breath. 'Here in this place a temple will be built to the glory of Yahweh and sacrifices will be offered up to him every day.'

'That's wonderful,' answered Isaac. 'Will it be built in our day?'

'No Isaac, it will not be built in our day. It will happen long after we have fallen asleep and we are returned to our fathers.' Abraham was not strong enough to reveal any more of the vision to Isaac. It disturbed him. Though Isaac pressed him for more news of the vision, Abraham held his tongue. When the sacrifice was over and Abraham had sufficiently recovered, Isaac assisted his father and they left the mountain of Moriah.

CHAPTER 37

Grief

Sarah revived later but she refused to eat and drink. Not a morsel would she let pass her lips. Rising up from her tent, with a renewed vigour, she made haste and took to the road to discover whatever news she could find about the fate of her son. She travelled on until she came to Hebron, where she stopped every traveller she met on the road to enquire of Isaac. But no one had any news concerning him. Some had seen him with Abraham a few days ago but no one had seen either of them recently.

When she came into Kireath-arba, which is Hebron, she remained there, making enquiries. She sent some of her servants on to Salem. The servants came back from Salem in haste. They were exhausted. They had no knowledge of Abraham and Isaac ever reaching Salem. Neither Shem nor Eber had seen them.

While Sarah was sitting in Hebron, a very old man approached her. Looking up she recognized him. This was the same man who had called upon her in Beersheba when she was sitting in the tent. 'Sarah,' he said.

'What is it? It's you again,' she accused him.

'Yes, it is I.'

The servants could hear and see Sarah speaking as if she were having a conversation with someone. But they could not see the old man. He was not visible to them. He only presented himself to Sarah. This old man was none other than Satan. Mastema he had called himself; this was another name that he used.

'What do you want with me, bearer of bad news?'

'I bear good news, Sarah.'

'Good news? What could be good news? There's no good news that can take away my grief.'

'I told you news previously about your son Isaac,' he paused. He enjoyed tormenting her in her sorrow. 'Well it was false. He didn't die at all. At this very moment he is returning home to you, to your tent in Beersheba.'

'Isaac. Isaac, my son,' she declared, sitting upright. 'He lives. He didn't die?'

'No he didn't die,' he watched her closely. 'He's alive and well and now he's on the road home, passing by Hebron as we speak.'

Leaping to her feet she shrieked, 'Is he dead or alive? How can I trust you? You might be lying now. Tell me the truth.'

'Truth,' he laughed, mocking her. 'What is truth? Don't you know that I'm the Father of Lies? How can I possibly tell the truth?'

Sarah swung her arms to strike the old man, 'Fall down, Satan,' she shrieked. 'Go away from me. May Yahweh, the Lord God, rebuke you. Leave me alone.' He vanished before her eyes.

One of the menservants came rushing up to Sarah, 'Good news, my Lady Sarah,' he gasped for breath. 'Abraham and Isaac have been seen by a man of Hebron. They were seen this day passing by the city, on their way home to Beersheba. He swears it is true.'

'Then it is true, he is alive. O, my son. O, my son,' she was overcome with joy. But the strain and the anxiety was too much for her and it burst her heart. She died there and then in the evening, in the city of Hebron. She was surrounded by her own faithful servants and they mourned for her.

Arriving in Beersheba, Abraham and Isaac returned to the tent expecting to find Sarah, but she was not there. The servants told Abraham, 'She has gone to Hebron looking for you. She heard bad news about Isaac and thinking that he was already dead went out to find you.'

On hearing this news Abraham was filled with dread. He left immediately with Isaac for Hebron. When they reached the city they were taken to the house where Sarah was staying and there they found her dead. With raised voices they wept bitterly over the death of Sarah. Isaac fell down on his knees beside his mother's body and hugged her, covering her face in kisses and tears. Abraham and Isaac were broken hearted and mourned deeply and their servants mourned with them.

Sarah had lived for one hundred and twenty-seven years when she died. It is recorded that Sarah died at Kireath-arba, also known as Hebron, in the land of Canaan. Rising up from mourning his wife Sarah, Abraham went out to seek a suitable burial place for her. He went out to speak to the Hittites, the sons of Heth.

Abraham went to the elders at the city gate and there he consulted with them. 'Behold my wife Sarah has died this day and I need a place to bury her body. I ask that I may receive from you a suitable sepulchre. Since I'm a nomad, I don't possess any land nor do I have a right to possess any. However, I appeal to you for a suitable cave in which to bury Sarah. What else can I do since she died in your city?'

The children of Heth, who knew and respected Abraham, said, 'You are a mighty and powerful man among us. Look at the land around you. You may choose wherever you desire and select the cave of your choice so that you may bury your dead.'

'I know of the Cave Machpelah,' answered Abraham. 'I ask that you go to Ephron, the son of Zohar, and entreat him on my behalf for this cave. Are you willing to go to him? The cave is in the end of his field and I will purchase the cave from him.'

The elders sought out Ephron, the son of Zohar, and he arrived and came before Abraham. 'I hear, Abraham, that your wife Sarah has died. I mourn with you at her loss. I'm also told that you're in need of a suitable cave in which to bury her body. You have expressed a desire to bury her in the Cave Machpelah. Abraham, it is my desire to give this cave to you. You're free to go and bury your dead wife Sarah there.'

'Ephron, I thank you for your most generous offer to give the Cave of Machpelah to me. But it's not right that I should receive it without acquiring it by legal means.'

'There is no need to pay for it, Abraham. I give it to you freely.'

'Again I thank you for your kindness. But I can't take the cave as a free gift from you. I want to pay you the true value for it. I will pay you for the cave and the field in which it is placed, so that it may be in my possession and be a place of burial for me and my family forever.'

'All that you've asked of me I'll do,' said Ephron. 'Give to me whatever you consider a good payment.'

'I will give to you the true value for it, according to the property values of the land.'

Turning to the elders, Ephron asked, 'What would be the true value of the field that has the Cave of Machpelah?'

Some of the elders had reservations regarding the selling of the cave to Abraham. 'This is most improper because it is not right to sell property to someone who is only sojourning in the land. This land cannot belong to him. He is an alien here.'

'But look. We all know and respect Abraham, he has been a

resident here for at least sixty years. And look how wealthy he is. He wants to buy a cave, not the city of Hebron. He's not going to displace us.'

'Very well. Do we all agree?'

They all agreed and so it was decided, 'In our own estimation we consider that the current value of the Cave of Machpelah and the field together is four hundred shekels of silver, to be placed in the hands of Ephron and his descendants.'

'And this is your true evaluation?' asked Abraham.

'It is,' answered the elders.

'And you, Ephron, are you agreeable to this transaction?'

'Yes Abraham, I am.'

There and then, Abraham had four hundred shekels of silver weighed out on the scales to Ephron the Hittite. Then Abraham wrote down the transaction between Ephron and himself regarding the purchase of the field and the Cave of Machpelah, for the current property value of four hundred shekels of silver.

This purchase was witnessed by four men who were present when the transaction took place. The names of these men were also written into the document and signed by them. These four witnesses were named Amigal the Hittite, son of Ashunach; Abdon the Gomerite, son of Achiram; Adichorom the Hivite, son of Ashunach and Bakdil the Zidonite, son of Abudish.

Finally the agreement was rolled and sealed before the elders and Abraham kept this sealed document with all of his most treasured possessions, for Isaac his son and for all future family descendants.

Abraham was taken by Ephron the Hittite to the field in which the Cave of Machpelah was situated. The field was to the east of Mamre, in the land of Hebron. There in the cave, Abraham laid down the body of his wife Sarah. She was the first to be buried in the sepulchre and she was buried in great pomp and ceremony. Dressed in a very beautiful garment she was entombed like a queen.

Shem and Eber received the news that Sarah had died and they came to mourn with Abraham and Isaac and they attended the burial. They helped Abraham and Isaac to carry Sarah's body into the sepulchre. Abraham's closest friends also carried her body into the tomb. Anar, Ashcol, and Mamre, the friends from Hebron, were there with Abimelech, the king of the Philistines. Sarah, according to the custom, was mourned for a period of seven days and all the people living nearby came to comfort Abraham and Isaac, because of their love for Sarah.

CHAPTER 38

Sceptre

After the period of mourning, Abraham and Isaac returned home to Beersheba and rounding up the flocks and the herds they left there and moved to Salem. Isaac entered the house of Shem and Eber to learn the ways of Yahweh, the Lord God. His father Abraham lived nearby in the fields with his cattle and sheep.

The following year the king of the Philistines, Abimelech, died. He died in the city of Gerar and he had lived for one hundred and ninety-three years. Abraham and Isaac and all of Abraham's people went to Gerar to comfort the Philistines in their time of grief. There the body of Abimelech was laid in the tomb and a large stone was rolled over the entrance to the sepulchre.

After the period of mourning the people of Gerar took the son of Abimelech and placed him on the throne, in the place of his father. The name of Abimelech's son was Benmalich and he was still only a boy of twelve years. When Benmalich sat down upon the throne of his father, the people of Gerar renamed him Abimelech. This was done according to the custom of the Philistines.

Lot, the son of Haran and the nephew of Abraham, died two years after the death of Sarah in the thirty-ninth year of the life of Isaac. Lot had lived for a total of one hundred and forty years. He was buried and he was mourned by his daughters and their sons Moab and Ben-Ammi. Abraham and Isaac mourned for him also. Moab had four sons: Ed, Mayon, Tarsus, and Kanvil. These Moabites lived to the east of the Salt Sea. Ben-Ammi's family, the Ammonites, lived to the north of the Moabites on the eastern side of the River Jordan.

News came to Abraham the year following the death of Lot that his own brother Nahor had died in the city of Haran, where he had been living. He died at the age of one hundred and seventy-two years and he was buried in the sepulchre in Haran in the land of Paddan Aram. He was mourned by his wife Milca and her son Bethuel and his son Laban and daughter Rebecca. Abraham was greatly saddened by this news and he grieved for his brother Nahor.

When the period of grieving was over Abraham called his servant Eliezer to him. 'Eliezer, I am old and well advanced in years and the death of my brother Nahor has grieved me greatly. I am considering the future for my son Isaac. I need to find him a suitable wife. I don't want him to marry a Canaanite woman. I want him to marry a woman from my own household. I want to continue the family of Shem.

'I'm sending you to my family who moved from the land of Ur of the Chaldeans to the city of Haran in the land of Paddan Aram in the upper regions of Mesopotamia. There, from my own relatives, I want you to find a wife for my son Isaac.'

'Abraham,' said Eliezer. 'What if the woman that I find for your son Isaac is unwilling to come back with me? If she doesn't trust me enough to travel back with me, must I then take Isaac with me to your family's household in the city of Haran?'

'No, Eliezer. Under no circumstances must you take Isaac away with you to the city of Haran. But don't be concerned, because Yahweh, the Lord God of heaven and earth, who brought me out of the land of my birth and my father's household and led me to this land that I'm now living in, will send an angel before you. He, the

Lord God, Yahweh, swore an oath to give this land to my offspring as an inheritance for all generations. He will prepare the path before you and you will be successful in finding Isaac a wife.'

'This, I will do for you,' said Eliezer.

'Come here then,' gestured Abraham. 'Place your hand under my thigh and swear an oath by Yahweh, the Lord God of heaven and earth, that you'll get a wife for Isaac from my own household in Haran and not from the daughters of the Canaanites.'

Eliezer did so. He placed his hand under the thigh of his master Abraham and swore an oath to do as Abraham requested. Then with haste Eliezer rose up and took ten camels and some men with him. These camels were laden with good things that Abraham wanted to be sent as a dowry for his daughter-in-law to her family. Eliezer set out for Paddan Aram and he prayed, 'O Yahweh, Lord God of heaven, prosper my journey to the city of Haran and show me the wife that you've selected for Isaac.'

When Eliezer and his men departed for the city of Haran, Abraham went to the house of Shem and Eber. Isaac had already spent three years studying there. While he was in the house of Shem, Abraham received a gift. 'Abraham, the time has come that I pass on this sceptre to you,' said Shem, holding out a staff to Abraham.

Abraham reached out his hand to receive it, 'I thank you for your gift, Shem.'

'This is no ordinary staff, Abraham,' said Shem. 'This staff was given to Adam by the hand of Yahweh, when Adam was banished from the Garden of Eden. This staff was given to Adam as the staff of authority in the Order of Melchizadek. He was the first king and priest and he received this holy order as a blessing from Yahweh. This holy order came not by the will of man, neither by father nor mother, neither by beginning of days nor the end of years, but of Yahweh. It was established in the creation of the earth by the Ancient of Days and it was delivered unto men from the beginning, by the calling of the voice of Yahweh according to his own will, unto as many as believed in his name.

'This anointing was passed down through the generations to my father Noah. He passed on the anointing to me and now I pass on the same anointing to you. Today El Elyon has anointed you and you have become a priest and king in the Order of Melchizadek. You will serve him and walk in his way. This Order of Melchizadek will never end. This order will last forever and the saviour of the world will be the greatest and the everlasting Melchizadek.

'Yahweh has given the authority to you. The Order of Melchizadek is both a civil and a heavenly authority. As priest and king you represent the presence of Yahweh among men. There will be many kings and there will be many priests and these will all pass away. But the Order of Melchizadek will never pass away, it will remain forever. You must not consider the order as an inheritance passed on to the first son. You must pray and consider wisely who should receive the staff of authority from you. The man must be appointed by Yahweh.'

'Gadol Adonai Yahweh,' said Abraham as he held the staff with conviction. 'Great is the Lord Yahweh. I will treasure this staff always and I will honour El Elyon to the end of my days. Yahweh will reveal the man to whom I must pass on this sceptre of authority. Perhaps he will tell me to pass it on to my son Isaac or he may tell me to pass it on to one of his children.'

'Stay close to Yahweh and listen to his voice,' said Shem. 'Do not fear, he will guide you.'

Abraham then took Isaac and his entire household and departed from the city of Salem and travelled back to the land of Beersheba.

CHAPTER 39

Rebecca

In the course of time Eliezer arrived at the city of Haran, the sun had fallen low in the sky. He stopped by the well of water outside the walls of the city and there he made his camels kneel down. It was at the time when the women went out to draw the water and he watched them approach the well.

Eliezer prayed, 'O Lord Yahweh, God of my master Abraham, show kindness to Abraham and grant me success this day. I'll ask one of these maidens for a drink of water and if she offers to give me a drink and also to provide water for my camels, then let her be the woman that you've chosen for your beloved Isaac.'

Before he had finished his prayer, his eyes fell upon a very beautiful young maiden. He watched her as she filled her jar with water from the well. She filled her jar and lifted it up onto her shoulder and turned to go home. Eliezer ran up to her and asked, 'Please young maiden, will you give me a drink of water from your jar?'

Lowering the jar she said, 'Yes my lord, drink your fill.' She gave the jar to Eliezer and he drank from it. Looking around her she asked, 'Do these camels belong to you, my lord?'

'Yes they are mine,' answered Eliezer.

Then pouring the remains of her jar into the trough she said, 'Let me water your camels as well. They look mighty thirsty.' Running back to the well again, she brought more water for them to drink. She supplied enough water until the camels finished drinking.

All this time Eliezer watched her in admiration. He could see that she carried out her duties well and with enthusiasm. Her manner was pleasant and he wondered if this was the girl that God had selected to be the wife of Isaac the son of Abraham. 'Tell me, young maiden, what is your name?'

'My name is Rebecca,' she answered. 'And my father is called Bethuel.'

'You're the daughter of Bethuel?' asked Eliezer. 'And who is your father's father? What is his name?'

'My grandfather's name is Nahor,' she answered with tears in her eyes.

'Why the tears, young girl?' asked Eliezer.

'My grandfather died last month. I miss him greatly and my grandmother still grieves his death.'

'What is your grandmother's name?'

'Her name is Milca and many years ago, long before I was born, she came to live in Haran with Nahor. They came originally from the city of Ur in Chaldea.'

'Then you would know my master Abraham, son of Terah.'

'I know of him. He lives in the land of Canaan,' she paused. 'I think that is true.'

'That's right,' said Eliezer, taking out a gold nose ring, weighing a beka. 'Take this, Rebecca,' he offered it to her and her eyes gleamed. 'Take these also,' he said and he took out two gold bracelets weighing ten shekels. She was delighted to receive them.

'Would there be room in your father's house for us all to spend the night, because it's getting late?'

'Yes. There's plenty of room in my father's house for you all and we have plenty of straw and fodder for your camels. Come with me,' she turned and ran home.

But Eliezer fell down on his knees to praise and worship Yahweh, 'Blessed be Yahweh, the Lord God of my master Abraham, who has shown steadfast faithfulness and mercy toward him. Thank you my Lord and God for leading me along the right path to find my master's family in this city of Haran.'

Rebecca ran into the house to tell her mother of all that had happened and Eliezer remained at the well with the camels. When Rebecca's brother Laban saw the nose ring and bracelets and heard the story he ran out and went to the well to meet Eliezer, who was waiting with the camels. 'You are Eliezer, the servant of Abraham, son of Terah?' asked Laban.

'Yes I am.'

'My name is Laban. I'm Rebecca's brother. Come with me, you who are blessed by Yahweh, the Lord God. Why are you still standing out here? The house is prepared for you and there's a place for your camels.'

'Lead on Laban,' said Eliezer and he followed him to his father's house. When they entered through the gate the camels were taken and were unloaded. Straw and fodder was provided for them. They were provided with plenty of water to drink.

Eliezer and his men followed Laban into his father's house where they were given water to wash their feet after the long and weary journey. Food was immediately set upon the table for them to eat but Eliezer refused to eat. He said, 'I will not eat until I first tell you why I'm here today.'

'Tell us your story,' said Laban.

'My name is Eliezer and I am originally from the city of Damascus. When I was a young child I was captured and enslaved to Nimrod, the King of Shinar. I was given to Abraham and he set me free from slavery. But because of my love for him I remained a servant to Abraham and have remained in his house for well over eighty years. Yahweh, the Lord God, has greatly blessed my master Abraham and he is well loved in the land of Canaan. Over the years, Yahweh has increased his flocks of sheep, herds of cattle, and has blessed him with many camels and donkeys. He's wealthy in silver and gold and has many menservants and maidservants. In her old age Yahweh, the Lord God, gave his wife Sarah a son and he will inherit all of his father's wealth.

'Abraham called me to him and made me swear an oath to find a wife for his son. He commanded me not to find a wife for his son from the daughters of the Canaanites, in whose land he is living. He told me to go to his own father's house in the land of Paddan Aram, to the city of Haran where he lived and find a wife from his father's family.

'I asked my master what I must do if the woman will not come back with me to the land of Canaan. He told me not to worry, because Yahweh, the Lord God, will go before me and prepare the way, to grant me success. When I find the woman, if she will not come back with me, then I am free from my oath to him.

'So how was I to find this woman in a strange land? I prayed to Yahweh, the Lord God, and asked him for help. I asked him to show me a sign, to point out the right woman to me. When I arrived at the city of Haran I rested at the well of water outside the city walls. I noticed the women and girls going down to the well in the evening time to collect water from the well with their jars.

'I said to Yahweh that if one of these women should grant my request then she would be the chosen wife for my master's son. If one of these maidens offers me a drink of water when I request it and also offers to water my camels without having been asked, then let her be the woman that is chosen as a wife for Isaac, the son of my master Abraham.

'In the midst of my prayer, my eyes fell upon this beautiful young maiden, your daughter Rebecca. I watched her fill up her jar with water and then lift it up onto her shoulder. Then I felt Yahweh, the Lord God, prompt me to approach her. As she left the well to go home I ran up to her and asked her for a drink from her jar.

'She immediately lowered her jar and offered me a drink. She asked me if these camels were mine and I answered her with a yes. Then she poured water from her jar into the trough for them to drink. Several times she collected water from the well and continued filling the trough until the camels were satisfied.

'I wondered at all that was happening and asked myself if this young maiden is the one that has been chosen for my master's son. So I asked her who her father was and she told me that his name was Bethuel, the son of Nahor that Milca his wife bore to him. Then I knew, and I gave her the gold ring for her nose and the gold bracelets for her arms. I then bowed my head and prayed, thanking God for leading my steps to your house. Here I have found your daughter Rebecca and ask that she may become the wife of Isaac, my master's son. I appeal to you now, Bethuel, will you grant the request of my master Abraham, your father's brother, and give your daughter Rebecca to his son Isaac in marriage?'

Both Laban and Bethuel answered, saying, 'This is truly from Yahweh, the Lord God. We can't question your sincerity.'

'Here is my daughter Rebecca,' answered Bethuel. 'Take her and go back to Canaan the land of Abraham and let it be done as God has directed. She will become the wife of Isaac your master's son.'

Hearing this response to his master's request, Eliezer bowed down and offered up a prayer of thanks to Yahweh. Then Eliezer took out gifts of gold, silver, and ornate jewels for Rebecca. He also gave her fine garments of clothing embroidered in many beautiful colours. He gave many gifts also to Rebecca's mother and father and he also had gifts for Laban.

Then a banquet was prepared by Bethuel and his household. The food was laid out before Eliezer and his men and they gave thanks to Yahweh before sitting down to eat. There was much feasting because of the celebration and there was plenty of wine to drink. The household of Bethuel sang and danced well into the night because of the betrothal of Rebecca to Isaac.

When they all rose up in the morning after celebrating the night before, Eliezer said to Bethuel and Laban, 'Send me on my way home and let me leave in order to return to my master Abraham this day, for he is very advanced in years.'

'Will you reconsider and allow Rebecca to remain with us for a few days more?' asked Bethuel.

'At least ten days,' suggested her mother. 'We are not ready to say farewell to her so soon. We rejoice for Rebecca, but at the same time we grieve that we may never see her again.'

'Do not delay me now,' said Eliezer. 'Can you not see that Yahweh has granted me success in my journey here, to find a wife for Isaac, the son of my master Abraham? Please give me your command to go on my way and begin my return journey today.'

'Let's call Rebecca,' said Bethuel. 'We'll see what she has to say about this matter.'

Rebecca came in when her mother and father called her and she stood before them in the company of Eliezer.

'Rebecca,' said her mother. 'Eliezer, the servant of Abraham, wants to leave today and return to his master. We have asked that you remain here for another ten days. It will be our last ten days together. What do you want to do?'

There was a glint in Rebecca's eyes and she was bursting with excitement. 'I'll go with Eliezer today. I'm eager to meet Isaac.'

So Eliezer was given the approval of Bethuel to go on his return journey. Preparations were made for the journey home. The camels were made ready and were loaded up with goods and provisions. All of Rebecca's gifts of silver and gold and rich garments were loaded up for her and many maidservants and menservants went with her along with her nurse Deborah, the daughter of her uncle Uz.

Her family said in blessing to Rebecca, 'Our daughter, become the mother of thousands upon ten thousands and may your descendants take possession of the gates of your enemies.'

Rebecca and her company mounted the camels and were led away from Haran by Eliezer and his men. Many tears were shed that day at her departure, both tears of sorrow and tears of great rejoicing. Rebecca was pleased to go.

It took many days to travel to the land of Canaan. Isaac at that time was living in the Negev and he came up from Lahai Roi. One evening Isaac felt a prompting in his spirit and went out into one of the fields to spend time waiting on Yahweh, the Lord God. After some time he looked up and in the distance he saw some camels approaching.

Rebecca, sitting on her camel, noticed a lone figure of a man standing in a field in the distance. He was watching the camels approach. Coming up close to Eliezer she asked, 'Who is that man standing in the field?'

'We'll know soon enough,' he answered. The man walked toward the camels and Eliezer recognized him. 'That's my master Isaac,' he said to Rebecca.

Taking her veil, Rebecca covered her face while Eliezer went up to Isaac and told him all that had happened. Then, taking Rebecca down from the camel, Isaac led her into the tent that had belonged to his mother Sarah. Rebecca and Isaac were married and she was glad to become his wife. Isaac loved Rebecca with all of his heart and she was a comfort to him after his mother's death.

CHAPTER 40

Persistence

Then Abraham in his old age took to himself another wife. Her name was Keturah and she was a woman from the land of Canaan. Over the course of time she bore six sons unto Abraham. These sons were named Zimran, Jokshan, Medan, Midian, Ishbak, and Shuach.

When the time came Abraham sent them on their way and they departed from their father Abraham, who lived in the land of Canaan. He gave them all rich gifts and they moved away from Abraham's son Isaac and they found a place of their own in which to live. Most of them moved to the mountains in the east where they lived in the cities that they built.

Those born to Sheba and Dedan, the sons of Jokshan, decided not to live in the cities but journeyed into the wilderness and they went from country to country settling nowhere. The Midianites went and settled in the land to the east of Cush where they found a valley which suited them. There they remained and built a city. Midian's sons had sons of their own and they grew in number and the land of Midian spread out.

Now Ishmael, the first son of Abraham, who was born to him by Hagar the handmaid of Sarah, had many children of his own.

Ishmael's wife from the land of Egypt was called Meribah, also known as Ribah. She bore four sons to Ishmael and they were named Nebayoth, Kedar, Adbeel, and Mibsam. She also gave birth to a daughter named Bosmath.

Ishmael was not pleased with the conduct of his wife Ribah and he sent her away from him. This is the wife who was bad mannered toward strangers and she was lazy and abusive to her children. Abraham had witnessed her bad conduct when she refused to give him some water to drink, even though the jar was full of water. So she left Ishmael's house and returned to her father's house in the land of Egypt.

After sending her away Ishmael went to the land of Canaan and he found another wife and her name was Malchuth. She bore eight sons and they were named Nishmah who was also known as Mishmah, Duma, Masa, Chadad, Tema, Yetur, Naphish, and Kedma. At that time Ishmael and his sons lived in the country in the wilderness of Paran, from Havilah to Shur. Ishmael had many grandchildren.

Eight years after Isaac married Rebecca the death occurred of Arphachsad the son of Shem, son of Noah. Arphachsad lived for a total of four hundred and thirty-eight years and he was the father of the Chaldeans. Rebecca was barren and was unable to conceive and she lived with Isaac in the land of Canaan.

'Isaac,' she said wearily. 'I'm not able to conceive and bear you any children. Your mother Sarah was also barren for many years. What's to become of me? Will I ever have a child of my own? Yahweh, the Lord God, blessed your mother and caused a miracle to take place, opening her womb so that she could conceive and bring you to birth. Even in her old age when childbirth was impossible, Yahweh made it happen. Rise up, Isaac, and lift up your hands and pray to Yahweh for me. May he listen to your prayer and be merciful to us.'

'Yahweh, the Lord God, has already promised my father that his seed will multiply and fill the earth, like the stars in the heavens and the grains of dust in the earth. This barrenness must be in you and not in me.'

'Whoever is barren does not matter. We can only have children if both of us are productive. You're my husband and you have the God-given authority in your own household to have children. Did Yahweh not command Adam and Eve to multiply and fill the earth? Are you not Adam in your own household? Will Yahweh not listen to your prayer?'

'Well,' considered Isaac. 'What you say is true.'

'Isaac, have you not walked in the way of Yahweh all the days of your life? Like your father Abraham before you, he has always walked in the ways of Yahweh, the Lord God, and has listened to his voice. Can you not listen to the voice of Yahweh? Ask him for help and listen to his reply.'

'But the prayer has already been made. We need to be patient, we need to wait for Yahweh, the Lord God, to act.'

'Sometimes we need to persist. We must not allow Yahweh to forget his promise, we must remind him. Likewise we must give no rest to ourselves, until the will of Yahweh has been fulfilled in our lives.'

Rising up Isaac said to Rebecca, 'I know what we must do. We must go, you and I, to the land of Moriah, to the mountain on which the fragrant burnt offering was sacrificed to Yahweh. I was the sacrifice on that day. There we will offer up our prayers to Yahweh. There we will remind him that I willingly offered up my life to him. Because of my love for Yahweh, the Lord God, he will listen to my prayer and because of my father's faithfulness and obedience he will open your womb to bear children.'

So Isaac and Rebecca went to the mountains of Moriah and they climbed up to the place that Yahweh had indicated to Abraham and Isaac for the fragrant burnt offering many years ago. There they found the remains of the altar that they had built and looking into the centre of the altar the ashes from the fire could still be seen.

Tears came to the eyes of both Isaac and Rebecca. 'It's here that Yahweh gave me new life,' said Isaac.

'And he didn't do that without good reason.'

'He gave me new life.'

'So that you could live it to the full. And he gave me to you to be your wife so that his promise would be fulfilled.'

'Now Rebecca, let us pray together.' Lifting up his hands Isaac prayed, 'O Adonai Yahweh, creator of heaven and earth, you are God and you are good and your mercies fill the earth. From the land of Ur of the Chaldeans you did call my father Abraham. From the land of his birth you did command him to leave. You told him to leave his father's house in Haran and to go to the land of Canaan. This is the land that he came to, in faithfulness to your command.

'This land is the land that you promised to give to him and to his seed forever. You told him that his seed would multiply and fill the earth and that his descendants would outnumber even the stars in the heavens. Now, as you gave me new life on this altar, give new life to the words of your covenant with my father Abraham.

'My eyes look to you, Yahweh, Lord God; both of us, Rebecca and I, look to you. We place our trust in you this day and forever. Look with kindness toward us and consider with favour our request. Grant us children. May your covenant be fulfilled in our lives, in our lifetime upon this earth. For you are a gracious God, you are kind and loving to all you have made. It's to you alone that we give glory and praise.'

There upon the mountain of Moriah, in that place of sacrifice, Isaac and Rebecca sang praises and danced to Yahweh, the Lord

God. And God's ears were opened and he listened to their prayer. God's eyes were open and he could see their love for each other and their love for him. There they sang and danced to Yahweh, the Lord God, and he showed them his mercy. Raising his hand in blessing Yahweh opened the womb of Rebecca so that she might conceive.

So she did conceive because Yahweh heard and answered her prayer and he was eager to fulfil his promise to Abraham. After about seven months into her pregnancy Rebecca experienced a lot of discomfort. The child within her womb became very active and it was like a battle taking place within her. This caused her great pain and she would scream on account of it. Neither sitting, lying down, nor even standing would ease her pain. She was unable to sleep and she became exhausted.

She made enquiries of the other women living in the land, 'Did such a thing happen to you when you were expecting your baby?'

They all answered, 'No.'

Crying out she complained, 'Why am I the only one in all the earth who has experienced such pain? I will ask for prayer.'

So Rebecca went to Abraham and asked him, 'Seek and ask Yahweh, the Lord God, for me, concerning my difficulty. Will all be well with me and my baby?'

Sending word to the city of Salem, to the house of Shem and Eber, she appealed for prayer, asking them to seek the counsel of Yahweh concerning her circumstances. All of these men prayed for Rebecca. Isaac remained by her side for most of the time now that she was struggling and he was praying constantly for her, both verbally and inwardly in his spirit.

One night when she was trying to sleep, Yahweh, the Lord God, came to her and appeared before her, 'Rebecca. Rebecca,' he called. 'Shema, Rebecca. Hear my voice.'

Hearing the voice of Yahweh she answered, 'Kadosh Yahweh,

hineni. Holy God, I'm here. I'm listening to your voice. Adonai Yahweh daber el libi. Lord God speak to my heart.'

'Rebecca, you're carrying two nations in your womb and two people born from your womb will be divided; one nation will be stronger than the other and the elder will serve the younger.'

'Thank you Holy God. You've heard and answered my prayer. I'm carrying two children. Praise Yahweh.'

In the course of time her waters broke and she knelt down to give birth. There were twins in her womb, just as Yahweh had told her. The first child came out and it was a boy. The boy was covered in red hair. 'He's like a red garment,' announced one of the women helping Rebecca. He was given the name Esau, which means hairy, but he was also known as Edom, which means red.

The second child came out of Rebecca's womb and when he was delivered he grasped hold of the heel of Esau. 'He shall be called Jacob,' said Rebecca. 'Because this means he grasps the heel.'

CHAPTER 41

Twins

At the birth of Esau and Jacob, their father Isaac was sixty years old and their grandfather Abraham was one hundred and sixty years old. The boys grew up and were a delight to their parents. Isaac favoured Esau who became a designing and deceitful man, an expert with the bow and a skilful hunter. But Jacob was favoured by his mother Rebecca. In contrast to his wild brother, Jacob was a quiet man who pondered upon Yahweh, the Lord God. He preferred living near the tents, tending his flock of sheep and was quick to obey his father and mother. Jacob listened to the instruction of Yahweh, the Lord God, and walked in his ways. But Esau refused to learn, preferring to fight and live in the wilderness.

Abraham observed the twins as they grew up into manhood and he knew that Isaac preferred Esau over Jacob. He knew also that Jacob would visit him and listen to instruction, whereas Esau would not. He prayed for his grandchildren, seeking the advice of Yahweh concerning them.

'Rebecca,' said Abraham one day. 'Since Isaac is not here, I want to speak to you. I don't want him to hear what I have to say to you.'

'Yes Abraham, what would you like to say to me?'

'I'm old and very advanced in years and I feel that my time here is nearly done. Do you remember what Yahweh, the Lord God, had to say to you when you were carrying the boys in your womb?'

'O yes I can remember it well. It is so clear, as if he said it to me yesterday.'

'Well I've been watching you and Isaac and the boys and I can see how Isaac favours Esau and you favour Jacob.'

'Yes that's true, though I love them both. I worry for Esau. He's gone most of the time, hunting for wild game that Isaac so loves. If only he wouldn't encourage him so much.'

'I agree with you, Rebecca. Did Yahweh not tell you that they would be divided from each other, going in different ways?'

'Yes he did.'

'And did he not tell you that the elder would serve the younger?'

'He did indeed.'

'Then I must tell you, Rebecca, to keep your eye on Jacob, because he is the one that has been chosen by Yahweh. It's through your son Jacob that the blessing of the covenant has been given. I can't say this to my son Isaac because his judgement is impaired by his taste for wild game. It is through Jacob that God will continue the whole house of Shem. A great nation will come through him and he will take possession of this land above all other nations. His people will grow and multiply and fill the earth. Everyone will know that there is a God because of him. He will be a blessing unto all the earth forever.

'All who bless Jacob will be blessed by Yahweh and if anyone should curse Jacob and his seed, then that man will be under the curse of Yahweh. In his descendants will my own name be remembered, for all time. Promise me, Rebecca, that Jacob will receive the blessing of the firstborn.'

'How can I promise that?' she asked, alarmed. 'It's not in my power to do so.'

'You must find a way. You know yourself that Jacob is the one favoured by God. He told you so before his birth.'

'That he did,' considered Rebecca. 'But you must pray for me so that I'll know how to act when the time comes.'

'You can be assured that I will,' answered Abraham.

'Then I promise,' answered Rebecca, 'that I will do all that is in my power to ensure that Jacob receives the blessing of the firstborn. May it be done, according to the will of Yahweh.'

CHAPTER 42

Abraham

Calling his servant Eliezer to his side Abraham said, 'Eliezer, my faithful servant, you have served me now for one hundred and twenty-five years. I've called you here to me now because my days on earth are almost done. Send servants into the earth and find my dispersed family. I need to speak to them before I die so that I can impart my final blessing upon them.'

With haste Eliezer dispatched servants to find the sons of Abraham. They were all given the news that Abraham was reaching the end of his days and he wanted them to come to him and receive his final blessing and so that they might place him in the sepulchre beside his beloved wife Sarah.

So his sons came from the lands in which they lived and they gathered around their aged father Abraham in the land of Canaan. There Abraham spoke to them all and all of his sons were present. Isaac came with his older brother Ishmael and their younger brothers, by their stepmother Keturah. They were all present: Zimran, Jokshan, Medan, Midian, Ishbak, and Shuach. Abraham was pleased that all of his sons were there to be with him in his last days. Raising his hands to heaven Abraham praised Yahweh and thanked him for all of his mercies. Laying his hands on the head of each of his sons he called upon Yahweh Elohim and he gave them his blessing.

Calling his son Isaac to him, he sent the others outside the tent. 'There is only one God, Isaac, and there is none like him. He's the one who took me out of the place of my birth, from the city of Ur of the Chaldeans. It's he who delivered me from the hands of the wicked, from the hands of those who tried to kill me. To the land of Haran he brought me with your mother Sarah, my father Terah, and my mother Amthelo. My brother Nahor and his wife Milca he also brought out with my nephew Lot. There we settled in the land of Paddan Aram in the city of Haran.

'From my father's house, he told me to depart with Sarah and Lot and go to the land of Canaan, this land in which we live. Because I placed my trust in him, I obeyed Yahweh and I came here to live in this land. A severe famine hit the land and we were compelled to go to Egypt, because there was grain in abundance there. In the land of Egypt, Yahweh gave me many blessings and I returned to Canaan a wealthy man.

'When the alliance of the four kings, led by Kedorlaomer, invaded the land and took Lot and his family as slaves, it was Elohei Tzeva'ot, the God of Hosts, who sent me to rescue him. Though our number was small he enabled the heavenly army of angels to fight with us and we were able to rescue Lot and his entire family from slavery.

'Then Yahweh came before me and he declared that his name is El-Shaddai. He called me to walk before him and be blameless and he would make an everlasting covenant between us, confirming that I would increase in number. He told me that I'd be the father of many nations and for all this he changed my name from Abram to Abraham, from exalted father to father of many nations.

'He promised to make me fruitful and told me that kings would come from me. He said that this covenant is for me and my descendants forever. He gave this land of Canaan to me and my descendants as an everlasting possession. He told me that I would no longer be a stranger here.

'For my part Elohim asked me to circumcise every male over eight days old. You, Isaac, were the first to be circumcised on the eighth day after your birth. Even the servants in my household I had to circumcise at the command of Elohim, otherwise they would be cut off from my people and the covenant would be broken.

'Elohim came to visit me and he promised that your mother Sarah would conceive and bear a son and this took place as he promised. You, Isaac, are the son of this promise. You are the Laughter of God. You brought us such great joy and your mother and I love you deeply.'

At this Abraham and Isaac embraced, 'I love you my father,' cried Isaac, the tears rolling down his face. They held each other in silence for a long time.

'My son,' said Abraham. 'Promise me that you'll always love Yahweh, the Lord God. Always walk in his ways. Never turn from his path to the left or to the right. Remain firm in your faith. Always trust in Yahweh. Esau and Jacob, your sons, never neglect them. Raise them and encourage them in the ways of Yahweh, the Lord God. Jacob, I see, walks in the ways of Yahweh but I fear for Esau.'

'I will do all that you ask,' answered Isaac. 'I will walk in the ways of Yahweh, the Lord God, and I will not depart from all of his commandments.'

Then Abraham blessed his son Isaac in the name of El-Elyon, God Most High. A short time after this Abraham died. He died in the fifteenth year of Esau and Jacob, the sons of Isaac. All the days of Abraham were one hundred and seventy-five years when he breathed his last. Isaac, Ishmael, and all of Abraham's sons came to bury him. Shem was with Abraham's sons to lay him in the tomb. The people living in Canaan came with their princes and kings to bury him and when the people of Haran heard the news they also came to console Isaac and his family in their grief.

Abraham was entombed alongside his beloved wife Sarah in the sepulchre, the Cave of Machpelah near Mamre, the one that he had purchased from Ephron, son of Zohar, the Hittite, as a place of burial. The mourning for Abraham was great. It lasted for a whole year because Abraham was well loved by many. He had been good to all and he lived a righteous life, both with God and with men.

Never was there a man like Abraham who loved Yahweh. Abraham loved the one true God from his early childhood and never deviated from Yahweh's path all of his days unto his death. He taught all the people of the land, whoever he had a chance to meet, the way and the love of Yahweh, the Lord God. He did this through his kindness and hospitality, he had a love for his neighbour and his love for Yahweh was always overflowing.

Esau

Nimrod, the king of Babel, who was also known as Amraphel since the fall of the Tower of Babel, was out in the field. He was out hunting with some of his men. Nimrod was renowned for his skill in hunting and there were none to compare to him. But he heard that another was better than him, 'Who is this man that is supposed to be better than me at hunting?'

'My Lord and King,' answered his companions, 'there is none greater than you in all the earth.'

'Nevertheless tell me his name and from where does he come?'

'We hear his name is Esau and he comes from the land of Canaan. He's only a boy.'

'Only a boy. How can a boy be a greater hunter than me? This is a lie. I invaded Shem's territory and conquered it. I have subdued all the kings in the land and I have governed them since my fortieth year. This brat of a boy can make no such claim.'

'You're right, O King. None can compare to you. You're the greatest hunter in all the earth.'

Nimrod feared that they were only placating him and this fuelled his jealousy toward the boy. He had made a decree stating that anyone heard speaking about the boy Esau being a better hunter than Nimrod was to be put to death. Even if his name was mentioned in conversation, the brick furnace would be the punishment for doing so.

Esau was a fierce hunter and he had a reputation for his skills, like none other in the land of Canaan. From an early age he was excited by the hunt and Isaac and Rebecca often had to send out servants to search for him because he would be gone for many days at a time, going deeper into the wilderness in search of his prey. He was cunning and he was extremely careful to avoid capture. Hiding in the fields and the mountains he would laugh to himself when his father's servant would walk right beside him and not be able to find him.

His mother and father were at first anxious for his safety but he always managed to return home, unscathed and heavily laden with wild game that he had managed to kill. He discovered through trial and error how to hunt without being discovered. He could make himself invisible to his prey. Most of all he had patience. Not for most things in life but when it came to stalking his prey, he could pause and lie in wait for that right moment. He could lie on his belly for hours without moving. Waiting to strike. He became very successful.

Esau desired to become the best hunter in the world. Most of his days were spent away from home. He was living like a wild beast. Like a wildcat with an insatiable appetite for wild game. He knew about Nimrod. All the earth knew about Nimrod. He was a wild, vicious, and brutal man and he lusted after his prey. But Esau was yearning to prove himself better than Nimrod.

Nimrod spent his life hunting and brutalizing men. Capturing and subduing kingdoms and nations was, for Nimrod, the thrill of the hunt. Forcing the vanquished to abandon God and God's way was his means of terrorizing and forcing them into obedience to him and his occult beliefs. He was an evil despot and the worship of the one true God was forbidden in all of the territory where he held control. His son Mardon was deified and Nimrod's subjects were forced to worship him. Human sacrifice was part of the worship ceremony and boys and girls were offered up to him on the altar.

'I will be greater than Nimrod,' declared Esau to himself.

'I will rid the world of this brat, Esau,' said Nimrod. 'I'll crush this little upstart. I'll encounter him at some time in the field. Then I'll strike and kill the impudent brat.'

One day Esau was in the field, hunting. He was a three days' journey away from home. He was enjoying himself because this was the life that he loved. Sitting down on the ground with his back leaning against a boulder, he closed his eyes. Using his sense of smell he could determine the time of day. The blistering heat of the day was gone and the cool of the day before the night had arrived. He could hear the gentle breeze and feel it blowing against his skin and playing with his hair. It reminded him of his mother singing whilst nurturing her son, passing her gentle fingers through his mop of wild red hair.

Lost, deep in thought for a moment, he was brought back to reality with a jolt. In the distance he heard voices, the voices of men. For the past two days he had encountered no one. The entire landscape was his and his alone, until now. As soon as he heard them, he dropped flat with his belly to the ground.

In the distance he could see the group of men talking with each other. He could not hear the words spoken. They were too far away but the wind carried the sound toward him. He looked about in all directions to make sure that he was not being observed. He did not want these men to be used as bait to distract him and throw him off his guard.

'They're not nomads,' said Esau to himself. 'There's no herd and no flock. They're not dressed like nomads.' The sun glinted on shiny metal and he noticed that they carried spears. 'They're hunters,' he said and he discovered that they carried bows and they had swords at their side.

Waiting and watching, that was the crucial requirement, and that is what Esau did. They had not seen him, he was sure of that and he was going to keep it that way. 'How many men are there?' he asked himself. 'I must count them.' Moving stealthily, he had to leave his hiding place in order to see them all clearly. He decided not to crawl because he might raise up a cloud of dust. The ground was powder dry. So he moved slowly on his hands and knees until he was satisfied with his new position.

'One, two, three, four,' he continued counting. 'Twelve. Where are they from?' he wondered. 'I can't tell from their clothes. They're no different than anyone else I've seen before. Their hair is different from the style in this part of the world and their beards are very ornately decorated.'

As the day approached its end, the sound carried much more clearly and Esau could hear their voices. 'I don't understand what they're saying to each other,' he complained to himself. 'They're speaking in a different language. If only the whole world spoke Hebrew,' he complained. 'So they're not from here. Are they from Ashur or Elam? They're not from Paddan Aram, my mother's homeland. They might be from Lower Mesopotamia, the land of Shinar, the city of Babel. Maybe Nimrod is here among them.'

He was not to find out because night closed in and he was surrounded by darkness. The men lit a fire and roasted wild game upon it. Esau kept watching them from a safe distance. He had nothing to eat and the wind was gently blowing the aroma of the roast meat toward him. The fragrance tormented his nostrils and the juices of his palate began to flow. His stomach growled, emitting gurgling noises which he thought would give him away if he was much closer to the men.

His desire for food was great but he was not going to reveal himself by lighting a fire. 'I've nothing to roast,' he complained. 'I've been too busy watching these men to stalk for game. I'll bide my time. I want to know if Nimrod is among these men.'

Esau had a fitful sleep that night. He was anxious not to lose sight of the men. He woke up several times in fright during the night, thinking that they had slipped away without his knowledge. But as dawn broke the men began to stir in the camp. The men got up and stretched themselves. That was a luxury Esau did not have. If he dared to stand up and stretch, he feared that he would be seen.

One of the men seemed to be the leader. The other men bowed to him and he gave all the orders to them. 'I must watch him carefully today,' said Esau. 'Maybe he is Nimrod.'

The men split up into smaller groups and went off in different directions to hunt. Esau kept his eyes fixed on this one figure. This man's group moved directly away from Esau. Two groups moved to Esau's left and another to his right. Esau was anxious not to lose sight of this man and he was moving away quickly. Esau had to move stealthily and in haste if he wanted to keep his eye on him.

In keeping his eye on his prey he had to ensure that the other groups of men did not notice him. It was not easy, but after a few hours he managed to gain on the group of men that he was following. There were three of them and he watched them as they hunted. There were times when they vanished from sight and he admired their skill in pursuing their prey. He watched them as they pounced and the scuffle was intense but at the same time was swift. Raising their voices, they roared with delight. They were successful in capturing their prey.

'Nimrod,' said Esau to himself. 'They congratulated Nimrod. I clearly heard his name. This man is Nimrod.' Esau's heart was beating wildly in his chest and the thrill sent waves of hot and cold up and down his spine. 'Today, Nimrod,' stated Esau, 'God has delivered you into my hands.'

Not satisfied with one beast, the men went on the hunt again.

This time Nimrod was moving in the direction toward Esau. With his heart pounding in his ears Esau crouched low in the grass. Nimrod and his men did not know that he was there. As Nimrod approached, Esau darted from his hiding place and thrust his sword through the throat of Nimrod. Falling to the ground, Nimrod convulsed as the blood poured from his throat, soaking the earth.

As Nimrod lay bleeding on the ground, he remembered his dream of long ago, when a young bird came out of the egg that Abram threw at him. This bird attacked him, pecking out his eyes. He remembered the words of Anuki the sage: 'You will be in great peril … The young bird that came out of the egg is none other than the seed of Abram. A young boy will strike and slay the king in days to come … If Abram is allowed to live then this will result in your downfall.'

Nimrod's two companions were stunned. Everything had happened so quickly that they were rooted to the spot. When they came to their senses they fell upon Esau with their swords. Esau released an arrow, piercing the chest of the first man but the second man was upon him before he could pull out another arrow.

Drawing the sword out of Nimrod's throat Esau lifted it to ward off the attack. A fierce battle ensued with this man who was experienced in battle. But this man's spirit faltered because his king, who was considered an invincible god, was now lying dead on the ground. With a strike of the sword to the knee, the man's legs buckled and Esau struck him with his sword on the side of the neck. He fell down dead.

Esau was trembling with excitement and fear. The impact of what he had done suddenly fell on him. He had killed men. Never before had he taken human life. His lips quivered and he began to cry, 'What have I done? What have I done?'

Covered in sweat, Esau turned, realising that the man pierced with the arrow was screaming for help, so he rushed forward and finished his life with one thrust of the sword. For good measure Esau swung the sword and removed Nimrod's head. This fulfilled the curse of Amthelo, the mother of Abram: 'May his head be sliced from his body.'

Esau noticed the skins that Nimrod always carried. These are the skins that his father Cush gave him, the garments that Yahweh made for Adam and Eve. These were the garments that endowed Nimrod with strength. Esau, desiring to possess them, picked them up and tied them around his waist.

Realising that the screams of the dying man had attracted the attention of his companions, Esau bolted from the scene. 'There are too many of them for me to fight. They are soldiers skilled in battle, the sons of warriors. I'm only the son of a shepherd. I'll flee to the mountains. Keep running.'

CHAPTER 44

Flight

So he ran for his life. The three groups of men that had separated, that had moved off in different directions to hunt, had heard the screams of the dying man. They turned and from a long distance they witnessed the sword fight between their companions and Esau. They all abandoned the hunt and ran to offer their assistance.

When they arrived at the scene of carnage they were horrified. There on the ground lay their king and two companions dead, lying in pools of blood. 'The king is dead,' they gasped. 'His head has been cut from his body.'

They trembled with fear and dismay. 'Our king, once so powerful, is no more. Who did this? Who is stronger than the king? Where is his killer?'

'Look,' pointed one of the hunters. 'There he is. Get him.'

One remained at the scene of the battle to keep the carrion from devouring the bodies of the dead men. Looking at the detached head of the king, this man said, 'So the mighty has fallen. Nimrod the god of Babylon is dead. What now of your kingdom? What fate is in store now for the rest of us? You were indeed a great and mighty king but your kingdom was built on terror and violence. You created many enemies. They'll now split your empire, each king taking back the control of his own kingdom.' He paused for thought, 'And we will all be thrown into slavery and all of our possessions will be taken from us.'

Esau was well ahead of his pursuers. But he kept running. There was no opportunity to rest. He knew that he would be no match for all who followed him. Looking back frequently, he had to know where they were and how many were pursuing him. 'There's only eight,' he said to himself. 'There should be nine. One is missing. Where is he?'

Quickly scanning the surrounding wilderness he tried to find him. But he was not able to see the man. 'Has he gone in a different direction? Is he planning a trap for me? I must outrun these men. I can't let them trap me or pass me out.' So, on he ran, gasping for breath. The back of his throat was sore and his breath was whistling through his teeth. The sweat ran through his eyebrows, stinging his eyes. Yet on he ran, weak at the knees. His life depended on him keeping ahead of his pursuers.

The midday heat was fierce and Esau's knees were weak. His legs trembled and he was not able to continue. Willpower was not enough. Exhaustion hit him. His knees buckled and down he fell. Gasping and panting, his vision turned black and lights floated before his eyes. He remained conscious but his head did spin. The dust of the earth stuck to his skin. 'I'm turning to dust,' he said to himself. 'Here I'll die.'

After lying in the dust for a few moments his head began to clear. Quickly he placed his arrows beside him on the ground and fitted one to the string of his bow. From a low position in the shelter of a clump of boulders he scanned the horizon, looking for his pursuers, but he could not see them. His eyes were stinging and he had to keep wiping the sweat from his brow.

The breeze was blowing toward him and he sniffed the air, 'Can I smell them?' he asked himself, sniffing the air again. 'Yes I can smell them. I can smell their sweat.' He doubted himself. 'Maybe it's myself that I can smell?' He was certainly pungent. 'I'll wait. I'll watch and listen.'

After what seemed an eternity he discerned the men in the distance. They could not see him but they were tracking him, following his marks in the earth. He knew what they were doing and he knew that before long, they would be upon him. 'I must move on. I can't stay here any longer.'

On he went, moving from one hiding place to another. They were relentless in their pursuit. The cat and mouse game continued throughout the day and well into the evening. As darkness fell Esau decided to change his direction and, as tired as he was, he went on his way through the night. 'They won't be able to track me through the night,' he said to himself.

When dawn arrived he changed direction again. 'This will make it more difficult to track me,' he assured himself. But he knew that there was no place for complacency. 'They're experienced trackers and if I don't keep ahead of them they will eventually find me. I must force myself on, altering my direction a few times during the day. I must be careful not to lose my own sense of direction or I will get lost. I must look out for familiar landmarks.'

CHAPTER 45

Jacob

Jacob was leaning over the pot, stirring his red lentil stew. Esau stumbled in upon him. Gripping Jacob's sleeve, Esau's knees buckled and down he fell, pulling Jacob down with him. Jacob gagged for breath because the pungent aroma from Esau violently assaulted his nostrils. Jacob quickly sprang up and stepped away, gulping in fresh air.

Looking down at his prostrate brother, Jacob could see that he was in a sorry state. He had never before seen his brother Esau like this. Clearly he was exhausted. The hair was matted to his skin and he was covered in dust. Like a man in mourning. He was also covered in blood. Jacob assumed that the blood was from the beast; the beast that had once lived in the skins tied around his brother's waist. He had no notion that Esau was covered in Nimrod's blood.

The servants, seeing his sorrowful state, gave Esau some water to drink and he gulped it down quickly. He drank it so fast that it hurt his throat. With one breath he was laughing and with the next he was wailing. He was hysterical. 'I'm dying,' he cried. 'I'm home at last but I'm about to die.' The tears rolled down his face, leaving streaks in his dust-covered cheeks.

'You're delirious,' said Jacob. 'A wild beast must have got the better of you.'

'I haven't eaten for days,' answered Esau, wiping the tears from his eyes. 'What's that you have in the pot?'

'It's stew. Red lentil stew.'

'Give me some. I'm dying from the hunger. Give me some before I die.'

'If you're going to die today you won't need your birthright.'

'My what?'

'Your birthright,' said Jacob. 'You're the firstborn son and you're entitled to everything from our father Isaac.'

'Well,' he answered, as his head spun, making him dizzy. 'What of it? I'm dying here from the hunger and all you want to do is talk about my birthright. Will you give me some of the stew?'

'I'll give you some stew,' answered Jacob. 'But first, sell me your birthright.'

'What do I care for my birthright?' answered Esau, considering that his pursuers would soon arrive to kill him. 'I'm about to die. Please feed me.'

'Give me your birthright and I'll feed you some stew.'

In frustration he gasped, 'Take my birthright. It means nothing to me.' He shouted, 'Take it.'

So it was agreed. Esau sold his birthright to Jacob and in exchange he received unleavened bread and a bowl of red lentil stew. He gulped down the stew in the blink of an eye and wiped his mouth with the back of his hand. Getting up and belching, he ran stumbling into his tent and hid the garments of Adam and Eve that he had stolen from Nimrod.

Rebecca sat silently in her tent. She overheard the exchange between her two sons. Remembering the advice from Abraham, she wondered how she would be able to deceive Isaac and ensure that Jacob would receive the blessing of the firstborn instead of Esau.

CHAPTER 46

Rejoice

Nimrod's men gave up the pursuit of Esau after the first day. Since their king was dead, a spirit of despair entered into them. They returned and lifted up Nimrod's body and carried him back, in sorrow, to the city of Babel. All of the days of the life of Nimrod numbered two hundred and fifteen years and he had invaded and ruled the land of Shinar for one hundred and seventy-five years.

At his death, the kingdom that Nimrod ruled was split up into many kingdoms, because there was no one like Nimrod to replace him. The Chaldeans, living in the land of Shinar under the oppression of Nimrod, rejoiced. 'The tyranny of Nimrod is over. The brutal beast is dead. We are free,' they declared. 'We are free. We rejoice in the man who slew the king.' They made up songs and, playing music, they danced in the streets. They drank beer and wine to celebrate, for they were now set free and the burden of fear was lifted from their shoulders.

The Bactrians, also known as the Gutians, were the first to drive out the Hamites and all those loyal to Nimrod from the land of Babel. The Bactrians were the descendants of Gether, son of Aram, son of Shem. Some of the Hamites fled to the land of Havilah, which is also called India, where they settled in the area of the Cophen

River. The sons of Yoktan who were already established in this area forced the Hamites to flee further into Havilah and they settled in the Indus Valley, where they became known as the Dravidians. All of the kings who had been subject to Nimrod took back the control of their own territories and they enslaved the entire household of Nimrod.

'So Nimrod died by the sword of Esau,' said one of Nimrod's wise men, who was slow to escape. Forced into slavery, and at the hand of his new master, he was being led away in sorrow to the land of Elam. He recognized another sage from the house of Nimrod. This man was also yoked to slavery. Crying out, he said, 'Remember when Nimrod told us of his dream many years ago? The dream of where a young bird came out of the egg and pecked out his eyes.'

'Yes, I remember the dream,' answered his companion.

'Did we not foresee his death?'

'I remember. Anuki told Nimrod that he would die at the hand of the seed of Abram, son of Terah.'

THE END

ABOUT THE AUTHOR

262

Brian J. Cahill has not always been a writer. For most of his working life he has been involved in the manufacturing and maintenance industries. In 2017 he gained a BA in Fine Art and enjoys the creative process of painting, drawing, and sculpture.

The desire to write has been brewing up inside him for many years and in August 2019 he began researching Abraham. The writing began in November 2019 and his first book, *Abram, son of Terah,* is now complete.

Brian currently lives in Ireland, in County Leitrim, with his wife and children.